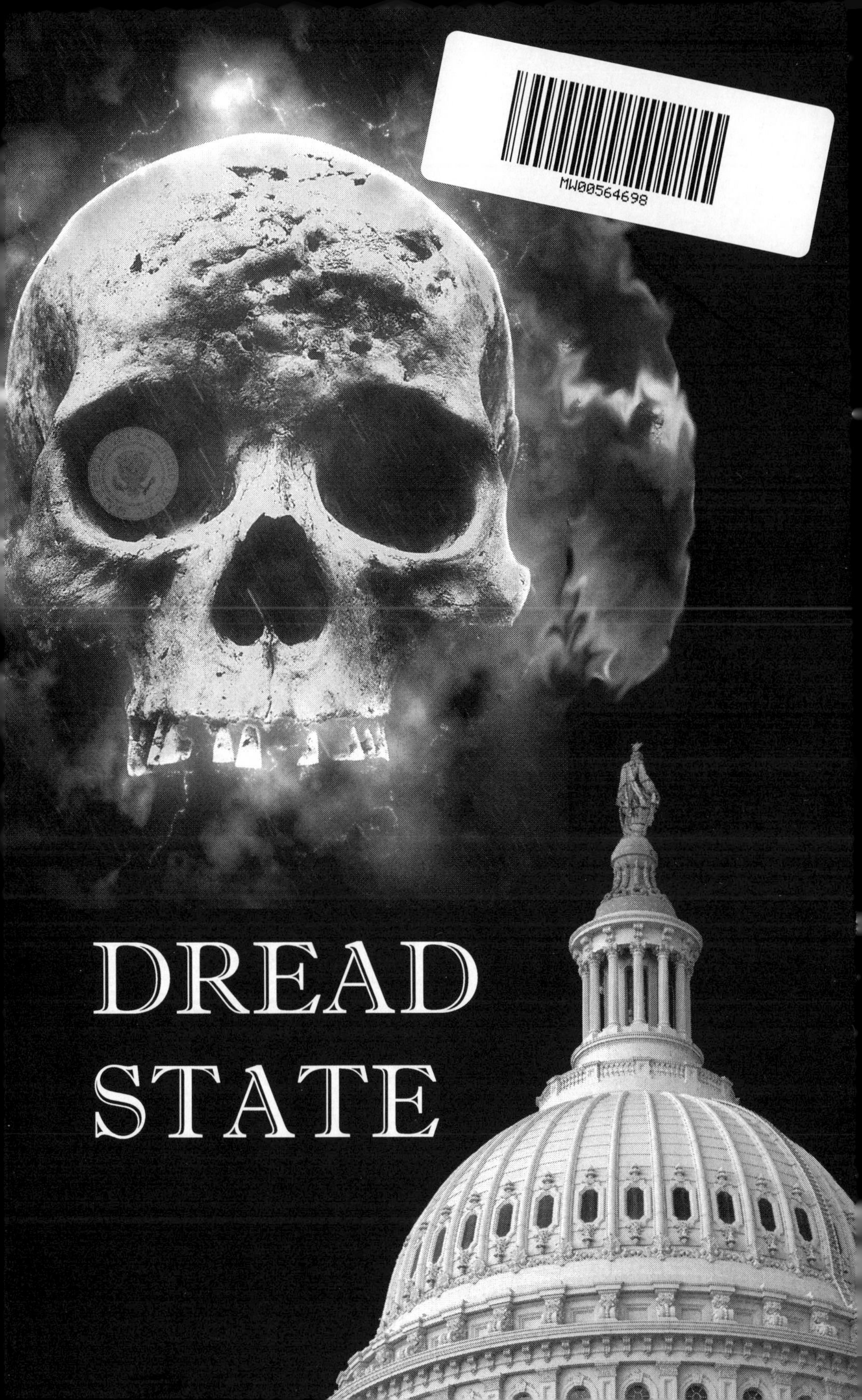
MW00564698
DREAD
STATE

Dread State - A Political Horror Anthology
c. 2016 ThunderDome Press
ISBN: 978-0692809686

Design and Typesetting by Michael Paul Gonzalez

Printed and Bound by CreateSpace

Cover Design by Michael Paul Gonzalez
(images acquired through Creative Commons License)

Interior Photography by Aleks Bieńkowska

REPRINT CREDITS
"Death and Suffrage" © 2002 Dale Bailey. First publication: The Magazine of Fantasy & Science Fiction, February 2002. Reprinted by permission of the author.

"Willow Tests Well", © Nick Mamatas, 2012. Originally published in Psychos: Serial Killers, Depraved Madmen, and the Criminally Insane, John Skipp, ed.

"Getting Out to Vote" © Hillary Lyon, 2011. Originally published in Flashes in the Dark.

"Love Perverts" © 2014 Sarah Langan. First publication: John Joseph Adams / Hugh Howey Apocalypse Tryptch, "The End Is Nigh," 2014.

"The Pedestrian" Reprinted by permission of Don Congdon Associates, Inc. © 1951 by the Fortnightly Publishing Company, renewed 1979 by Ray Bradbury

This book will be released in electronic format, but its primary goal in design is to remind the reader of the simple pleasure of holding the printed work in hand. It's small enough to take with you to spread the word far and wide: the paper book is not dead.
Show it. Share it. Help it survive.

Bonus Print Story exclusive to print edition:
THE CRAWL: Story Framework by Michael Paul Gonzalez with contributions from Lauren Candia (Burn it all down/Maira's Last Letter), Amanda Gowin (Marc in Chillicothe), James Chambers (Everything's going tits up...), Linda Nagle (This may be the last...), Elizabeth Massie (Listen Up, World!), Thom Erb (Hey Emma), Tim Waggoner (The Confession p.122-159), and John Skipp (Last Drunk Note)

DREAD STATE

A Political Horror Anthology

Edited by
Michael Paul Gonzalez
and
Eugene Johnson

TABLE OF CONTENTS

Introduction - Jeff Strand 1
The War Room by Paul Moore 5
The Blood of Patriots and Tyrants by Ray Garton 25
Return of the Gipper by Jason V Brock 37
Death and Suffrage by Dale Bailey 46
The Governor's Executions by G. Ted Theewen 86
GOTV by Tom Breen 100
The Fool on the Hill by Lisa Morton 105
How I Learned to Stop Worrying and Love the Wall by Simon McCaffery 116
Willow Tests Well by Nick Mamatas 127
Seeds by John Palisano 139
The Tie-Breaker by Kevin Holton 150
Year of the Mouse by William F. Nolan 156
Your Own Damned Fault by David Perlmutter 164
Love Perverts by Sarah Langan 168
Gadu Yansa by Sunni K Brock 193
Feast by Joseph Rubas 202
Hyper-Pluralism by Bobby Wilson 208
That Hot Summer Night in Healey's Bar
Two Weeks Before the Election by Anthony Ambrogio 216
Everybody Listens to Buck by Nicholas Manzolillo 230
Getting Out to Vote by Hillary Lyon 240
Take Me to Your Cheerleader by Mark Allan Gunnells 244
The Sixth Street Bus Holds an Election by Curtis VanDonkelaar 250
The Candidate by Luke Styer and Skip Johnson 255
The Pedestrian by Ray Bradbury 260
Afterword - David Wellington 266

INTRODUCTION
by Jeff Strand

I wrote the first draft of this introduction a few days before the 2016 United States presidential election. It was not remotely bipartisan (and neither is this draft, so reader beware!) and toyed around with the horrors of a Trump victory that I knew deep in my heart would never actually happen.

The editors, wisely, asked if I'd consider writing something more general. What I'd given them would most likely be out of date before the book was actually published. I considered going with "How dare you?!? Do you know who I am?!? I rewrite for nobody!!!" but ultimately settled on, "Sure, no problem."

So I said I'd have it done on Election Day, figuring that I could write this introduction while I watched the live coverage. Perfect, right? I could multi-task and not give the TV my full attention; this wasn't an episode of Lost. (Lost started off great and ended with incoherent chaos, much like the 2016 election, minus the "started off great" part.)

Spoiler alert: I didn't finish this on Election Day.

It was like thinking I'd been reading a romance novel, where there'd be some conflict but a happy ending was inevitable, only to realize that somebody had swapped out the covers and instead I was reading the latest work by Jack Ketchum. I started to feel a little sick to my stomach. This was supposed to be an inspirational comedy! What the hell was happening? I was watching a slasher flick, but instead of shouting "Don't go in the basement!" I was shouting "Don't turn that state red!"

In the end, we had my worst presidential nightmare and I hadn't written a damn word on this introduction.

The next day, I got as much writing done as I would on a

day where a madman wearing a mask of human skin was chasing me with a chainsaw. My contribution to the national discussion consisted of a couple of amusing tweets that I deleted after deciding that lighthearted fun was not the way to go at the moment.

The day after that, today, I chugged some Pepto-Bismol and got back to work. My stomach isn't hurting as much. I have taken (false?) solace in some articles about how this isn't necessarily going to lead to a post-apocalyptic hellscape. As you read this, I might not be subsiding on a diet of radioactive vermin! Gosh, that would be swell.

So, this isn't really the general "politics and horror" introduction I meant to write, but my mind is engulfed by thoughts of politics, and I'm scared. Sadly, this is going to be timely for much longer than my other draft...

I'm writing this introduction in scary times. The authors in this anthology had their work cut out for them in trying to come up with politically themed material that's scarier than the real world, right now.

Maybe things worked out okay. Maybe this anthology is a collection of horror stories. Tales to keep you up at night. Tales to send a shiver down your spine.

Or maybe these stories have become the equivalent of a romance novel. Quaint tales to distract you from the outside world, to immerse yourself in fantasies of better times.

You already know.

I don't yet, so I'll be hiding under the bed.

DIE!

THE WAR ROOM

by Paul Moore

It was a small moment. Minuscule, quiet. A soft tap on the shoulder delivered in passing. An afterthought. A casual gesture like so many made during a busy day. One more insignificant connection amid the gestures, expressions and acknowledgments that punctuated the flurries of chaos and celebration that spun, unfurled and dissipated in the War Room.

The War Room.

It was a silly name perpetuated by a pompous sense of importance and popular zeitgeist. Elections were not wars. They barely qualified as battles. At best, they were skirmishes decided by men who lived in ivory towers consorting with men of shadow, in underground networks designed to increase profit and power from the sediment of eroded trust and virtue. A cycle of abuse that would one day end when these men of ill-intent eventually carved away enough of the nation's bedrock and the entire system collapsed.

But that would be then, and then was far from Kara's mind. She was in the War Room and in that room the only thing that mattered was now. And though she had not considered it until now, there were no insignificant connections in the War Room.

Kara glanced up from the computer monitor as Burke passed. She caught his eye, confirming she had not imagined the tap. Despite appearing absorbed with his phone, Burke was ready to speak with her. Outside of the public arena. Outside of the War Room.

And that was what people called a big deal. Burke was an important man. A very important man. A kingmaker. The real power behind many thrones; the kind of thrones whose existence was unknown to most people.

Kara tapped two keys and an expanding bar flickered at the bottom of the screen as her progress was saved. Interesting concept, saving progress, but the time for such thoughts was late at night after a few glasses of wine. At the moment, her thoughts could be summed up in two sentences.

Burke tapped you for a reason. Whatever it is, do not fuck it up.

Kara moved with efficient speed. A stride that communicated, I know where I am going, why I am going there, and anything impeding my progress will be met with a reckoning most men would wish to avoid. It was one of the many talents she had developed in graduate school and the workplace beyond.

It was also a lie.

Kara rarely knew where she was going, or why, as she moved from hotel to hotel based on the whims of her many bosses. Questions beyond bare logistics strained their tolerance and were never answered. They only communicated their need.

As for her reckoning with the men in her life, they were like freckles, or warts. After awhile, you just stopped counting; you never started caring. Burn them, freeze them or camouflage them; just never acknowledge them.

Long ago, she had given herself to the political machine. A collection of vast, rusting gears that mercilessly ground anything remotely human into dust. Soulless or not, this was the world she chose to inhabit and had committed herself to rule. It was an ambitious promise, one she pledged to herself to keep. A lofty goal for anyone.

Anyone who was not Kara Jefferson.

It was her turn. Whatever came next, it was hers to embrace and reject. Opportunities were like men, she seldom rejected them; milked them until they were dry husks wilting beneath the sun that burned in her rear view mirror.

Burke was still engrossed in his phone and Kara felt a sense of self-satisfaction as she tapped his shoulder. He made no attempt to suppress his irritation as he turned and glanced at her. Kara opened her mouth to speak, but Burke had a finger already in the air to give her pause as the thumb on his other hand danced with surprising skill across the phone's screen, finishing its practiced routine with a definitive slap against the Send icon. Satisfied, Burke palmed his phone and addressed Kara. By her reckoning, the man had spoken directly to her less than a dozen times in the two years she had been working with him.

"Follow me."

Once again Kara opened her mouth to ask a few basic questions. Burke simply turned and walked away. Kara followed dutifully, but casually. Urgency would imply need. Any implication of need was a fatal mistake in the War Room.

Two flights of stairs, three hallways and four fire doors later, Burke and Kara stepped onto the loading dock. No words or glances had been exchanged during their short journey. Whatever was about to happen, it would define the course of Kara's life before the sun set. She should have been frightened.

She was excited. She had been waiting for that tap on her shoulder her entire adult life. She did not know how she knew it, but she was about to receive the keys to a kingdom known only to the select few.

"A car will be here in a few minutes," Burke announced as he checked his watch; inconspicuous, expensive. "Four to be exact."

He turned and made genuine eye contact with her for the first time.

"If you choose to take this ride, they will put a hood over your head, drive you to a place you will never find again and present you with an offer."

A single sentence that raised as many questions as it sparked fears. Kara knew not to fall into the obvious traps of where and why. But she also knew that asking nothing did not imply fearlessness, but blind obedience. Men of substance had no use for the blind in the courts of their kings. Blind devotion was a quality only prized in soldiers destined to die on hills that history quickly forgot.

Kara was not a soldier. She was a gun for hire, and like any good mercenary she wanted the bottom line.

"What kind of offer?"

Burke took a moment either to size her up or to consider his answer. Either way, his cloud gray eyes were inscrutable.

"The kind of offer you accept."

Kara did not hesitate.

"I'll be the judge of that. It's still my life."

"It is," Burke noted without a hint of emotion, "And you'll accept if you want to keep it that way."

He glanced at his watch.

"Two minutes, forty-eight seconds." He pinned her once again with his eyes. "Go ahead."

The smug permission under any other circumstances would be infuriating. But Kara knew from experience that those one hundred and sixty-eight seconds were a rare gift from a man like Burke.

She chose not to waste them with faux indignation.

"And if I don't?" Kara asked as she decided to play along with Burke's obvious game of follow- the-leader.

"Your desk will be cleaned out, your hotel room, phone, social media accounts, et cetera will be scrubbed, altered and deleted as necessary. An explanation for your death has already been written, printed and sealed," Burke stated with no more gravitas than someone reciting a grocery list might use. "You will disappear. Your body will resurface at whatever time and place deemed necessary for the purposes of your former employers."

Kara should have been shocked, frightened, outraged. She should have turned away, tendered her resignation, packed her bags and caught the first flight out of town. But she was not only resolute in her ambition, she was curious. She was about to roam the halls of power. True power. Some part of her needed more than anything to know the price of that privilege.

Once again, Burke consulted his watch.

"Thirty-two seconds," Burke announced. "Not too late to go back to your desk."

They both knew how the scenario would unfold.

"Not enough time for Twenty Questions." Kara joked, dryly.

"No. But time enough for one more."

"Are you coming along for the ride?"

"No. I will be there later tonight if everything goes as predicted."

"Predicted," Kara mused. "You're all very sure of yourselves."

"Elections are not won with uncertainty, Miss Jefferson," Burke observed. "They are won with the knowledge that whoever spills the most blood controls the tide."

A black SUV turned into the alley as Burke turned toward her for a final time. It was the last time she would see him in the daylight.

"Last chance."

"I know," she responded, "That's why I'm still here."

Burke's lips curled upward in the the slightest hint of a smile.

"You do not disappoint, Kara."

Burke's use of her first name was enough to cause her breath to catch in her throat. Whatever was coming, whatever happened after she climbed into the SUV, whatever this was all about, it was big. Bigger than anything she had dared consider up to this point.

Burke extended his hand, palm facing upward, as the black SUV rolled to a stop next to the loading dock.

"Surrender your phone."

Kara pulled it from her pocket and laid it in his outstretched palm.

"Is there anything else I'll be required to surrender?"

"Yes." Burke answered as he pocketed her phone. "It was an honor working with you, Miss Jefferson. I wish you well."

The doors to the SUV opened and two goons who looked like

they had been sent from Central Casting approached the loading dock. Burke did not acknowledge them, or Kara. He simply turned and reentered the building.

Somewhere in Kara's brain, primitive cells flared; a single word splashing across the screen in the theater of her mind.

RUN!

However it was only a flicker. An overlooked frame by an editor who had worked too long and too late on his magnum opus; a movie too many years in the making, with too much blood in the bins. Whatever happened now was of no importance. What was important was completing the final reel. Seeing the last act through to the end.

Is that what this is? Kara thought, the final act?

She did not know. On a more immediate level, she did not care.

Kara nodded to the men as she descended the steps and climbed into the waiting vehicle. Moments later, the door closed behind her as a black hood was slipped over her head.

Kara held her breath as darkness swallowed her world.

The ride was long and silent. No music from the radio, no idle chatter among the three men in the SUV, no sound whatsoever excepting the occasional squeak of someone's weight shifting against the leather seats.

Kara noted it was also a smooth ride. A few stops and starts as they navigated the city, but once they found the open road any changes in direction were subtle. Every turn was economic and precise.

Her sense of time was stunted beneath the hood; it felt like they had been driving for eons. In the absence of any stimulation, Kara had taken to quietly counting the seconds. They stretched into minutes, grew into hours. Two and a half by her count. Kara gave herself a plus-or-minus margin of error of thirty minutes, but regardless, they were well outside of Washington. Maybe Maryland, maybe Virginia. There was even the outside possibility they had driven to the West Virginian panhandle or southern Pennsylvania.

None of it mattered. Kara was certain that wherever they were, she would never find it again and there would be nobody within ten miles without top level security clearance. She was alone. The men in the car with her were killers. No, killers was the wrong word. They were...

Assassins.

A wave of regret rippled beneath her skin. Sucking stale air through thick burlap, Kara realized there was no way out of the situation. Her option was to survive it. And to survive it, she would have to go through it.

Kara wondered what her odds at survival were. After a moment of consideration, she decided they were alarmingly low no matter which way she zigged or zagged. Dead or alive, Kara was in the briar patch.

Without warning, the thin air inside the hood evaporated. Kara struggled to control her breathing. Any sign of weakness would doom her.

She clenched her hands against her thighs, tightened her muscles. She focused intently and attempted to calm her body as it threatened hysterics. Pulses of blistering air funneled past her lips. In a matter of moments, the realization of her foolish choice seized her. She was going to die. Alone. No explanation. No body.

No Kara. It would be as if she never existed. She considered her options. Decided her best chance for a painless...

The SUV rolled to a stop. A moment later, a faint whine penetrated her canvas hood; the sound of a window opening. Cool air rushed into the SUV. That same air carried faint noises of chirping insects and the echo of a purring engine.

"Cards and papers."

Rustling.

"Thank you."

A few beeps. Something like a bar code scanner at a

supermarket.

"Umm..." a few clicks "How should I log this, sir?"

"However you want," the voice was as cold as a January morning, "It's not my fucking problem."

"Yessir," said the man who had shifted into complete subservience.

Kara knew the guy guarding the gate was military, and probably no slouch. Wherever they had taken her, it was no minimum security facility, and critical facilities were never manned by the bottom of the class.

The fact that he acquiesced so quickly to such a dismissive tone told Kara that she was riding with some very formidable men. She had no doubt that other people had taken this ride, and she was also certain it had not ended well for many of them.

And how does it end for you? Kara thought.

She declined to answer herself. That ship had sailed as soon as she had entered the SUV.

The driver rolled up the window as soon as they cleared the gate. Kara began her count again and by her estimation, they traveled four minutes at a low speed before they stopped. No one said a word as the doors opened and the men exited the vehicle.

A moment later, Kara's door opened. A firm hand gripped her upper arm as someone guided her out of the SUV.

"This way," a voice commanded, devoid of emotion. Kara realized that she had been reduced to something less than human; a package. Something to be delivered. Nothing more.

Kara did her best to walk steadily as the gripping hand led her forward. The man who was assisting her was patient, but unforgiving. She felt a slight, painful twist every time she threatened to veer off course.

The sounds of the footsteps around her informed her that her escort consisted of two men. Perhaps the driver stayed behind, or had fallen back in the event Kara had a change of heart. Sweat began to bead beneath the hood. Kara was beginning to believe that perhaps she had not been selected for a special assignment.

Perhaps she had inadvertently crossed someone who should not have been crossed.

Burke?

No. Burke would not go to such lengths to dismiss her. The information she had processed was sensitive, but not critical. If he wanted her off the campaign, he would have simply pink-slipped her. This was something bigger.

She took another step and the hand restrained her as she came to an awkward stop. Seconds later, Kara heard a beep and a click.

Key card, she thought.

Moments later, she was in a corridor, concrete by the sound of the echoing footsteps. The cool air was a relief, the air inside her hood stifling. Kara knew better than to reach for it. Any sign of weakness would be fatal at this point.

Just because she had entered the belly of the beast, it did not mean all of the teeth were behind her. Like all secret installations, Kara was sure this one had levels. And the further one descended, the darker those levels became. A verse from Dante's Inferno flashed through her mind.

In the middle of the journey of our life, I found myself within a dark woods where the straight way was lost.

Had her ambition delivered her to the Nine Circles? And if so, how far down was she required to go? And what would she find?

On cue, the guiding hand halted her. A moment later, there was a soft ding followed by the sound of elevator doors sliding open. The firm hand urged her forward and turned her. A few seconds passed and the doors slid shut. A gentle thrum could be felt through the floor as the elevator descended.

Well that's a little on the nose, Kara mused.

Kara had stopped counting steps and seconds, but the ride felt like a minute.

How many floors in a minute? Kara queried herself. She realized she had no answer. It was not one of those things people typically pondered.

Another ding, more sliding doors and another long walk through another cold hallway. Kara had decided that enough was now officially enough. If her journey did not end at the next doorway, she was going to remove the hood and start asking questions. She understood that would most likely be a fatal action, but she had determined that if her head was to be laid on the chopping block, she would look her executioner in the eyes.

A door opened and closed and the echo of their footsteps disappeared. They were in a much smaller space. Her handler, for lack of better word, stayed her.

"Wait here," he ordered.

Kara did not think about it. She simply acted.

She reached up and peeled the hood from her head. Cool air rushed across her face as she sucked it into her lungs. The lights in the room were dim, but Kara still found herself blinking them away. She focused on the two men before her, the same men who she had met at the loading dock.

They stared back at her. She read alarm, indecision. She had broken the rules; they were weighing their options. Kara decided she would help them make up their minds.

"If you're going to do it," she stated, "then do it. None of us are getting any younger."

The two men glanced at one another as they passed a nearly imperceptible communique. The moment hung between all three of them.

"Wait here," the taller of the two men repeated.

Without waiting for a response, he turned, tapped a code into a keypad and exited through the room's other door. Kara turned to face her remaining escort, who still wore his cliched sunglasses.

"Too bright for you?" she quipped.

He ignored her.

"Strong, silent type, huh?"

Silence.

"I guess you wouldn't want to break character," she observed, trying to elicit a response. Any response. She needed information. as much information as she could acquire before stepping through the next door. So far, she was failing dismally.

His silence did tell her a few things. He was under orders and he was intent on following them. That made him disciplined and resolute. It also meant he would have no compunction about carrying out orders that were less than favorable to Kara's health and well being.

These men were trained killers. There would be no negotiating or pleading if the situation devolved into a dark place.

If it gets any darker than standing with murders in a subterranean bunker, Kara thought, the only thing I'm going to need is a priest or an exorcist.

She was just beginning to reflect on the concept that those two things were one and the same, only differentiated by the light in which they were cast, when the coded door opened and the taller handler returned.

He held the door open.

"Walk to the end of the corridor and stand in front of the door. Touch nothing and wait. Are we clear?"

Everything about his tone implied that any deviation from those directives would have nothing less than fatal consequences.

What have I done?

Kara did not bother to answer as she nodded. She was through the looking glass and any further reflection was academic. She had gone all in without seeing the cards, and that only ever worked in the movies.

But she had been invited to the big table and she knew that only power players were allowed a seat. And they did not tolerate weakness or fear. Weakness was an accusation that had never been leveled at Kara. As for fear, that was an essential element of survival.

And Kara was nothing if not a survivor.

There was a cold, definitive clack as the door closed behind her.

It was the longest walk of Kara's life. The hallway was nothing more than concrete and recessed lights. Each step was the tick of a slowing metronome. The temperature in the corridor bordered on uncomfortably cold and yet, sweat was soaking through Kara's clothes and slicking her face.

A steel door loomed ahead.

As she grew closer, she saw it had no handle, knob or keypad. An additional shiver ran through her and it had nothing to do with her cool surroundings. It had to do with intuition.

Entering that door was a one way trip.

Kara arrived and followed the taller goon's instructions to the word. Standing in a pool of stark light she felt her stomach knot and her bowels loosen.

This is it.

After an interminable moment, a click echoed along the concrete. The door opened to reveal Burke.

"You broke the rules."

No fear, no weakness, Kara reminded herself.

"You rigged the game."

The corners of Burke's lips twitched upward.

"You're half right," he responded. "Are you ready?"

"I'm here."

He swept his arm toward the darkness behind him.

"After you," he informed.

Of all the things that Kara would later try to forget, the look in his eyes would always be at the top of the list.

It was a long walk, and like Dante following Virgil, she saw, heard and felt too many things to be processed in the moment. Her body became more numb with each step and the more she heard and saw; the more her mind resisted.

No, that's not right...

The more her soul resisted. In truth, her mind had nearly

succumbed and was just waiting for her soul to get the memo.

"Kara, what would you say are the most divisive issues in American politics?"

"In this election, or overall?"

"Good question. Overall."

"Who's in charge?"

A few steps of silence as hollow footsteps echoed past increasingly bizarre scenes unfolding behind glass walls that were several feet thick.

"I have to admit, I don't completely understand your answer, because I know you're not talking about the President."

"No. I'm not."

More footsteps. Intermittent darkness.

"I'm talking about God."

"Explain."

"Most people vote their beliefs. Some defer to the spiritual, others to the logical. Some see themselves as saving the world, others see themselves as shaping it, changing it into something better,"

"Which side is right?"

"Who knows and who cares? You said I was half-right."

"I did."

"And that's because the game is rigged. You're just not the one who rigged it."

A few more hollow steps. Things pulsed and undulated behind the impenetrable glass.

"I knew selecting you was the right call."

"I suppose we'll know soon enough."

'"Drop the tough act. Tell me about God."

"Never met Him."

"Does he exist?"

"Like I said, never met Him."

"Do we have souls? Because that is really the core of your argument."

"I'll leave that to the theologians. My position changes with my employer. That's politics."

"So you have no conviction on the subject."

"I didn't say that. You're confusing the words 'conviction' and 'position.'"

"No..."

Wet, slurping sounds. Muffled by the glass, but unmistakable.

"...I was making sure that you weren't confused."

"What is confusing me is what I'm seeing."

"Processing. Those men in the hazmat suits are handling our nation's most precious resource. Preparing it to remove impurities and begin distillation."

"Those containers are all marked as medical waste. How do you purify broken needles and tainted gauze?"

"I wouldn't know."

They arrived at a large steel door that looked as if it were built to withstand a nuclear blast at ground zero. Formidable and imposing, built to keep out an army.

Or imprison one.

"Purification here is about one thing, and one thing only."

"And that is...?"

Burke looked at her for the first time since they had entered the corridor. His eyes had all of the emotion of a glacier.

"Deboning."

As if on cue, gears ground as the steel doors began to separate. Kara's breath caught in her throat as she realized the gravity of her situation. Every conceivable scenario evaporated in her mind and dispersed like ash in the wind.

"After you."

Kara's feet moved independently of her shattered mind as she stepped over the threshold and sealed her fate.

There were hundreds of them crouched in the darkness beneath the catwalk. Leathery, translucent skin rippled and pulsed. Bony, elongated hands flexed as black talons plucked bits of gelatinous flesh from the slow moving slurry of grue flowing through the troughs that stretched before them. Saliva dripped from irregular fangs as their tongues dipped into the stream of liquefied flesh.

No, Kara's mind stated as it struggled to make sense of the otherworldly scene beneath her, not tongues... proboscises.

Fluid traveled upward through the translucent, pulsing tubes as veined bellies throbbed. Eyes, overgrown with cataracts, fluttered behind thin lids. With the exception of the slurps and sucking sounds, the room was silent. Kara dared not speak as fear coursed through her own veins.

Burke had no such reservations.

"The first time is always a bit..." he scanned his inner lexicon for the least alarming word, "Unsettling."

"What are they?"

"Republicans, Democrats, House, Senate..." Burke said, "And the next two presidential candidates, of course."

Somewhere deep in Kara's brain the pieces were starting to come together, but the shock of witnessing the macabre menagerie below her had numbed her brain. She was still processing questions and answers in simple binary chunks.

"No," Kara said as she locked eyes with Burke, "What are they?"

He disengaged his eyes from hers and returned his attention to the feeding monstrosities below. For the first time in Kara's entire time of knowing Burke, she witnessed true emotion on his face. The sight was so alien, that she had trouble recognizing what he was expressing. After a moment, it came to her. It was not one emotion;

it was two.

Fear and awe.

"They're an ancient race," he started, "predating mankind. From our communications with them, we've learned that they age in millennia, not years. We also learned through centuries of conflict that they are nearly indestructible. Our distant ancestors were able to coexist with them, much in the way that water buffaloes learned to live with tigers."

"And how is that?"

"Sacrificing a few at a time for the good of the herd."

Kara noticed his expression had changed from awe to reverence as he continued.

"But that was when the world was big, and we went and made it small. War was inevitable. A war we would have lost. It would have destroyed humanity, so a truce was struck. As best as we could tell, the truce was put into effect shortly after Nero fiddled his closing number."

"What was the truce?"

Burke leaned his elbows against the catwalk's rail and licked his lips. It was a jarring moment for Kara. She had never seen so much expression from Burke.

"We would be spared as long as they were allowed to rule us. They're changelings. They can assume the form of creatures that they consume. As long as those creatures are roughly the same size and shape, of course."

The pieces were falling into place quickly for Kara. She was no longer stunned. She was horrified.

"You mean..."

"Every king, queen, czar, prime minster, dictator, Pope or president has been one of them. Candidates are chosen and consumed and then after an incubation period, one of them emerges and ascends to its designated position."

A flash of shadowy movement caught the corner of Kara's eye. She glanced below, but nothing else moved.

"For the benefit of humans, the illusion of free will must be maintained. The truth would be too much. So we keep the elections, the due process, but none of it means anything. The results are predetermined and many of those creatures have served as the leaders of men more than once. We just repackage and recycle them. But in the end, it's all the same. The illusion of choice."

"And what do they get out of all this?" Kara asked. She could feel the beginnings of anger bubbling inside her. Anger that would become rage.

She had spent her entire adult life devoted to the concept of channeling power through choice. The idea of changing society through manipulation and barter. Now she was being told that her lifelong pursuit was nothing more than a charade. A house of cards.

"What do they get?" Burke repeated, "They get fed. And they have a very particular diet."

A shuffling sound whispered from the shadows to Kara's left. She turned her head, but again, nothing moved.

"And that diet is us." Kara surmised.

"Sort of."

Kara turned her attention away from the shadows and back to Burke.

"They can sustain themselves on fully developed humans, but according to them, we don't taste all that great. They prefer their meals a little less developed. A little more tender."

The sounds in the corridor, the processing behind the glass, the medical waste containers... The pieces were slamming into place inside Kara's aching brain. The anger had coalesced into rage and Kara was barely containing it.

"What is in those troughs?" Kara demanded.

"Umm..." Burke sighed, "Stillborns from hospitals, the occasional abandoned newborn, but mostly fetal tissue from clinics. I'm told they're most fond of anything that was harvested in the second trimester."

Burke's response was so matter of fact that it chilled Kara's veins, the fury inside her freezing. Behind her, a soft scraping sound echoed along the catwalk as a shape emerged from the shadows. Something large and inhuman.

Kara did not have to turn to look. She knew what it was.

"Why did you show me this?"

"Because I've been watching you for years. You're efficient, you're resolute, highly intelligent, capable of making logical decisions devoid of emotion, and easy on the eyes. Everything we need."

The soft sounds of creaking metal and shifting muscle continued behind her. The thing was growing closer. Kara kept her eyes pinned on Burke.

"Everything you need for what?"

"I have good news and bad news, Kara," Burke began. "The good news is that you are going to be the next President of the United States..."

For the first time in Kara's life, she saw Burke smile. His lips peeled away from his teeth in a wide grin. Despite all she had seen and heard, it was Burke's grin that terrified her the most.

"The bad news," Burke said, grinning, "is that you won't be alive to see it."

Kara closed her eyes as darkness consumed her.

Taking a pledge against
END HOMELESSNESS.
The Co-operative
PROSECUTED, SUPPRESSED, OR B
OUR VIEW
WE HAVE FAR WORSE
THAN A DEBT CRISIS
This is dawning of demographic poverty
shelter to close
INDEPENDENT
poor gap
on focus
be not
FEDERAL RESE
Smaller Shelters and Persuasion Coax Homeless Off Bronx Streets
THAN A DEBT CRISIS
Ever More Homeless Families
poverty

THE BLOOD OF PATRIOTS AND TYRANTS

by Ray Garton

Duncan's eyelids peeled apart and light punched his eyeballs so hard that he pressed the lids together again. He was lying on his back in a cool bed with crisp sheets in a room filled with the gentle humming of machinery and the smell of alcohol and other chemicals. He tried opening his eyes again, slowly this time.

The light that had stabbed his eyes a moment ago turned out to be not very bright after all. It was soft and diffuse and everything seemed to have a gray look to it. Duncan was not sure if that was caused by whatever drugs he had been given or if the room was truly gray. He did not care.

He felt floaty and kind of transparent, as if he were still in the process of taking on, once again after what seemed so long, the form of Duncan Hauser, a thirteen-year-old paperboy for the Norrington News, who had been dragged into a van...how long ago? Was he still thirteen? He could not think clearly enough at the moment to figure any of it out.

When he tried to move his weak arms, he found that they were shackled to the railings at the wrists. Tape on his right arm held fast a narrow, worm-like tube that clearly contained his blood.

His neck was stiff, but he turned his head slowly to the right, pressing his ear into the pillow. The head of his bed was slightly elevated, just like the bed beside him. A rather mountainous figure seemed to be scrunched beneath the sheet, shoulders hunched. His head was on the pillow: a long forehead that curved down from short, wavy tufts of white hair; brown plastic-frame glasses on a large, beak-like nose that became bulbous at the end; a small mouth that ended abruptly in a fat cheek, a chin lost in folds, and no visible neck, only the shoulder hunched up to his ear and that round torso that made a great dome of the white sheet. His unshackled left arm, which appeared too short for his body, lay limp beside him like a lumpy, pale slug, and also had a slender, red tube taped to it. His eyes were closed. Duncan wondered if the man was dead. The flabby skin of his face was as gray as the room.

He straightened his head and looked up at the ceiling again, only vaguely wondering where he was. He was more concerned about what would happen to him next. What would be done to him next.

When he looked to his left, he saw only a gray wall. He appeared to be in a hospital, but there were none of the usual sounds of bustling movement and activity, no sign at all that there were other people around.

Duncan started to speak, but his voice was a dry croak, so he cleared his throat, then tried again.

"Where am I?"

He heard movement in the bed beside him, then a low, gravelly voice.

"Yuddavake."

Duncan squinted at him. "What?"

The man repeated himself, "You're awake," and Duncan realized that he spoke with a grave German accent and pronounced his Ws like Vs.

Duncan said, "Yes, I'm awake."

"What is your name, young man?"

"Duncan Hauser."

"Hauser. A good German name. Your parents are German?"

"No, they're locals. My dad's an alcoholic, if that counts."

The man looked at the ceiling as his body shook silently with laughter. After a while, he said, "You're very funny, Duncan. But you should never volunteer information. Wait until someone asks for it, then decide if you want to share it or lie. How old are you?"

"That depends. What's the date?"

He shook with laughter again. "You kill me."

"No, really. I'm serious. What's the date?"

"December twenty-one."

"Almost Christmas," Duncan muttered. "What year?" The man frowned at him for a moment, then told him. He said, "I'm fourteen. And a half. How old are you?"

Another silent, shaking laugh. "Far older than I feel, I'm happy to say."

"You aren't dying?"

"Far from it. Fourteen and a half. You're the oldest I've had so far."

"Oldest you've had for what?"

"Most of them are younger. And unconscious. You're a bright boy. Do you get high marks in school?"

"Not lately. I haven't been in school for a while. I've spent some time in a cage, though."

"A cage. Well, now. Life is full of unexpected turns, Duncan. We must learn to take them as gracefully as possible."

He did not know what that meant and did not really care. Duncan was more interested in talking to someone in charge, someone not in a bed attached to tubes. But when he looked around, he saw no one, and when he listened, he heard no sounds of others nearby. But he heard the old man in the other bed mumbling. He had the back of his head turned to Duncan as he spoke quietly, his voice like rocks shifting underground. Was he talking to himself or was there someone on the other side of his bed? It was impossible to tell from Duncan's vantage point.

When the mumbling stopped, Duncan said, "Where are we?"

The man turned to him again. "The New World Clinic." It came out Da New Verld Clinic.

"What are we doing here?"

"Just a procedure, nothing more. I never get to talk to the donors because they're always sedated."

"Donors?"

"Tell me about yourself, Duncan."

"Like what?" Donors? What kind of donors? Duncan would

have to come back to that and ask.

"Oh, I don't know. You can tell me about your family, or about school. Or about how you got here. It's up to you. We're not going anywhere." He chuckled and it sounded like two bricks being rapidly struck together. "I'm not, anyway."

"I got here...in a van. A big white van with no windows."

It was a sunny but chilly October morning filled with orange leaves, the smell of wood smoke, and pumpkins on porches. He'd had the paper route since the beginning of summer and had sharpened his aim, rarely missing the porches now.

The paper route took Duncan out of the dingy trailer park where he lived and sent him on his bike through lovely neighborhoods with manicured lawns and shrubbery and American flags waving majestically in the breeze. Colorful cutouts of witches and ghosts were taped to windows and crepe skeletons swayed from tree limbs. On some of the lawns, elaborate animatronic decorations went through their dances or large, inflated monsters towered over rosebushes and birdbaths.

The homes looked solid and safe and somehow happy. Whatever went on inside, they looked happy. But Duncan knew better. Most of them probably were not happy at all and just had good paint jobs or nice siding.

The trailer park wasn't so bad, really. It did not hold up well when compared with his paper route neighborhood, but on its own it made a good home. They had lived in a house once, but then the furniture factory where Dad had worked his whole life had laid off a lot of people, including Dad, then, just a couple of months later, closed its doors for good to move to China. Later that year, he had fallen off the roof stringing up the Christmas lights and broken his back. He had walked with a cane ever since. And he had been drunk ever since.

They lost the house and moved to Sunny Oaks Mobile Home Park, where Dad began to drink. It softened him, made him funny, but he cried easily and usually fell asleep in his chair. Duncan suspected it had been sinking him deeper into depression, but he kept those thoughts to himself. If Dad mixed liquor with painkillers, which he had been doing with increasing frequency, he became mean. As soon as he saw Dad reach for the pill bottle, Duncan went to his room or left the trailer. His sister Susan usually stuck around to watch some dumb singing competition on TV, or something. She was a lot better than Duncan at tuning out everything around her.

After dad's surgery, Mom had to go to work and took whatever jobs she could. On the day that Duncan made what was unknowingly his final delivery run, she was working two jobs: Target during the day and cleaning medical offices at night. While he was tossing papers, Susan was probably eating breakfast in the kitchen, probably one of the hot cereals she liked so much. Dad would, no doubt, still be in bed. He liked to be up in time to watch the last segment of *Today*, hosted by Kathie Lee Gifford and Hoda Kotb, while he had his Pop Tarts and beer. He was fond of the hosts because they drank wine during the show, which was broadcast live, and he said as far as he was concerned, any women who drank before noon five days a week were worth paying attention to.

Duncan was on the last block of his route when the van pulled over in front of him and came to an abrupt stop. He stopped his bike, then was about to go around the van when the door opened and a heavy guy in a dark blue jumpsuit got out.

"Hey, kid, can you give me a hand for a second?" he said.

"Well, I've gotta finish my paper on—"

"It'll just take a second, I swear. All I need is for you to hold open the back door for me. Otherwise it'll swing closed. Come on, take a second, give me a hand, and I'll give you five bucks."

"Really?"

"Sure."

Duncan got off his bike, pulled it over to the curb, and dropped the kickstand. He went to the van as the man opened the two back doors.

"You need to climb inside so you'll be out of the way, then reach out and hold this door open," he said of the door on the right.

Duncan climbed up into the van and that was the last thing he could remember from that whole day.

As he finished telling the German man about himself, Duncan realized that whatever drug he had been under was not wearing off. It seemed, instead, to be regaining its effectiveness. He felt a growing heaviness in his eyes. And in his head.

"You have to be ready for surprises, Duncan," the man said. "Do you think I saw Woodward and Bernstein coming?" He looked at the ceiling again. "They were onto a story, sure, and it was big, but what happened was absurd. They virtually became movie stars while some good men were destroyed. Well. Maybe not *good* men. But still. Ridiculous. Fortunately, I managed to get through that difficulty unscathed."

Duncan continued to look at him, but the man stopped talking. A moment later, he turned to Duncan again.

"You have no idea what I'm talking about, of course," he said.

"No, I don't." He wondered if the man had heard anything he had said about being kidnapped by a guy in a van.

"You're too young, much too young to remember any of that nonsense. Forgive me. I tend to ramble at times. But I'm an old man, so I'm entitled. Of course I'm an old man, or I wouldn't be here." He chuckled. "Tell me, Duncan, in school do you ever fight? With other boys?"

"No."

"Never?"

"No, never."

"Because you are afraid?"

"Of pain, yeah. I'd rather settle things in other ways."

"Ah, yes." His small mouth broke open in a smile. "A boy after my own heart. Avoid the pain. Just as I did back then. But you will find, Duncan, that in life fighting is at times a necessity. Perhaps not with your fists, but still fighting nonetheless. You must fight for what you believe in, for what you stand for."

There was something Duncan was going to ask him, but he could not remember what it was. Instead, he stayed with the present discussion. "What do you believe in and stand for?" Duncan said.

"Myself, mostly. Just as you do when you avoid the pain, when you find other ways of settling things. In my case, of course, there are always vast sums of money involved, but the principle is the same. Have you ever settled a fight between two other boys?"

"No."

"Mm. You're better off. You should try negotiating peace between the Arabs and Israelis. That will make you want to do something else in a hurry, I can tell you."

Neither of them spoke for a while and the machinery hummed along. Duncan did not feel good. He was beginning to feel somehow...hollow. He had felt a growing hollowness ever since he had been picked up by the man in the van, ever since his life had abruptly ended, to be replaced by a perverted nightmare. But that was a spiritual hollowness. This was different. He felt like his bones were actually hollowing out and he was growing lighter, less substantial. From the inside.

He had always been able to avoid fights at school, but he would happily trade years of them for the battle he had been waging for the past year. He would prefer to have taken dozens of punches to the face than a single silver-haired politician in his mouth or a movie star or televangelist in his ass. He would rather be ganged up on by an army of bullies than be gangbanged by a bunch of rich men at another afterparty, or after-afterparty, where they would insist that he snort their powders with them, take their pills, drink their liquor. Meanwhile, there would be cameras and microphones everywhere, recording everything from every possible angle. It didn't matter whether it was in Washington or Beverly Hills, everything was recorded. Nothing was missed and nothing would be forgotten. And Duncan did as he was told or, he had been assured, his entire family would be killed. And so would he.

"What do you like to do for fun, Duncan?" the man said.

Not that, he thought. His chest felt heavy as he took in a breath. "I like baseball. And books, I like to read. I want to be a writer."

"Ah. My advice is to get rich first. Then be a writer."

"What's happening to me?"

"Beg pardon?"

"I feel, um...funny. I don't know. Weird."

"Ah, yes. That happens."

"What happens? What is it?"

"It's called parabiosis."

"That sounds scary."

"No, it's quite extraordinary. Quite recently, the procedure has been marketed publicly. Of course, the price is so exorbitant that only the very wealthy can afford it. But it has been in use for some time now. Twenty years or so. Very quietly."

"But what does it...you know, do?"

"It is a transfusion, Duncan, a blood transfusion. Do you know what that is?"

"I'm...not sure."

"Your blood is being transfused into my body."

Duncan felt a chill and a sinking feeling of dread pulling him downward. "Why?"

"Young blood rejuvenates old bodies, Duncan. The heart, the liver, the lungs, the brain, all are strengthened. The process extends life, and improves the quality of life in those extended years."

"How...old are you?"

"I am about to turn one hundred years old." He smiled. "Can you believe it? I have this done twice a year and I have the health of a man in his thirties. Of course, my body still shows the effects of aging. I have arthritis, a few things like that. All the wrinkles and sags, of course. But inside, my organs are strong and healthy because of this procedure. Most importantly, my brain functions excellently. I can think clearly, and therefore, I can continue my work."

"What kind of...work?"

"I'm a diplomat, a political consultant. I have single-handedly, Duncan, brought peace to warring nations, negotiated treaties. I have dealt with international crises and tense face-offs between nations. After I left government, I worked as a consultant to multinational corporations, governments. I served on the boards of directors of enormous, world-moving companies. I have, in fact, made colossal fortunes for some of the world's most important men. I was appointed by the president to chair a committee to investigate the September 11 attacks. You know about 9/11?"

Duncan was a little surprised by how slowly he responded, by the slurred sound of his own words. "I've seen videos on YouTube."

"Yes. Terrible thing. Anyway, I accepted the appointment, but they wanted me to release a complete list of all my clients. Had they not insisted on that, there would have been no problem. None at all. But they insisted I release the list, which would have suddenly brought on cries of conflicts of interest, and a lot of unpleasant press and public difficulty that I chose to avoid by ultimately stepping down. Such unnecessary nonsense. But my point is that, in all humility, Duncan, I am a very important man. Some might say a great man. The world needs me. That's why it is important that I have access to this procedure, so that I can continue my work and go on making the world a better place for so many. And thanks to young people like you, I can."

Duncan slowly took in deep breath, then let it out in a weary sigh. "That's what they've got me doing now?" he said. "Donating blood to you guys?"

"I'm sorry, I don't understand, Duncan. What do you mean?"

He spoke slowly. "First I'm...forced to have sex with all these old rich guys...while it's all secretly caught on video...and I'm forced to make porn movies with old men...and now I've gotta...donate fucking blood to you people? I just want to...go home. I don't feel good. What's happening to me?"

"Just a natural reaction to the procedure. Nothing to worry about. What do you mean, Duncan, when you say you were forced to have sex with people. When? By whom?"

"Over a year. Since I was taken by that...guy in the van I told you about." Duncan turned his head slowly to the right.

The man frowned and his tall forehead became a corrugated knot of gray flesh. "A year and a half? That cannot be right. What have you been doing in all that time?"

Duncan looked up at the ceiling and told him.

The man's frown became angry as he lifted his head from the pillow and turned to his right. He said something, and a figure stood on the other side of the bed, a slender, stern-looking woman, who quickly said, "Yes, sir," and hurried away.

"This is outrageous," the man said, his voice angry now as he muttered to himself. Then he turned again to Duncan and smiled. "I apologize for the interruption, Duncan."

"What's happening to me?" he said, his voice weak. "It's getting...worse."

"Duncan, you are making a tremendous contribution to the betterment of the world, I assure you."

"Contri...bution?"

The woman returned with a man in black pants, a white shirt, and a long, white coat with a stethoscope around his neck.

The man in the bed lifted his head again. He raised his voice only slightly, but his anger was clear. "I signed a contract assuring me that you would use only untouched donors. No sex, no drugs. And you specified children. He is over fourteen years old. He was taken more than a year ago and has been in active circulation the entire time."

"Sir, I don't understand," the man in the white coat said, suddenly tense as he looked at Duncan. "He's not even supposed to be conscious."

"We've been talking for some time now and it has been quite revealing. I demand a full refund with compensation for the risks incurred by this transfusion, and our contract is canceled. That won't be necessary, though, because I will have this clinic shut down before you can draft a letter of apology."

"But sir, I don't even—"

"We are finished here, Dr. Wallace."

When the doctor tried to continue, the woman put her hands on his shoulders, turned him back the way he came, and sent him on his way. She returned to her post on the other side of the old man's bed.

The man turned to Duncan and smiled again.

"Are we...almost done?" Duncan said.

"Yes, we are. You've done very well, Duncan. As I said, you have made a tremendous contribution to the good of the world in which your family lives. You should be proud."

He seemed like a nice enough man. Duncan tried to smile, but got only halfway before he could no longer keep his eyes open.

Suspended in blackness, with no physical sensations or any sense of himself, he could still hear the machinery humming quietly on and on. Until it stopped.

LEGISLATIVE
INFLUENCE

THE RETURN OF THE GIPPER

by Jason V Brock

I.

"I'm getting a little tired of everybody quoting Ronald Reagan."

—Son/Radio Host Michael Reagan

The road was long, but he was finally ready. The time had arrived, and no one was going to stop him—not God, not Satan, not Gorbachev, not anyone.

"News conferences are the only chance the American public has to see Ronald Reagan use his mind."

—Reporter Sam Donaldson

The hardest part had been the digging. After that, everything was easy. The distance did not matter.

He was on a mission.

"Nothing is going to change the fact that I believe Ronald Reagan is the greatest president in my lifetime—[and] may well be the greatest president this nation ever had."

—Lt. Col. Oliver North

It had taken him months to cross the country on foot. Longer than he anticipated. But, he had been summoned, and—this time—he was going to heed the call.

He was needed as never before.

"What we can borrow from Ronald Reagan... is that great sense of optimism. He led by building on the strengths of America, not running America down."

—NYC Mayor Rudy Giuliani

The heat of late July was stifling, but it did not bother him. He maintained his focus, plodding one foot in front of the other. He had endured the cold rains of November, the icy frosts of January, the cutting winds of March.

Nothing on Earth mattered to him but reaching his final goal, his ultimate destiny.

"The words spoken by the leader of the free world can expand the frontiers of freedom or shrink them. When Ronald Reagan called on Gorbachev to 'tear down this wall', a surge of confidence rose that would ultimately breach the bounds of the evil empire."

—Gov. Mitt Romney

He paused, swaying in the twilight. A rictus slowly twisted his features. There, gleaming on the misty horizon, the great city on a hill: Washington, D.C.

He was nearly home.

"Ronald Reagan became, you know, not only a Republican but a pretty conservative Republican—not the most. But a pretty conservative Republican. And he's somebody that I actually knew and liked. And he liked me. And I worked with him and helped him."

—Donald J. Trump

He loped by the hallowed Lincoln Memorial, ran past iconic Capitol Hill, and scaled the fence to 1600 Pennsylvania Avenue with the gusto of a man possessed.

And Hell followed with him.

II.

Despite of the hail of bullets the Secret Service had pumped into him, Ronald Reagan finally made it to the front door of the White House.

Tearing the first agent's head off with a savage and terrifyingly quick explosion of energy from his rotting hands, the former president broke the door down and was over the threshold before other agents could arrive to stop him. Once they were on-scene, Reagan dispatched one after another in an equally spectacular and gruesome manner—evisceration, dismemberment, crushing heads, gouging eyes, keening at them as he overwhelmed the agents in a supernatural display of speed, agility, and strength. In the nauseating aftermath, like some Three Stooges skit gone terribly awry, the corridors of power were running redder than the hallways of the Overlook Hotel, body parts littering the Grand Foyer.

Reagan's perfectly fixed pompadour, black and shiny, remained amazingly intact, clinging to the desiccated patches of skin still adhering to his skull. His ragged tuxedo—worm-eaten, stiffened by exposure to the elements—flapped in body-fluid stained glory as he moved with the ferocity of Bruce Lee in a blender: red, white, blue, like some sickening approximation of the American flag. Gore now freshly streaked his funerary outfit—gray brain matter, pink vomit, green bile—as he stalked his former abode, sunken eyes unblinking, clouded with decay. Ribbons of bluish flesh hung in fluttering strips from his hideously grinning face, the teeth yellowed and broken from escaping the confines of his grave in California.

"I'm... from the government and... I'm here to help. I am... the Gipper... and I have returned!" he declared, raising a bony fist into the air and shaking it in ominous triumph. He gurgled in amusement, his laughter deep and croaky as it rose from the putrid recesses of his dirt-clotted throat.

Standing once again in the antechamber of his former residence, the reanimated corpse of Reagan surveyed the chaotic scene. Before turning to leave, he used a skeletal finger to trace a message in the lake of blood staining the marble floor—the bone skittering and squealing against the stone as he wrote. In the distance, his deadened eardrums detected the wails of emergency vehicles approaching. Message delivered, he exited the demolished front door, running across the front lawn like a madman and leaping over the perimeter fence in one bound.

The journey had been long, but well worth it: The power of belief had brought him back from the dead, and just in time.

III.

There were no survivors in the brutal White House attack: Only the savagery captured by the security cameras.

"My *God*," the President said, watching the tape. "Pause it right there." Leaning in: "Is... Is that... Ronald *Reagan*?"

The Secretary of State shifted uncomfortably in her chair. The Situation Room was tense, and all of Washington had been put on High Alert. She cleared her throat.

"Yes. It appears to be. His cadaver, at least." Sensing the absurdity of her remark, she quietly added: "This is highly irregular."

The POTUS looked at her, eyes wide, and simply nodded in agreement, mouth agape. "You can say that again!" As Reagan raised his fist in defiance on the video, the President observed: "Mm, mm, *mm*. He always was a ham, wasn't he? Okay. Well, I *sure* as hell don't want the media getting wind of this—just chalk up raising the Alert Level to a terrorist threat or something." The President leveled an intense glare at the gathered members of the National Security Council while the footage looped silently in the background. "And no *leaks* for God's sake! Keep it *out* of the news cycle until after the Republican National Convention to give us a chance to create a good cover story. Damn guy's turned into some kind of conservative version of… *Jesus Christ* or something as it is. Now this. The nerve! Returning from the dead. Such a cliché, too. What's next? Walking on water?" The President made a temple with their fingers, bemused, arching an eyebrow in thought. "Of course, maybe President Reagan doesn't realize he's dead. And not just his brain, either!"

The SoS glanced at the other NSC members around the table—the glum Vice President, the constipated Secretary of Defense, the bewildered Chairman of the Joint Chiefs of Staff, the nervous Director of National Intelligence—flattening her hands as she parsed her words with care. "It must have taken *months* to shamble back to D.C. from California…" She looked at the President. "The video doesn't show one thing… There was… something written in the blood at the crime scene. A message of sorts."

The President regarded her intently. "Message? What message, Madam Secretary?"

She lowered her gaze to the table. "It read 'The Gipper will see All the President's Men at the RNC, MOTHERFUCKERS.'"

Incredulous, the President slumped back into the seat.

"Shit… *That's tomorrow!*"

IV.

Security at the 20,000-plus seat Verizon Center had never been more vigilant. The Republican National Convention commenced as scheduled to a packed house of power players, assembled delegates, and other GOP faithful.

Backstage, the mood was more sombre than the Trump rallies of the 2016 Election cycle. Participants of the RNC paced nervously behind-the-scenes, jumping at the slightest technical glitch, or the tightening of a security detail's jawline. At last, the hour to convene was at hand. As the Invocation ceremony started, everyone's guard relaxed for a few moments; the mysterious and unsettling notices from the White House to "be aware of one's surroundings" due to a "highly unusual, credible threat" of a "terrorist nature" faded into the background.

A little over two hours into the convention, there was a commotion at the celebrity entrance backstage. At first it was difficult to ascertain what was happening; a guard ran by an aged Sen. Ted Cruz, who was about to be wheeled onstage by a wizened Sen. Marco Rubio, nearly causing Gov. Jeb Bush's oxygen line to be pulled from his nose. Henry Kissinger and Sec. Condoleezza Rice hobbled over to where Sec. Donald Rumsfeld and former Speaker of the House Paul Ryan were wiping a silvery slick of spittle from Dick Cheney's chin as a gaunt Gen. Colin Powell thumbed his suspenders. Cheney made a high-pitched sound like a squeaky dog toy, motioning his arms as though skeet shooting.

Speaker Ryan beamed down at the former Vice President, his waxy complexion resembling an older version of Eddie Munster, and pat the ancient politico on his sweaty pate. "Now Uncle Dick—you be good and keep your diapers clean and we'll let you fondle your shotgun before your keynote! Right now we have a little issue, it appears…"

"Fuck! I sure hope it's not that *asshole* from the War Crimes Tribunal again!" Rumsfeld thundered, anxiously stroking his breastbone.

"We'll protect you, Don, not a problem," Kissinger wheezed subsonically. "No one makes us pay. *Ever*!"

"Y'all slow down, now! Hmm," Sen. Lindsey Graham drawled, clutching Sen. John McCain's hand to his breast. "Hope ever'thang's alri—"

A terrible smell—inhuman, ripe—crept molecule-by-molecule into the air, enveloping everyone and everything. Ryan clutched his throat before suddenly keeling over, dead. Graham and McCain embraced each other, eyes streaming tears, locking in a last passionate kiss before their bowels evacuated, commingling with the sharp reek of urine puddling beneath Kissinger, Rice, Cruz, and Rubio, ratcheting up what seemed to be the stink from thousands of anonymous desert graves...

Cheney's crooked grin dissolved into his floppy jowls as he comprehended what was happening with a sudden, alarming insight, and he mustered a phlegmy scream—

Reagan slashed through the grouping of untried war criminals and charlatans—a ghastly, putrefying dervish—sporing his filth like some titanic, death-dealing fungus from another universe. He grabbed Cheney's head, pulling the old man up like a huge potato and raking his skin off in a single stroke, holding it next to him like a fleshy suit from a drawing by Vesalius. For an instant, Cheney's innards quivered wetly—even delicately—in space before glopping in a steaming, bloody heap all over the floor. Reagan tossed him aside like a used enema. Gunfire erupted in the darkness, punctuating the mindless jabbering of a speaker in the front of the house. The bullets tore away chunks of Reagan, ripping his suit, exposing his ribs, throwing great clouds of grave dust and mold into the air, which only compounded the soul-crushing stink of decay, briefly igniting blue flashes of light in a stroboscopic display. The former president made quick work of his armed assailants—either ripping them limb-from-limb, stripping their spines from their bodies, or biting their throats out and bathing in arterial sprays of jetting blood.

In a primal howl of angst, pulled from the great open pit of evil underlying reality, he shouted: "I'm... from the government and... I'm here to help. I am... the Gipper... and I have returned!" The entire hall grew silent in an instant. Another great volley of shooting exploded the night—there was an electricity in the air.

In the audience, there was a gradually building murmur of nervous confusion.

"Ladies and gentlemen, please remain calm," one of the speakers, a young woman—perhaps a Congressional aide—intoned into a microphone on the stage. "We'll send security to investigate the disturbance backstage... Remain calm. Please stay seated—" She began to cough then, holding her throat: "*Gha*! Can't... *breathe*!" The woman promptly collapsed, already turning blue, cooling in death.

Then, in spite of every effort to stop him, Ronald Reagan exploded onto the stage like a rotting, strutting pumpkin. The smell of him alone created a wave of gagging, barfing hysteria that resulted in a panicked stampede: men, women, and children were crushed and trampled underfoot in a mad paroxysm of desperation as the foul cloud of Rotten Ronnie expanded into the cavernous space, robbing it of breathable air. Many more would die of asphyxiation as the odiferous fog settled on the throngs who had congregated to hear the lineup of conservative speakers—unaware of the horror that had unfolded backstage.

President Reagan leapt into the hapless crowd, mauling and rendering young and old alike into tiny, bloody pieces—a furious tempest of ex-Commander-in-Chief exuding a greenish haze from his disintegrating carcass. Screams of agony and shock reverberated throughout the venue as Reagan plowed through the assembled humanity, becoming Death and laying waste to all. CNN captured the gruesome mayhem in a live stream, even as Wolf Blitzer and Anderson Cooper—slavishly reporting every excruciatingly obvious detail—were ripped to shreds by the unbridled fury of the dead president; over at MSNBC's booth, Rachel Maddow and James Carville drowned in the overflow of Chris Matthews's saliva as the disgusting odor of Reagan overwhelmed his olfactory apparatus, dehydrating him to the point of an Egyptian mummy. Fox News anchors seemed strangely immune to the distressingly fetid miasma, succumbing instead to the violence unleashed by the fleeing convention-goers.

"I'm... from the government and... I'm here to help. I am... the Gipper... and I have returned!" he shrieked into the cameras, broadcasting his message across the airwaves to the unsuspecting outside world. The former POTUS gnashed, clawed, and plundered his way all through the convention, well past the night and into the wee small hours of the dawn. Finally at the public entryway to the Verizon Center—a place now reduced to a shambles, piled high with the dead and dying—he paused, admiring the scene outside the hall. The sun was cresting the skyline; his visage once more twisted into the approximation of a smile: It was morning in America.

And he understood, deep within the awful folds of his Alzheimer's-riddled brain, that he must now continue his rampaging destruction throughout the rest of this godless land—even if that meant killing every man, woman, and child in the country—in order to save it.

As he scampered into this new day, this new era, Reagan had no other thoughts, no other dreams. He was nothing, and everything. He was beyond the reach of the past, and incapable of a future. He was an eternal now, implacable, insatiable, mindless, unstoppable—a force of nature without conscience, or hate, or love, or caring, or malice. He was not human, not inhuman. He was simply a tool of the universe, a strand of cosmic filament unthreading the momentarily intertwined lives of a group of people who thought they had answers, and rarely asked questions—a few of whom were even named Nancy.

Sometimes, invoking history creates complications for the present… and the future.

DEATH AND SUFFRAGE

by Dale Bailey

It's funny how things happen, Burton used to tell me. The very moment you're engaged in some task of mind-numbing insignificance–cutting your toenails, maybe, or fishing in the sofa for the remote–the world is being refashioned around you. You stand before a mirror to brush your teeth, and halfway around the planet flood waters are on the rise. Every minute of every day, the world transforms itself in ways you can hardly imagine, and there you are, sitting in traffic or wondering what's for lunch or just staring blithely out a window. History happens while you're making other plans, Burton always says.

I guess I know that now. I guess we all know that.

Me, I was in a sixth-floor Chicago office suite working on my résumé when it started. The usual chaos swirled around me–phones braying, people scurrying about, the televisions singing exit poll data over the din–but it all had a forced artificial quality. The campaign was over. Our numbers people had told us everything we needed to know: when the polls opened that morning, Stoddard was up seventeen points. So there I sat, dejected and soon to be unemployed, with my feet on a rented desk and my lap-top propped against my knees, mulling over synonyms for directed. As in directed a staff of fifteen. As in directed public relations for the Democratic National Committee. As in directed a national political campaign straight into the toilet.

Then CNN started emitting the little overture that means somewhere in the world history is happening, just like Burton always says.

I looked up as Lewis turned off the television.

"What'd you do that for?"

Lewis leaned over to shut my computer down. "I'll show

you," he said.

I followed him through the suite, past clumps of people huddled around televisions. Nobody looked my way. Nobody had looked me in the eye since Sunday. I tried to listen, but over the shocked buzz in the room I couldn't catch much more than snatches of unscripted anchor-speak. I didn't see Burton, and I supposed he was off drafting his concession speech. "No sense delaying the inevitable," he had told me that morning.

"What gives?" I said to Lewis in the hall, but he only shook his head.

Lewis is a big man, fifty, with the drooping posture and hangdog expression of an adolescent. He stood in the elevator and watched the numbers cycle, rubbing idly at an acne scar. He had lots of them, a whole face pitted from what had to be among the worst teenage years in human history. I had never liked him much, and I liked him even less right then, but you couldn't help admiring the intelligence in his eyes. If Burton had been elected, Lewis would have served him well. Now he'd be looking for work instead.

The doors slid apart, and Lewis steered me through the lobby into a typical November morning in Chicago: a diamond-tipped wind boring in from the lake, a bruised sky spitting something that couldn't decide whether it wanted to be rain or snow. I grew up in southern California–my grandparents raised me–and there's not much I hate more than Chicago weather; but that morning I stood there with my shirt-sleeves rolled to the elbow and my tie whipping over my shoulder, and I didn't feel a thing.

"My God," I said, and for a moment, my mind just locked up. All I could think was that not two hours ago I had stood in this very spot watching Burton work the crowd, and then the world had still been sane. Afterwards, Burton had walked down the street to cast his ballot. When he stepped out of the booth, the press had been waiting. Burton charmed them, the consummate politician even in defeat. We could have done great things.

And even then the world had still been sane.

No longer.

It took me a moment to sort it all out–the pedestrians shouldering by with wild eyes, the bell-hop standing dumbfounded before the hotel on the corner, his chin bobbing at half-mast. Three taxis had tangled up in the street, bleeding steam, and farther up the block loomed an overturned bus the size of a beached plesiosaur. Somewhere a woman was screaming atonally, over and over and over, with staccato hitches for breath. Sirens wailed in the distance. A t.v. crew was getting it all on tape, and for the first time since I blew Burton's chance to hold the highest office in the land, I stood in the presence of a journalist who wasn't shoving a mike in my face to ask me what had come over me.

I was too stunned even to enjoy it.

Instead, like Lewis beside me, I just stared across the street at the polling place. Dead people had gathered there, fifteen or twenty of them, and more arriving. Even then, there was never any question in my mind that they were dead. You could see it in the way they held their bodies, stiff as marionettes; in their shuffling gaits and the bright haunted glaze of their eyes. You could see it in the lacerations yawning open on the ropy coils of their guts, in their random nakedness, their haphazard clothes–hospital gowns and blood-stained blue jeans and immaculate suits fresh from unsealed caskets. You could see it in the dark patches of decay that blossomed on their flesh. You could just see that they were dead. It was every zombie movie you ever saw, and then some.

Goose flesh erupted along my arms, and it had nothing to do with the wind off Lake Michigan.

"My God," I said again, when I finally managed to unlock my brain. "What do they want?"

"They want to vote," said Lewis.

The dead have been voting in Chicago elections since long before Richard J. Daley took office, one wag wrote in the next morning's Tribune, but yesterday's events bring a whole new meaning to the tradition.

I'll say.

The dead had voted, all right, and not just in Chicago. They had risen from hospital gurneys and autopsy slabs, from open coffins and embalming tables in every precinct in the nation, and they had cast their ballots largely without interference. Who was going to stop them? More than half the poll-workers had abandoned ship when the zombies started shambling through the doors, and even workers who stayed at their posts had usually permitted them to do as they pleased. The dead didn't threaten anyone–they didn't do much of anything you'd expect zombies to do, in fact. But most people found that inscrutable gaze unnerving. Better to let them cast their ballots than bear for long the knowing light in those strange eyes.

And when the ballots were counted, we learned something else as well: They voted for Burton. Every last one of them voted for Burton.

"It's your fault," Lewis said at breakfast the next day.

Everyone else agreed with him, I could tell, the entire senior staff, harried and sleep-deprived. They studied their food as he ranted, or scrutinized the conference table or scribbled frantic notes in their day-planners. Anything to avoid looking me in the eye. Even Burton, alone at the head of the table, just munched on a bagel and stared at CNN, the muted screen aflicker with footage of zombies staggering along on their unfathomable errands. Toward dawn, as the final tallies rolled in from the western districts, they had started to gravitate toward cemeteries. No one yet knew why.

"My fault?" I said, but my indignation was manufactured. About five that morning, waking from nightmare in my darkened hotel room, I had arrived at the same conclusion as everyone else.

"The goddamn talk show," Lewis said, as if that explained everything.

And maybe it did.

The goddamn talk show in question was none other than Crossfire and the Sunday before the polls opened I got caught in it. I had broken the first commandment of political life, a commandment I had flogged relentlessly for the last year. Stay on message, stick to the talking points.

Thou shalt not speak from the heart.

The occasion of this amateurish mistake was a six-year-old girl named Dana Maguire. Three days before I went on the air, a five-year-old boy gunned Dana down in her after-school program.

The kid had found the pistol in his father's night stand, and just as Dana's mother was coming in to pick her up, he tugged it from his insulated lunch sack and shot Dana in the neck. She died in her mother's arms while the five-year-old looked on in tears.

Just your typical day in America, except the first time I saw Dana's photo in the news, I felt something kick a hole in my chest. I can remember the moment to this day: October light slanting through hotel windows, the television on low while I talked to my grandmother in California. I don't have much in the way of family. There had been an uncle on my father's side, but he had drifted out of my life after my folks died, leaving my mother's parents to raise me. There's just the two of us since my grandfather passed on five years ago, and even in the heat of a campaign, I try to check on Gran every day. Mostly she rattles on about old folks in the home, a litany of names and ailments I can barely keep straight at the best of times. And that afternoon, half-watching some glib CNN hardbody do a stand-up in front of Little Tykes Academy, I lost the thread of her words altogether.

Next thing I know, she's saying, "Robert, Robert–" in this troubled voice, and me, I'm sitting on a hotel bed in Dayton, Ohio, weeping for a little girl I never heard of. Grief, shock, you name it–ten years in public life, nothing like that had ever happened to me before. But after that, I couldn't think of it in political terms. After that, Dana Maguire was personal.

Predictably, the whole thing came up on Crossfire. Joe Stern, Stoddard's campaign director and a man I've known for years, leaned into the camera and espoused the usual line–you know, the one about the constitutional right to bear arms, as if Jefferson had personally foreseen the rapid-fire semi-automatic with a sixteen-round clip. Coming from the mouth of Joe Stern, a smug fleshy ideologue who ought to have known better, this line enraged me.

Even so, I hardly recognized the voice that responded to him. I felt as though something else was speaking through me–as though a voice had possessed me, a speaker from that broken hole in the center of my chest.

What it said, that voice, was: "If Grant Burton is elected, he'll see that every handgun in the United States is melted into pig iron. He'll do everything in his power to save the Dana Maguires of this nation."

Joe Stern puffed up like a toad. "This isn't about Dana Maguire–"

The voice interrupted him. "If there's any justice in the universe, Dana Maguire will rise up from her grave to haunt you," the voice said. It said, "If it's not about Dana Maguire, then what on earth is it about?"

Stoddard had new ads in saturation before the day was out: Burton's face, my words in voice-over. If Grant Burton is elected, he'll see that every handgun in the United States is melted into pig iron. By Monday afternoon, we had plummeted six points and Lewis wasn't speaking to me.

I couldn't seem to shut him up now, though.

He leaned across the table and jabbed a thick finger at me, overturning a styrofoam cup of coffee. I watched the black pool spread as he shouted. "We were up five points, we had it won before you opened your goddamn–"

Angela Dey, our chief pollster, interrupted him. "Look!" she said, pointing at the television.

Burton touched the volume button on the remote, but the image on the screen was clear enough: a cemetery in upstate New York, one of the new ones where the stones are set flush to the earth to make mowing easier. Three or four zombies had fallen to their knees by a fresh grave.

"Good God," Dey whispered. "What are they doing?"

No one gave her an answer and I suppose she hadn't expected one. She could see as well as the rest of us what was happening. The dead were scrabbling at the earth with their bare hands.

A line from some old poem I had read in college–

—ahh, who's digging on my grave—

–lodged in my head, rattling around like angry candy, and for the first time I had a taste of the hysteria that would possess us all by the time this was done. Graves had opened, the dead walked the earth. All humanity trembled.

Ahh, who's digging on my grave?

Lewis flung himself back against his chair and glared at me balefully. "This is all your fault."

"At least they voted for us," I said.

Not that we swept into the White House at the head of a triumphal procession of zombies. Anything but, actually. The voting rights of the dead turned out to be a serious constitutional question, and Stoddard lodged a complaint with the Federal Election Commission. Dead people had no say in the affairs of the living, he argued, and besides, none of them were legally registered anyway. Sensing defeat, the Democratic National Committee counter-sued, claiming that the sheer presence of the dead may have kept legitimate voters from the polls.

While the courts pondered these issues in silence, the world convulsed. Church attendance soared. The president impaneled experts and blue-ribbon commissions, the Senate held hearings. The CDC convened a task force to search for biological agents. At the UN, the Security Council debated a quarantine against the United States; the stock market lost fifteen percent on the news.

Meanwhile, the dead went unheeding about their business. They never spoke or otherwise attempted to communicate, yet you could sense an intelligence, inhuman and remote, behind their mass resurrection. They spent the next weeks opening fresh graves, releasing the recently buried from entombment. With bare hands, they clawed away the dirt; through sheer numbers, they battered apart the concrete vaults and sealed caskets. You would see them in the streets, stinking of formaldehyde and putrefaction, their hands torn and ragged, the rich earth of the grave impacted under their fingernails.

Their numbers swelled.

People died, but they didn't stay dead; the newly resurrected kept busy at their graves.

A week after the balloting, the Supreme Court handed down a decision overturning the election. Congress, meeting in emergency session, set a new date for the first week of January. If nothing else, the year 2000 debacle in Florida had taught us the virtue of speed.

Lewis came to my hotel room at dusk to tell me.

"We're in business," he said.

When I didn't answer, he took a chair across from me. We stared over the fog-shrouded city in silence. Far out above the lake, threads of rain seamed the sky. Good news for the dead. The digging would go easier.

Lewis turned the bottle on the table so he could read the label. I knew what it was: Glenfiddich, a good single malt. I'd been sipping it from a hotel tumbler most of the afternoon.

"Why'nt you turn on some lights in here?" Lewis said.

"I'm fine in the dark."

Lewis grunted. After a moment, he fetched the other glass. He wiped it out with his handkerchief and poured.

"So tell me."

Lewis tilted his glass, grimaced. "January fourth. The president signed the bill twenty minutes ago. Protective cordons fifty yards from polling stations. Only the living can vote. Jesus. I can't believe I'm even saying that." He cradled his long face in his hands. "So you in?"

"Does he want me?"

"Yes."

"What about you, Lewis? Do you want me?"

Lewis said nothing. We just sat there, breathing in the woodsy aroma of the scotch, watching night bleed into the sky.

"You screwed me at staff meeting the other day," I said. "You hung me out to dry in front of everyone. It won't work if you keep cutting the ground out from under my feet."

"Goddamnit, I was right. In ten seconds, you destroyed everything we've worked for. We had it won."

"Oh come on, Lewis. If Crossfire never happened, it could have gone either way. Five points, that's nothing. We were barely outside the plus and minus, you know that."

"Still. Why'd you have to say that?"

I thought about that strange sense I'd had at the time: another voice speaking through me. Mouthpiece of the dead.

"You ever think about that little girl, Lewis?"

He sighed. "Yeah. Yeah, I do." He lifted his glass. "Look. If you're angling for some kind of apology–"

"I don't want an apology."

"Good," he said. Then, grudgingly: "We need you on this one, Rob. You know that."

"January," I said. "That gives us almost two months."

"We're way up right now."

"Stoddard will make a run. Wait and see."

"Yeah." Lewis touched his face. It was dark, but I could sense the gesture. He'd be fingering his acne scars, I'd spent enough time with him to know that. "I don't know, though," he said. "I think the right might sit this one out. They think it's the fuckin Rapture, who's got time for politics?"

"We'll see."

He took the rest of his scotch in a gulp and stood. "Yeah. We'll see."

I didn't move as he showed himself out, just watched his reflection in the big plate glass window. He opened the door and turned to look back, a tall man framed in light from the hall, his face lost in shadow.

"Rob?"

"Yeah?"

"You all right?"

I drained my glass and swished the scotch around in my mouth. I'm having a little trouble sleeping these days, I wanted to say. I'm having these dreams.

But all I said was, "I'm fine, Lewis. I'm just fine."

I wasn't, though, not really.

None of us were, I guess, but even now–maybe especially now–the thing I remember most about those first weeks is how little the resurrection of the dead altered our everyday lives. Isolated incidents made the news–I remember a serial killer being arrested as his victims heaved themselves bodily from their shallow backyard graves–but mostly people just carried on. After the initial shock, markets stabilized. Stores filled up with Thanksgiving turkeys; radio stations began counting the shopping days until Christmas.

Yet I think the hysteria must have been there all along, like a swift current just beneath the surface of a placid lake. An undertow, the kind of current that'll kill you if you're not careful. Most people looked okay, but scratch the surface and we were all going nuts in a thousand quiet ways.

Ahh, who's digging on my grave, and all that.

Me, I couldn't sleep. The stress of the campaign had been mounting steadily even before my meltdown on Crossfire, and in those closing days, with the polls in California–and all those lovely delegates–a hair too close to call, I'd been waking grainy-eyed and yawning every morning. I was feeling guilty, too. Three years ago, Gran broke her hip and landed in a Long Beach nursing home. And while I talked to her daily, I could never manage to steal a day or two to see her, despite all the time we spent campaigning in California.

But the resurrection of the dead marked a new era in my insomnia. Stumbling to bed late on election night, my mind blistered with images of zombies in the streets, I fell into a fevered dream. I found myself wandering through an abandoned city. Everything burned with the tenebrous significance of dreams–every brick and stone, the scraps of newsprint tumbling down high-rise canyons, the darkness pooling in the mouths of desolate subways. But the worst thing of all was the sound, the lone sound in all that sea of silence: the obscurely terrible cadence of a faraway clock, impossibly magnified, echoing down empty alleys and forsaken avenues.

The air rang with it, haunting me, drawing me on at last into a district where the buildings loomed over steep, close streets, admitting only a narrow wedge of sky. An open door beckoned, a black slot in a high, thin house. I pushed open the gate, climbed the broken stairs, paused in the threshold. A colossal grandfather clock towered within, its hands poised a minute short of midnight. Transfixed, I watched the heavy pendulum sweep through its arc, driving home the hour.

The massive hands stood upright.

The air shattered around me. The very stones shook as the clock began to toll. Clapping my hands over my ears, I turned to flee, but there was nowhere to go. In the yard, in the street–as far as I could see–the dead had gathered. They stood there while the clock stroked out the hours, staring up at me with those haunted eyes, and I knew suddenly and absolutely–the way you know things in dreams–that they had come for me at last, that they had always been coming for me, for all of us, if only we had known it.

I woke then, coldly afraid.

The first gray light of morning slit the drapes, but I had a premonition that no dawn was coming, or at least a very different dawn from any I had ever dared imagine.

Stoddard made his run with two weeks to go.

December fourteenth, we're 37,000 feet over the midwest in a leased Boeing 737, and Angela Dey drops the new numbers on us.

"Gentleman," she says, "we've hit a little turbulence."

It was a turning point, I can see that now. At the time, though, none of us much appreciated her little joke.

The resurrection of the dead had shaken things up–it had put us on top for a month or so–but Stoddard had been clawing his way back for a couple of weeks, crucifying us in the farm belt on a couple of ag bills where Burton cast deciding votes, hammering us in the south on vouchers. We knew that, of course, but I don't think any of us had foreseen just how close things were becoming.

"We're up seven points in California," Dey said. "The gay vote's keeping our heads above water, but the numbers are soft. Stoddard's got momentum."

"Christ," Lewis said, but Dey was already passing around another sheet.

"It gets worse," she said. "Florida, we're up two points. A statistical dead heat. We've got the minorities, Stoddard has the seniors. Everything's riding on turnout."

Libby Dixon, Burton's press secretary, cleared her throat. "We've got a pretty solid network among Hispanics–"

Dey shook her head. "Seniors win that one every time."

"Hispanics never vote," Lewis said. "We might as well wrap Florida up with a little bow and send it to Stoddard."

Dey handed around another sheet. She'd orchestrated the moment for maximum impact, doling it out one sheet at a time like that. Lewis slumped in his seat, probing his scars as she worked her way through the list: Michigan, New York, Ohio, all three delegate rich, all three of them neck-and-neck races. Three almost physical blows, too, you could see them in the faces ranged around the table.

"What the hell's going on here?" Lewis muttered as Dey passed out another sheet, and then the news out of Texas rendered even him speechless. Stoddard had us by six points. I ran through a couple of Alamo analogies before deciding that discretion was the better part of wisdom. "I thought we were gaining there," Lewis said.

Dey shrugged. I just read the numbers, I don't make them up.

"Things could be worse," Libby Dixon said.

"Yeah, but Rob's not allowed to do Crossfire any more," Lewis said, and a titter ran around the table. Lewis is good, I'll give him that. You could feel the tension ease.

"Suggestions?" Burton said.

Dey said, "I've got some focus group stuff on education. I was thinking maybe some ads clarifying our–"

"Hell with the ads," someone else said, "we've gotta spend more time in Florida. We've got to engage Stoddard on his ground."

"Maybe a series of town meetings?" Lewis said, and they went around like that for a while. I tried to listen, but Lewis's little icebreaker had reminded me of the dreams. I knew where I was–37,000 feet of dead air below me, winging my way toward a rally in Virginia–but inside my head I hadn't gone anywhere at all. Inside my head, I was stuck in the threshold of that dream house, staring out into the eyes of the dead.

The world had changed irrevocably, I thought abruptly.

That seems self-evident, I suppose, but at the time it had the quality of genuine revelation. The fact is, we had all–and I mean everyone by that, the entire culture, not just the campaign–we had all been pretending that nothing much had changed. Sure, we had UN debates and a CNN feed right out of a George Romero movie, but the implications of mass resurrection–the spiritual implications–had yet to bear down upon us. We were in denial. In that moment, with the plane rolling underneath me and someone–Tyler O'Neill I think it was, Libby Dixon's mousy assistant–droning on about going negative, I thought of something I'd heard a professor mention back at Northwestern: Copernicus formulated the heliocentric model of the solar system in the mid-1500s, but the Church didn't get around to punishing anyone for it until they threw Galileo in jail nearly a hundred years later. They spent the better part of a century trying to ignore the fact that the fundamental geography of the universe had been altered with a single stroke.

And so it had again.

The dead walked.

Three simple words, but everything else paled beside them–social security, campaign finance reform, education vouchers. Everything.

I wadded Dey's sheet into a noisy ball and flung it across the table. Tyler O'Neill stuttered and choked, and for a moment everyone just stared in silence at that wad of paper. You'd have thought I'd hurled a hand grenade, not a two paragraph summary of voter idiocy in the Lonestar state.

Libby Dixon cleared her throat. "I hardly thin–"

"Shut up, Libby," I said. "Listen to yourselves for Christ's sake. We got zombies in the street and you guys are worried about going negative?"

"The whole . . ." Dey flapped her hand. ". . . zombie thing, it's not even on the radar. My numbers–"

"People lie, Angela."

Libby Dixon swallowed audibly.

"When it comes to death, sex, and money, everybody lies. A total stranger calls up on the telephone, and you expect some soccer mom to share her feelings about the fact that grandpa's rotten corpse is staggering around in the street?"

I had their attention all right.

For a minute the plane filled up with the muted roar of the engines. No human sound at all. And then Burton–Burton smiled.

"What are you thinking, Rob?"

"A great presidency is a marriage between a man and a moment," I said. "You told me that. Remember?"

"I remember."

"This is your moment, sir. You have to stop running away

from it."

"What do you have in mind?" Lewis asked.

I answered the question, but I never even looked Lewis's way as I did it. I just held Grant Burton's gaze. It was like no one else was there at all, like it was just the two of us, and despite everything that's happened since, that's the closest I've ever come to making history.

"I want to find Dana Maguire," I said.

I'd been in politics since my second year at Northwestern. It was nothing I ever intended–who goes off to college hoping to be a senate aide?–but I was idealistic, and I liked the things Grant Burton stood for, so I found myself working the phones that fall as an unpaid volunteer. One thing led to another–an internship on the Hill, a post-graduate job as a research assistant–and somehow I wound up inside the beltway.

I used to wonder how my life might have turned out had I chosen another path. My senior year at Northwestern, I went out with a girl named Gwen, a junior, freckled and streaky blonde, with the kind of sturdy good looks that fall a hair short of beauty. Partnered in some forgettable lab exercise, we found we had grown up within a half hour of one another. Simple geographic coincidence, two Californians stranded in the frozen north, sustained us throughout the winter and into the spring. But we drifted in the weeks after graduation, and the last I had heard of her was a Christmas card five or six years back. I remember opening it and watching a scrap of paper slip to the floor. Her address and phone number, back home in Laguna Beach, with a little note. Call me some time, it said, but I never did.

So there it was.

I was thirty-two years old, I lived alone, I'd never held a relationship together longer than eight months. Gran was my closest friend, and I saw her three times a year if I was lucky. I went to my ten year class reunion in Evanston, and everybody there was in a different life-place than I was. They all had kids and homes and churches.

Me, I had my job. Twelve hour days, five days a week. Saturdays I spent three or four hours at the office catching up. Sundays I watched the talk shows and then it was time to start all over again. That had been my routine for nearly a decade, and in all those years I never bothered to ask myself how I came to be there. It never even struck me as the kind of thing a person ought to ask.

Four years ago, during Burton's re-election campaign for the Senate, Lewis said a funny thing to me. We're sitting in a hotel bar, drinking Miller Lite and eating peanuts, when he turns to me and says, "You got anyone, Rob?"

"Got anyone?"

"You know, a girl friend, a fiancée, somebody you care about."

Gwen flickered at the edge of my consciousness, but that was all. A flicker, nothing more.

I said, "No."

"That's good," Lewis said.

It was just the kind of thing he always said, sarcastic, a little mean-hearted. Usually I let it pass, but that night I had just enough alcohol zipping through my veins to call him on it.

"What's that supposed to mean?"

Lewis turned to look at me.

"I was going to say, you have someone you really care about–somebody you want to spend your life with–you might want to walk away from all this."

"Why's that?"

"This job doesn't leave enough room for relationships."

He finished his beer and pushed the bottle away, his gaze steady and clear. In the dim light his scars were invisible, and I saw him then as he could have been in a better world. For maybe a moment, Lewis was one step short of handsome.

And then the moment broke.

"Good night," he said, and turned away.

A few months after that–not long before Burton won his second six-year Senate term–Libby Dixon told me Lewis was getting a divorce. I suppose he must have known the marriage was coming apart around him.

But at the time nothing like that even occurred to me.

After Lewis left, I just sat at the bar running those words over in my mind. This job doesn't leave much room for relationships, he had said, and I knew he had intended it as a warning. But what I felt instead was a bottomless sense of relief. I was perfectly content to be alone.

Burton was doing an event in St. Louis when the nursing home called to say that Gran had fallen again. Eighty-one year old bones are fragile, and the last time I had been out there–just after the convention–Gran's case manager had privately informed me that another fall would probably do it.

"Do what?" I had asked.

The case manager looked away. She shuffled papers on her desk while her meaning bore in on me: another fall would kill her.

I suppose I must have known this at some level, but to hear it articulated so baldly shook me. From the time I was four, Gran had been the single stable institution in my life. I had been visiting in Long Beach, half a continent from home, when my family–my parents and sister–died in the car crash. It took the state police back in Pennsylvania nearly a day to track me down. I still remember the moment: Gran's mask-like expression as she hung up the phone, her hands cold against my face as she knelt before me.

She made no sound as she wept. Tears spilled down her cheeks, leaving muddy tracks in her make-up, but she made no sound at all. "I love you, Robert," she said. She said, "You must be strong."

That's my first true memory.

Of my parents, my sister, I remember nothing at all. I have a snapshot of them at a beach somewhere, maybe six months before I was born: my father lean and smoking, my mother smiling, her abdomen just beginning to swell. In the picture, Alice–she would have been four then–stands just in front of them, a happy blond child cradling a plastic shovel. When I was a kid I used to stare at that photo, wondering how you can miss people you never even knew. I did though, an almost physical ache way down inside me, the kind of phantom pain amputees must feel.

A ghost of that old pain squeezed my heart as the case manager told me about Gran's fall. "We got lucky," she said. "She's going to be in a wheelchair a month or two, but she's going to be okay."

Afterwards, I talked to Gran herself, her voice thin and querulous, addled with pain killers. "Robert," she said, "I want you to come out here. I want to see you."

"I want to see you, too," I said, "but I can't get away right now. As soon as the election's over–"

"I'm an old woman," she told me crossly. "I may not be here after the election."

I managed a laugh at that, but the laugh sounded hollow even in my own ears. The words had started a grim little movie unreeling in my head–a snippet of Gran's cold body staggering to its feet, that somehow inhuman tomb light shining out from behind its eyes. I suppose most of us must have imagined something like that during those weeks, but it unnerved me all the same. It reminded me too much of the dreams. It felt like I was there again, gazing out into the faces of the implacable dead, that enormous clock banging out the hours.

"Robert–" Gran was saying, and I could hear the Demerol singing in her voice. "Are you there, Ro–"

And for no reason at all, I said:

"Did my parents have a clock, Gran?"

"A clock?"

"A grandfather clock."

She was silent so long I thought maybe she had hung up.

"That was your uncle's clock," she said finally, her voice thick and distant.

"My uncle?"

"Don," she said. "On your father's side."

"What happened to the clock?"

"Robert, I want you to come out he–"

"What happened to the clock, Gran?"

"Well, how would I know?" she said. "He couldn't keep it, could he? I suppose he must have sold it."

"What do you mean?"

But she didn't answer.

I listened to the swell and fall of Demerol sleep for a moment, and then the voice of the case manager filled my ear. "She's drifted off. If you want, I can call back later--"

I looked up as a shadow fell across me. Lewis stood in the doorway.

"No, that's okay. I'll call her in the morning."

I hung up the phone and stared over the desk at him. He had a strange expression on his face.

"What?" I said.

"It's Dana Maguire."

"What about her?"

"They've found her."

Eight hours later, I touched down at Logan under a cloudy midnight sky. We had hired a private security firm to find her, and one of their agents–an expressionless man with the build of an ex-athlete–met me at the gate.

"You hook up with the ad people all right?" I asked in the car, and from the way he answered, a monosyllabic "Fine," you could tell what he thought of ad people.

"The crew's in place?"

"They're already rigging the lights."

"How'd you find her?"

He glanced at me, streetlight shadow rippling across his face like water. "Dead people ain't got much imagination. Soon's we get the fresh ones in the ground, they're out there digging." He laughed humorlessly. "You'd think people'd stop burying em."

"It's the ritual, I guess."

"Maybe." He paused. Then: "Finding her, we put some guys on the cemeteries and kept our eyes open, that's all."

"Why'd it take so long?"

For a moment there was no sound in the car but the hum of tires on pavement and somewhere far away a siren railing against the night. The agent rolled down his window and spat emphatically into the slipstream. "City the size of Boston," he said, "it has a lot of fucking cemeteries."

The cemetery in question turned out to be everything I could have hoped for: remote and unkempt, with weathered gothic tombstones right off a Hollywood back lot. And wouldn't it be comforting to think so, I remember thinking as I got out of the car–the ring of lights atop the hill nothing more than stage dressing, the old world as it had been always. But it wasn't, of course, and the ragged figures digging at the grave weren't actors, either. You could smell them for one, the stomach-wrenching stench of decay. A light rain had begun to fall, too, and it had the feel of a genuine Boston drizzle, cold and steady toward the bleak fag end of December.

Andy, the director, turned when he heard me.

"Any trouble?" I asked.

"No. They don't care much what we're about, long as we don't interfere."

"Good."

Andy pointed. "There she is, see?"

"Yeah, I see her."

She was on her knees in the grass, still wearing the dress she had been buried in. She dug with single-minded intensity, her arms caked with mud to the elbow, her face empty of anything remotely human. I stood and stared at her for a while, trying to decide what it was I was feeling.

"You all right?" Andy said.

"What?"

"I said, are you all right? For a second there, I thought you were crying."

"No," I said. "I'm fine. It's the rain, that's all."

"Right."

So I stood there and half-listened while he filled me in. He had several cameras running, multiple filters and angles, he was playing with the lights. He told me all this and none of it meant anything at all to me. None of it mattered as long as I got the footage I wanted. Until then, there was nothing for me here.

He must have been thinking along the same lines, for when I turned to go, he called after me: "Say, Rob, you needn't have come out tonight, you know."

I looked back at him, the rain pasting my hair against my forehead and running down into my eyes. I shivered. "I know," I said. A moment later, I added: "I just–I wanted to see her somehow."

But Andy had already turned away.

I still remember the campaign ad, my own private nightmare dressed up in cinematic finery. Andy and I cobbled it together on Christmas Eve, and just after midnight in a darkened Boston studio, we cracked open a bottle of bourbon in celebration and sat back to view the final cut. I felt a wave of nausea roll over me as the first images flickered across the monitor. Andy had shot the whole thing from distorted angles in grainy black and white, the film just a hair over-exposed to sharpen the contrast. Sixty seconds of derivative expressionism, some media critic dismissed it, but even he conceded it possessed a certain power.

You've seen it, too, I suppose. Who hasn't?

She will rise from her grave to haunt you, the opening title card reads, and the image holds in utter silence for maybe half a second too long. Long enough to be unsettling, Andy said, and you could imagine distracted viewers all across the heartland perking up, wondering what the hell was wrong with the sound.

The words dissolve into an image of hands, bloodless and pale, gouging at moist black earth. The hands of a child, battered and raw and smeared with the filth and corruption of the grave, digging, digging. There's something remorseless about them, something relentless and terrible. They could dig forever, and they might, you can see that. And now, gradually, you awaken to sound: rain hissing from a midnight sky, the steady slither of wet earth underhand, and something else, a sound so perfectly lacking that it's almost palpable in its absence, the unearthly silence of the dead. Freeze frame on a tableau out of Goya or Bosch: seven or eight zombies, half-dressed and rotting, laboring tirelessly over a fresh grave.

Fade to black, another slug line, another slow dissolve.

Dana Maguire came back.

The words melt into a long shot of the child, on her knees in the poison muck of the grave. Her dress clings to her thighs, and it's a dress someone has taken some care about–white and lacy, the kind of dress you'd bury your little girl in if you had to do it–and it's ruined. All the care and heartache that went into that dress, utterly ruined. Torn and fouled and sopping. Rain slicks her blond hair black against her skull. And as the camera glides in upon Dana Maguire's face, half-shadowed and filling three-quarters of the screen, you can glimpse the wound at her throat, flushed clean and pale. Dark roses of rot bloom along the high ridge of her cheekbone. Her eyes burn with the cold hard light of vistas you never want to see, not even in your dreams.

The image holds for an instant, a mute imperative, and then, mercifully, fades. Words appear and deliquesce on an ebon screen, three phrases, one by one:

The dead have spoken.

Now it's your turn.

Burton for president.

Andy touched a button. A reel caught and reversed itself. The screen went gray, and I realized I had forgotten to breathe. I sipped at my drink.

The whiskey burned in my throat, it made me feel alive.

"What do you think?" Andy said.

"I don't know. I don't know what to think."

Grinning, he ejected the tape and tossed it in my lap. "Merry Christmas," he said, raising his glass. "To our savior born."

And so we drank again.

Dizzy with exhaustion, I made my way back to my hotel and slept for eleven hours straight. I woke around noon on Christmas day. An hour later, I was on a plane.

By the time I caught up to the campaign in Richmond, Lewis was in a rage, pale and apoplectic, his acne scars flaring an angry red. "You seen these?" he said, thrusting a sheaf of papers at me.

I glanced through them quickly–more bad news from Angela Dey, Burton slipping further in the polls–and then I set them aside. "Maybe this'll help," I said, holding up the tape Andy and I had cobbled together.

We watched it together, all of us, Lewis and I, the entire senior staff, Burton himself, his face grim as the first images flickered across the screen. Even now, viewing it for the second time, I could feel its impact. And I could see it in the faces of the others as well–Dey's jaw dropping open, Lewis snorting in disbelief. As the screen froze on the penultimate image–Dana Maguire's decay-ravaged face–Libby Dixon turned away.

"There's no way we can run that," she said.

"We've got–" I began, but Dey interrupted me.

"She's right, Rob. It's not a campaign ad, it's a horror movie." She turned to Burton, drumming his fingers quietly at the head of the table. "You put this out there, you'll drop ten points, I guarantee it."

"Lewis?" Burton asked.

Lewis pondered the issue for a moment, rubbing his pitted cheek with one crooked finger. "I agree," he said finally. "The ad's a frigging nightmare. It's not the answer."

"The ad's revolting," Libby said. "The media will eat us alive for politicizing the kid's death."

"We ought to be politicizing it," I said. "We ought to make it mean something."

"You run that ad, Rob," Lewis said, "every redneck in America is going to remember you threatening to take away their guns. You want to make that mistake twice?"

"Is it a mistake? For Christ's sake, the dead are walking, Lewis. The old rules don't apply." I turned to Libby. "What's Stoddard say, Libby, can you tell me that?"

"He hasn't touched it since election day."

"Exactly. He hasn't said a thing, not about Dana Maguire, not about the dead people staggering around in the street. Ever since the FEC overturned the election, he's been dodging the issue–"

"Because it's political suicide," Dey said. "He's been dodging it because it's the right thing to do."

"Bullshit," I snapped. "It's not the right thing to do. It's pandering and it's cowardice–it's moral cowardice–and if we do it we deserve to lose."

You could hear everything in the long silence that ensued–

cars passing in the street, a local staffer talking on the phone in the next room, the faint tattoo of Burton's fingers against the formica table top. I studied him for a moment, and once again I had that sense of something else speaking through me, as though I were merely a conduit for another voice.

"What do you think about guns, sir?" I asked. "What do you really think?"

Burton didn't answer for a long moment. When he did, I think he surprised everyone at the table. "The death rate by handguns in this country is triple that for every other industrialized nation on the planet," he said. "They ought to be melted into pig iron, just like Rob said. Let's go with the ad."

"Sir–" Dey was standing.

"I've made up my mind," Burton said. He picked up the sheaf of papers at his elbow and shuffled through them. "We're down in Texas and California, we're slipping in Michigan and Ohio." He tossed the papers down in disgust. "Stoddard looks good in the south, Angela. What do we got to lose?"

We couldn't have timed it better.

The new ad went into national saturation on December 30th, in the shadow of a strange new year. I was watching a bowl game in my hotel room the first time I saw it on the air. It chilled me all over, as though I'd never seen it before. Afterwards, the room filled with the sound of the ball game, but now it all seemed hollow. The cheers of the fans rang with a labored gaiety, the crack of pads had the crisp sharpness of movie sound effects. A barb of loneliness pierced me. I would have called someone, but I had no one to call.

Snapping off the television, I pocketed my key-card.

Downstairs, the same football game was playing, but at least there was liquor and a ring of conversation in the air. A few media folks from Burton's entourage clustered around the bar, but I begged off when they invited me to join them. I sat at a table in the corner instead, staring blindly at the television and drinking scotch without any hurry, but without any effort to keep track either. I don't know how much I drank that night, but I was a little unsteady when I stood to go.

I had a bad moment on the way back to my room. When the elevator doors slid apart, I found I couldn't remember my room number. I couldn't say for sure I had even chosen the right floor. The hotel corridor stretched away before me, bland and anonymous, a hallway of locked doors behind which only strangers slept. The endless weary grind of the campaign swept over me, and suddenly I was sick of it all–the long midnight flights and the hotel laundries, the relentless blur of cities and smiling faces. I wanted more than anything else in the world to go home. Not my cramped apartment in the District either.

Home. Wherever that was.

Independent of my brain, my fingers had found my key-card. I tugged it from my pocket and studied it grimly. I had chosen the right floor after all.

Still in my clothes, I collapsed across my bed and fell asleep. I don't remember any dreams, but sometime in the long cold hour before dawn, the phone yanked me awake. "Turn on CNN," Lewis said. I listened to him breathe as I fumbled for the remote and cycled through the channels.

I punched up the volume.

"–unsubstantiated reports out of China concerning newly awakened dead in remote regions of the Tibetan Plateau–"

I was awake now, fully awake. My head pounded. I had to work up some spit before I could speak.

"Anyone got anything solid?" I asked.

"I'm working with a guy in State for confirmation. So far we got nothing but rumor."

"If it's true–"

"If it's true," Lewis said, "you're gonna look like a fucking genius."

Our numbers were soft in the morning, but things were looking up by mid-afternoon. The Chinese weren't talking and no one yet had footage of the Tibetan dead–but rumors were trickling in from around the globe. Unconfirmed reports from U.N. Peace-keepers in Kosovo told of women and children clawing their way free from previously unknown mass graves.

By New Year's Day, rumors gave away to established fact. The television flickered with grainy images from Groznyy and Addis Ababa. The dead were arising in scattered locales around the world. And here at home, the polls were shifting. Burton's crowds grew larger and more enthusiastic at every rally, and as our jet winged down through the night towards Pittsburgh, I watched Stoddard answering questions about the crisis on a satellite feed from C-SPAN. He looked gray and tired, his long face brimming with uncertainty. He was too late, we owned the issue now, and watching him, I could see he knew it, too. He was going through the motions, that's all.

There was a celebratory hum in the air as the plane settled to the tarmac. Burton spoke for a few minutes at the airport, and then the Secret Service people tightened the bubble, moving us en masse toward the motorcade. Just before he ducked into the limo, Burton dismissed his entourage. His hand closed about my shoulder. "You're with me," he said.

He was silent as the limo slid away into the night, but as the downtown towers loomed up before us he turned to look at me. "I wanted to thank you," he said.

"There's no–"

He held up his hand. "I wouldn't have had the courage to run that ad, not without you pushing me. I've wondered about that, you know. It was like you knew something, like you knew the story was getting ready to break again."

I could sense the question behind his words–Did you know, Rob? Did you?–but I didn't have any answers. Just that impression of a voice speaking through me from beyond, from somewhere else, and that didn't make any sense, or none that I was able to share.

"When I first got started in this business," Burton was saying, "there was a local pol back in Chicago, kind of a mentor. He told me once you could tell what kind of man you were dealing with by the people he chose to surround himself with. When I think about that, I feel good, Rob." He sighed. "The world's gone crazy, that's for sure, but with people like you on our side, I think we'll be all right. I just wanted to tell you that."

"Thank you, sir."

He nodded. I could feel him studying me as I gazed out the

window, but suddenly I could find nothing to say. I just sat there and watched the city slide by, the past welling up inside me. Unpleasant truths lurked like rocks just beneath the visible surface. I could sense them somehow.

"You all right, Rob?"

"Just thinking," I said. "Being in Pittsburgh, it brings back memories."

"I thought you grew up in California."

"I did. I was born here, though. I lived here until my parents died."

"How old were you?"

"Four. I was four years old."

We were at the hotel by then. As the motorcade swung across two empty lanes into the driveway, Gran's words–

—that was your uncle's clock, they couldn't keep it—

–sounded in my head. The limo eased to the curb. Doors slammed. Agents slid past outside, putting a protective cordon around the car. The door opened, and cold January air swept in. Burton was gathering his things.

"Sir–"

He paused, looking back.

"Tomorrow morning, could I have some time alone?"

He frowned. "I don't know, Rob, the schedule's pretty tight–"

"No, sir. I mean–I mean a few hours off."

"Something wrong?"

"There's a couple of things I'd like to look into. My parents and all that. Just an hour or two if you can spare me."

He held my gaze a moment longer.

Then: "That's fine, Rob." He reached out and squeezed my shoulder. "Just be at the airport by two."

That night I dreamed of a place that wasn't quite Dana Maguire's daycare. It looked like a daycare–half a dozen squealing kids, big plastic toys, an indestructible grade of carpet--but certain details didn't fit: the massive grandfather clock, my uncle's clock, standing in one corner; my parents, dancing to big band music that seemed to emanate from nowhere.

I was trying to puzzle this through when I saw the kid clutching the lunch sack. There was an odd expression on his face, a haunted heart-broken expression, and too late I understood what was about to happen. I was trying to move, to scream, anything, as he dragged the pistol out of the bag. But my lips were sealed, I couldn't speak. Glancing down, I saw that I was rooted to the floor. Literally rooted. My bare feet had grown these long knotted tendrils. The carpet was twisted and raveled where they had driven themselves into the floor.

My parents whirled about in an athletic fox-trot, their faces manic with laughter. The music was building to an awful crescendo, percussives bleeding seamlessly together, the snap of the snare drums, the terrible booming tones of the clock, the quick sharp report of the gun.

I saw the girl go over backwards, her hands clawing at her throat as she convulsed. Blood drenched me, a spurting arterial fountain–I could feel it hot against my skin–and in the same moment this five-year-old kid turned to stare at me. Tears streamed down his cheeks, and this kid–this child really, and that's all I could seem to think–

—he's just a child he's only a child—

–he had my face.

I woke then, stifling a scream. Silence gripped the room and the corridor beyond it, and beyond that the city. I felt as if the world itself were drowning, sunk fathoms deep in the fine and private silence of the grave.

I stood, brushing the curtains aside. An anonymous grid of lights burned beyond the glass, an alien hieroglyph pulsing with enigmatic significance. Staring out at it, I was seized by an impression of how fragile everything is, how thin the barrier that separates us from the abyss. I shrank from the window, terrified by a sense that the world was far larger–and immeasurably stranger–than the world I'd known before, a sense of vast and formless energies churning out there in the dark.

I spent the next morning in the Carnegie Library in Oakland, reeling through back issues of the Post-Gazette. It didn't take long to dig up the article about the accident–I knew the date well enough–but I wasn't quite prepared for what I found there. Gran had always been reticent about the wreck–about everything to do with my life in Pittsburgh, actually–but I'd never really paused to give that much thought. She'd lost her family, too, after all–a granddaughter, a son-in-law, her only child–and even as a kid, I could see why she might not want to talk about it.

The headline flickering on the microfilm reader rocked me, though. Two die in fiery collision, it read, and before I could properly formulate the question in my mind–

—there were three of them—

–I was scanning the paragraphs below. Disconnected phrases seemed to hover above the cramped columns–bridge abutment, high speed, alcohol-related–and halfway through the article, the following words leapt out at me:

Friends speculate that the accident may have been the product of a suicide pact. The couple were said to be grief-stricken following the death of their daughter, Alice, nine, in a bizarre shooting accident three weeks ago.

I stood, abruptly nauseated, afraid to read any further. A docent approached–

"Sir, are you all–"

–but I thrust her away.

Outside, traffic lumbered by, stirring the slush on Forbes Avenue. I sat on a bench and fought the nausea for a long time, cradling my face in my hands while I waited for it to pass. A storm was drifting in, and when I felt better I lifted my face to the sky, anxious for the icy burn of snow against my cheeks. Somewhere in the city, Grant Burton was speaking. Somewhere, reanimated corpses scrabbled at frozen graves.

The world lurched on.

I stood, belting my coat. I had a plane to catch.

I held myself together for two days, during our final campaign swing through the midwest on January 3 and the election that followed, but I think I had already arrived at a decision. Most of the senior staff sensed it, as well, I think. They congratulated me on persuading Burton to run the ad, but they didn't come to me for advice much in those final hours. I seemed set-apart somehow, isolated, contagious.

Lewis clapped me on the back as we watched the returns roll in. "Jesus, Rob," he said, "you're supposed to be happy right now."

"Are you, Lewis?"

I looked up at him, his tall figure slumped, his face a fiery map of scars.

"What did you give up to get us here?" I asked, but he didn't answer. I hadn't expected him to.

The election unfolded without a hitch. Leaving off their work in the grave yards, the dead gathered about the polling stations, but even they seemed to sense that the rules had changed this time around. They made no attempt to cast their ballots. They just stood behind the cordons the National Guard had set up, still and silent, regarding the proceedings with flat remorseless eyes. Voters scurried past them with bowed heads, their faces pinched against the stench of decay. On Nightline, Ted Koppel noted that the balloting had drawn the highest turn-out in American history, something like ninety-three percent.

"Any idea why so many voters came out today?" he asked the panel.

"Maybe they were afraid not to," Cokie Roberts replied, and I felt an answering chord vibrate within me. Trust Cokie to get it right.

Stoddard conceded soon after the polls closed in the west. It was obvious by then. In his victory speech, Burton talked about a mandate for change. "The people have spoken," he said, and they had, but I couldn't help wondering what might be speaking through them, and what it might be trying to say. Some commentators speculated that it was over now. The dead would return to the graves, the world would be the old world we had known.

But that's not the way it happened.

On January 5th, the dead were digging once again, their

numbers always swelling. CNN was carrying the story when I handed Burton my resignation. He read it slowly and then he lifted his gaze to my face.

"I can't accept this, Rob," he said. "We need you now. The hard work's just getting underway."

"I'm sorry, sir. I haven't any choice."

"Surely we can work something out."

"I wish we could."

We went through several iterations of this exchange before he nodded. "We'll miss you," he said. "You'll always have a place here, whenever you're ready to get back in the game."

I was at the door when he called to me again.

"Is there anything I can do to help, Rob?"

"No, sir," I said. "I have to take care of this myself."

I spent a week in Pittsburgh, walking the precipitous streets of neighborhoods I remembered only in my dreams. I passed a morning hunting up the house where my parents had lived, and one bright, cold afternoon I drove out 76 and pulled my rental to the side of the interstate, a hundred yards short of the bridge where they died. Eighteen wheelers thundered past, throwing up glittering arcs of spray, and the smell of the highway enveloped me, diesel and iron. It was pretty much what I had expected, a slab of faceless concrete, nothing more.

We leave no mark.

Evenings, I took solitary meals in diners and talked to Gran on the telephone–tranquil gossip about the old folks in the home mostly, empty of anything real. Afterwards, I drank Iron City and watched cable movies until I got drunk enough to sleep. I ignored the news as best I could, but I couldn't help catching glimpses as I buzzed through the channels. All around the world, the dead were walking.

They walked in my dreams, as well, stirring memories better left forgotten. Mornings, I woke with a sense of dread, thinking of Galileo, thinking of the Church. I had urged Burton to engage this brave new world, yet the thought of embracing such a fundamental transformation of my own history–of following through on the article in the Post-Gazette, the portents within my dreams–paralyzed me utterly. I suppose it was by then a matter mostly of verifying my own fears and suspicions–suppose I already knew, at some level, what I had yet to confirm. But the lingering possibility of doubt was precious, safe, and I clung to it for a few days longer, unwilling to surrender.

Finally, I could put it off no longer.

I drove down to the Old Public Safety Building on Grant Street. Upstairs, a grizzled receptionist brought out the file I requested. It was all there in untutored bureaucratic prose. There was a sheaf of official photos, too, glossy black and white prints. I didn't want to look at them, but I did anyway. I felt it was something I ought to do.

A little while later, someone touched my shoulder. It was the receptionist, her broad face creased with concern. Her spectacles swung at the end of a little silver chain as she bent over me. "You all right?" she asked.

"Yes, ma'am, I'm fine."

I stood, closing the file, and thanked her for her time.

I left Pittsburgh the next day, shedding the cold as the plane nosed above a lid of cloud. From LAX, I caught the 405 South to Long Beach. I drove with the window down, grateful for the warmth upon my arm, the spike of palm fronds against the sky. The slipstream carried the scent of a world blossoming and fresh, a future yet unmade, a landscape less scarred by history than the blighted industrial streets I'd left behind.

Yet even here the past lingered. It was the past that had brought me here, after all.

The nursing home was a sprawl of landscaped grounds and low-slung stucco buildings, faintly Spanish in design. I found Gran in a garden overlooking the Pacific, and I paused, studying her, before she noticed me in the doorway. She held a paperback in her lap, but she had left off reading to stare out across the water. A salt-laden breeze lifted her gray hair in wisps, and for a moment, looking at her, her eyes clear in her distinctly boned face, I could find my way back to the woman I had known as a boy.

But the years intervened, the way they always do. In the end, I couldn't help noticing her wasted body, or the glittering geometry of the wheelchair that enclosed her. Her injured leg jutted before her.

I must have sighed, for she looked up, adjusting the angle of the chair. "Robert!"

"Gran."

I sat by her, on a concrete bench. The morning overcast was breaking, and the sun struck sparks from the wave-tops.

"I'd have thought you were too busy to visit," she said, "now that your man has won the election."

"I'm not so busy these days. I don't work for him anymore."

"What do you mean–"

"I mean I quit my job."

"Why?" she said.

"I spent some time in Pittsburgh. I've been looking into things."

"Looking into things? Whatever on earth is there to look into, Robert?" She smoothed the afghan covering her thighs, her fingers trembling.

I laid my hand across them, but she pulled away. "Gran, we need to talk."

"Talk?" She laughed, a bark of forced gaiety. "We talk every day."

"Look at me," I said, and after a long moment, she did. I could see the fear in her eyes, then. I wondered how long it had been there, and why I'd never noticed it before. "We need to talk about the past."

"The past is dead, Robert."

Now it was my turn to laugh. "Nothing's dead, Gran. Turn on the television sometime. Nothing stays dead anymore. Nothing."

"I don't want to talk about that."

"Then what do you want to talk about?" I waved an arm at the building behind us, the ammonia-scented corridors and the endless numbered rooms inhabited by faded old people, already ghosts of the dead they would become. "You want to talk about Cora in 203 and the way her son never visits her or Jerry in 147 whose emphysema has been giving him trouble or all the–"

"All the what?" she snapped, suddenly fierce.

"All the fucking minutia we always talk about!"

"I won't have you speak to me like that! I raised you, I made you what you are today!"

"I know," I said. And then, more quietly, I said it again. "I know."

Her hands twisted in her lap. "The doctors told me you'd forget, it happens that way sometimes with trauma. You were so young. It seemed best somehow to just . . . let it go."

"But you lied."

"I didn't choose any of this," she said. "After it happened, your parents sent you out to me. Just for a little while, they said. They needed time to think things through."

She fell silent, squinting at the surf foaming on the rocks below. The sun bore down upon us, a heartbreaking disk of white in the faraway sky.

"I never thought they'd do what they did," she said, "and then it was too late. After that . . . how could I tell you?" She clenched my hand. "You seemed okay, Robert. You seemed like you were fine."

I stood, pulling away. "How could you know?"

"Robert–"

I turned at the door. She'd wheeled the chair around to face me. Her leg thrust toward me in its cast, like the prow of a ship. She was in tears. "Why, Robert? Why couldn't you just leave everything alone?"

"I don't know," I said, but even then I was thinking of Lewis, that habit he has of probing at his face where the acne left it pitted–as if someday he'll find his flesh smooth and handsome once again, and it's through his hands he'll know it. I guess that's it, you know: we've all been wounded, every one of us.

And we just can't keep our hands off the scars.

#

I drifted for the next day or two, living out of hotel rooms and haunting the places I'd known growing up. They'd changed like everything changes, the world always hurrying us along, but I didn't know what else to do, where else to go. I couldn't leave Long Beach, not till I made things up with Gran, but something held me back.

I felt ill at ease, restless. And then, as I fished through my wallet in a bar one afternoon, I saw a tiny slip of paper eddy to the floor. I knew what it was, of course, but I picked it up anyway. My fingers shook as I opened it up and stared at the message written there, Call me some time, with the address and phone number printed neatly below.

I made it to Laguna Beach in fifty minutes. The address was a mile or so east of the water, a manicured duplex on a corner lot. She had moved no doubt–five years had passed–and if she hadn't moved she had married at the very least. But I left my car at the curb and walked up the sidewalk all the same. I could hear the bell through an open window, footsteps approaching, soft music lilting from the back of the house. Then the door opened and she was there, wiping her hands on a towel.

"Gwen," I said.

She didn't smile, but she didn't close the door either.

It was a start.

The house was small, but light, with wide windows in the kitchen over-looking a lush back lawn. A breeze slipped past the screens, infusing the kitchen with the scent of fresh-cut grass and the faraway smell of ocean.

"This isn't a bad time, is it?" I asked.

"Well, it's unexpected to say the least," she told me, lifting one eyebrow doubtfully, and in the gesture I caught a glimpse of the girl I'd known at Northwestern, rueful and wry and always faintly amused.

As she made coffee, I studied her, still freckled and faintly gamine, but not unchanged. Her eyes had a wary light in them, and fresh lines caged her thin upper lip. When she sat across from me at the table, toying with her coffee cup, I noticed a faint pale circle around her finger where a ring might have been.

Maybe I looked older too, for Gwen glanced up at me from beneath a fringe of streaky blonde bangs, her mouth arcing in a crooked smile. "You look younger on television," she said, and it was enough to get us started.

Gwen knew a fair bit of my story–my role in Burton's presidential campaign had bought me that much notoriety at least–and hers had a familiar ring to it. Law school at UCLA, five or six years billing hours in one of the big LA firms before the cutthroat culture got to her and she threw it over for a job with the ACLU, trading long days and a handsome wage for still longer ones and almost no wage at all. Her marriage had come apart around the same time. "Not out of any real animosity," she said. "More like a mutual lack of interest."

"And now? Are you seeing anyone?"

The question came out with a weight I hadn't intended.

She hesitated. "No one special." She lifted the eyebrow once again. "A habit I picked up as a litigator. Risk aversion."

By this time, the sky beyond the windows had softened into twilight and our coffee had grown cold. As shadows lengthened in the little kitchen, I caught Gwen glancing at the clock.

She had plans.

I stood. "I should go."

"Right."

She took my hand at the door, a simple handshake, that's all, but I felt something pass between us, an old connection close with a kind of electric spark. Maybe it wasn't there at all, maybe I only wanted to feel it–Gwen certainly seemed willing to let me walk out of her life once again–but a kind of desperation seized me.

Call it nostalgia or loneliness. Call it whatever you want. But suddenly the image of her wry glance from beneath the slant of hair leaped into mind.

I wanted to see her again.

"Listen," I said, "I know this is kind of out of the blue, but you wouldn't be free for dinner would you?"

She paused a moment. The shadow of the door had fallen across her face. She laughed uncertainly, and when she spoke, her voice was husky and uncertain. "I don't know, Rob. That was a long time ago. Like I said, I'm a little risk aversive these days."

"Right. Well, then, listen–it was really great seeing you."

I nodded and started across the lawn. I had the door of the rental open when she spoke again.

"What the hell," she said. "Let me make a call. It's only dinner, right?"

I went back to Washington for the inauguration.

Lewis and I stood together as we waited for the ceremony to begin, looking out at the dead. They had been on the move for days, legions of them, gathering on the mall as far as the eye could see. A cluster of the living, maybe a couple hundred strong, had been herded onto the lawn before the bandstand–a token crowd of warm bodies for the television cameras–but I couldn't help thinking that Burton's true constituency waited beyond the cordons, still and silent and unutterably patient, the melting pot made flesh: folk of every color, race, creed, and age, in every stage of decay that would allow them to stand upright. Dana Maguire might be out there somewhere. She probably was.

The smell was palpable.

Privately, Lewis had told me that the dead had begun gathering elsewhere in the world, as well. Our satellites had confirmed it. In Cuba and North Korea, in Yugoslavia and Rwanda, the dead were on the move, implacable and slow, their purposes unknown and maybe unknowable.

"We need you, Rob," he had said. "Worse than ever."

"I'm not ready yet," I replied.

He had turned to me then, his long pitted face sagging. "What happened to you?" he asked.

And so I told him.

It was the first time I had spoken of it aloud, and I felt a burden sliding from my shoulders as the words slipped out. I told him all of it: Gran's evasions and my reaction to Dana Maguire that day on CNN and the sense I'd had on Crossfire that something else, something vast and remote and impersonal, was speaking through me, calling them back from the grave. I told him about the police report, too, how the memories had come crashing back upon me as I sat at the scarred table, staring into a file nearly three decades old.

"It was a party," I said. "My uncle was throwing a party and Mom and Dad's baby-sitter had canceled at the last minute, so Don told them just to bring us along. He lived alone, you know. He didn't have kids and he never thought about kids in the house."

"So the gun wasn't locked up?"

"No. It was late. It must have been close to midnight by then. People were getting drunk and the music was loud and Alice didn't seem to want much to do with me. I was in my uncle's bedroom, just fooling around the way kids do, and the gun was in the drawer of his night stand."

I paused, memory surging through me, and suddenly I was there again, a child in my uncle's upstairs bedroom. Music thumped downstairs, jazzy big band music. I knew the grown-ups would be dancing and my dad would be nuzzling Mom's neck, and that night when he kissed me good night, I'd be able to smell him, the exotic aromas of bourbon and tobacco, shot through with the faint floral essence of Mom's perfume. Then my eyes fell upon the gun in the drawer. The light from the hall summoned unsuspected depths from the blued barrel.

I picked it up, heavy and cold.

All I wanted to do was show Alice. I just wanted to show her. I never meant to hurt anyone. I never meant to hurt Alice.

I said it to Lewis–"I never meant to hurt her"–and he looked away, unable to meet my eyes.

I remember carrying the gun down stairs to the foyer, Mom and Dad dancing beyond the frame of the doorway, Alice standing there watching. "I remember everything," I said to Lewis. "Everything but pulling the trigger. I remember the music screeching to a halt, somebody dragging the needle across the record, my mother screaming. I remember Alice lying on the floor and the blood and the weight of the gun in my hand. But the weird thing is, the thing I remember best is the way I felt at that moment."

"The way you felt," Lewis said.

"Yeah. A bullet had smashed the face of the clock, this big grandfather clock my uncle had in the foyer. It was chiming over and over, as though the bullet had wrecked the mechanism. That's what I remember most. The clock. I was afraid my uncle was going to be mad about the clock."

Lewis did something odd then. Reaching out, he clasped my shoulder–the first time he'd ever touched me, really touched me, I mean–and I realized how strange it was that this man, this scarred, bitter man, had somehow become the only friend I have. I realized something else, too: how rarely I'd known the touch of another human hand, how much I hungered for it.

"You were a kid, Rob."

"I know. It's not my fault."

"It's no reason for you to leave, not now, not when we need you. Burton would have you back in a minute. He owes this election to you, he knows that. Come back."

"Not yet," I said, "I'm not ready."

But now, staring out across the upturned faces of the dead as a cold January wind whipped across the mall, I felt the lure and pull of the old life, sure as gravity. The game, Burton had called it, and it was a game, politics, the biggest Monopoly set in the world and I loved it and for the first time I understood why I loved it. For the first time I understood something else, too: why I had waited years to ring Gwen's doorbell, why even then it had taken an active effort of will not to turn away. It was the same reason: Because it was a game, a game with clear winners and losers, with rules as complex and arcane as a cotillion, and most of all because it partook so little of the messy turmoil of real life. The stakes seemed high, but they weren't. It was ritual, that's all–movement without action, a dance of spin and strategy designed to preserve the status quo. I fell in love with politics because it was safe. You get so involved in pushing your token around the board that you forget the ideals that brought you to the table in the first place. You forget to speak from the heart. Someday maybe, for the right reasons, I'd come back. But not yet.

I must have said it aloud for Lewis suddenly looked over at me. "What?" he asked.

I just shook my head and gazed out over the handful of living people, stirring as the ceremony got underway. The dead waited beyond them, rank upon rank of them with the earth of the grave under their nails and that cold shining in their eyes.

And then I did turn to Lewis. "What do you think they

want?" I asked.

Lewis sighed. "Justice, I suppose," he said.

"And when they have it?"

"Maybe they'll rest."

A year has passed, and those words–justice, I suppose–still haunt me. I returned to D.C. in the fall, just as the leaves began turning along the Potomac. Gwen came with me, and sometimes, as I lie wakeful in the shelter of her warmth, my mind turns to the past.

It was Gran that brought me back. The cast had come off in February, and one afternoon in March, Gwen and I stopped by, surprised to see her on her feet. She looked frail, but her eyes glinted with determination as she toiled along the corridors behind her walker.

"Let's sit down and rest," I said when she got winded, but she merely shook her head and kept moving.

"Bones knit, Rob," she told me. "Wounds heal, if you let them."

Those words haunt me, too.

By the time she died in August, she'd moved from the walker to a cane. Another month, her case manager told me with admiration, and she might have relinquished even that. We buried her in the plot where we laid my grandfather to rest, but I never went back after the interment. I know what I would find.

The dead do not sleep.

They shamble in silence through the cities of our world, their bodies slack and stinking of the grave, their eyes coldly ablaze. Baghdad fell in September, vanquished by battalions of revolutionaries, rallying behind a vanguard of the dead. State teems with similar rumors, and CNN is on the story. Unrest in Pyongyang, turmoil in Belgrade.

In some views, Burton's has been the most successful administration in history. All around the world, our enemies are falling. Yet more and more these days, I catch the president staring uneasily into the streets of Washington, aswarm with zombies. "Our conscience," he's taken to calling them, but I'm not sure I agree. They demand nothing of us, after all. They seek no end we can perceive or understand. Perhaps they are nothing more than what we make of them, or what they enable us to make of ourselves. And so we go on, mere lodgers in a world of unpeopled graves, subject ever to the remorseless scrutiny of the dead.

THE GOVERNOR'S EXECUTIONS

by G. Ted Theewen

"Who taught you to mix a White Russian, Wilson?"

"My uncle, sir. He used to tend bar at a supper club up in Wisconsin."

"Wisconsin is famous for their supper clubs."

"Yes, sir," said Wilson as he knelt down to wipe up a small puddle off the hardwood floor.

"I didn't make too big of a mess, did I?"

"Not at all, Governor," said Wilson. "Just some water."

The governor licked his lips and smiled slightly.

"This study is incredible, Governor. I mean, dang!"

"You've been in here before, Wilson."

"Yes sir, but we interns are usually in and out quickly. I've never read the titles before and I can't believe you have so many poetry collections!"

"You're not like the other interns. And you actually like poetry?" He made a face.

"Yes, sir," he said. "My mother is a librarian back home. You have every book written by a Poet Laureate of our state since statehood in 1839. She would fall in love with this!"

"I'm sure there are more than a few books in here she wouldn't believe."

"Yes, sir?"

"Behind the bust of Chief Blackhawk, you'll find a black leather-bound ledger. Open that."

Wilson gently set the book on an antique oak table and opened it up.

"I see names and dates that go all the way back to before we were a state."

"Keep reading."

Wilson looked, then looked again. The governor had silently risen from the leather sofa and was observing the intern. His face was expressionless.

"Wait," he said. "I see some names that look familiar. Joseph Phillip Boone, Fredrick Augustus Boone, Enoch Micheal Boone," he drifted off to silence. Then a whisper. "The Boone Brothers!"

"Our state's most notorious band of outlaws. They murdered over forty men, women, and children before they were captured by the militia."

"They were executed right out there, sir." Wilson pointed out a large window covered in heavy burgundy drapes to the public park across the street.

"You are holding my Execution Ledger, Wilson. The names of every man and woman to have been executed by the state." Governor Newton continued to stare at Wilson.

The young intern closed the book.

"No," said the large, elder man in a terse voice.

"No?"

"No. Open it to the bookmark."

Wilson licked his lips and did as he was told and looked up at the governor.

"Read the last three names out loud."

"Richard Leroy Allen, lethal injection. Brett Eugene Siegel, lethal injection. Rufus Obadiah Parks, electric chair." Wilson's voice trembled slightly.

"I wrote those names in myself."

"Yes, sir." They were ornately written in black ink.

"Next month, I will write another. Ask me if I care."

"Sir?"

"Ask me if I care about writing more names in the Governor's

Execution Ledger." His bloodshot eyes were hard and fixated on the kid, who was wearing a suit that was half a size too big for him and a few years out of fashion.

"Governor Newton," he began, pausing to clear his throat. "Do you care if you write more names in the state's Execution Ledger?"

"No." He stared a hole into the intern. "Do you know why?"

"No, sir."

"Because sometimes you just have to kill somebody."

A fire engine drove past the mansion and for a few seconds red lights swirled over the tops of the drapes as the muted sirens faded to silence.

"Can you understand that?"

"Yes, sir."

"Now kindly put that book back and pour me another." The governor sat down on the sofa, watching the wrap-up of all of that day's games. The volume had been muted.

Wilson put the drink in his hand. He took a sip and sighed in contentment.

"Your uncle taught you well, kid."

"Thank you, sir."

"Those brandy old-fashioneds during the game packed a punch, too."

"Too bad we ran out of brandy."

The governor took a deep breath and yawned, followed by a giant exhale.

"State really got 'em tonight, didn't they?"

"They sure did, Governor. It was all over before the end of the first half."

"Southern hasn't had a good team in years. That game used to always be close."

"Kind of like Alabama and Auburn, sir?"

"Exactly. Back when I played for State, the games always

came down to the final play, and once we even went into overtime."

"You were a defensive end, sir?"

"Sure was. All-Conference my senior year."

He inhaled deeply before finishing his drink.

"Show me the Wink of Confidence again, Kid."

Wilson pointed, smiled and winked with a slight nod just as he'd been instructed earlier in the day.

The governor laughed. "Keep practicing, Kid. We'll make you a ladies man yet."

"Yes, sir," said Wilson as he handed the Governor a fresh drink.

"The wife and daughters are shopping with her sister in Chicago. We've got the whole Governor's Mansion to ourselves."

"We're a couple of bachelors then, sir." Wilson wiped down the trunk bar, taking his time on the ornate carvings of white-tailed deer and pheasants. The oak inside was inlaid with various duck species made from cherry and fit so perfectly the intern couldn't feel the joints or seams.

"I love these White Russians but they're dangerous."

"Yes, sir," said Edgar. Edgar Wilson. Yet for some reason, everybody on Governor Newton's staff called him by his last name, which he liked. It just seemed to fit and it made him feel like he was more than just the paid intern working as the Governor's go-fer.

"You know what? Enough of this 'sir' bullshit. Call me Joe."

"Thanks, Joe."

"Yeah," said Joe with a belch. "Ain't nobody around here anyways."

"We're bachelors," Wilson repeated with a wince. "But just for tonight."

"Wilson, do you have a girlfriend?"

"Not right now, Joe. No time."

Joe laughed. "How old are you, kid?"

"I turned twenty-one last month, Ss—Joe."

"I've got shoes older than you, kid."

Wilson snorted.

Joe stood up and began weaving right away, then sat back down with a laugh.

"Here," said Wilson as he walked up next to Joe. "Let me help you."

"Fuck," he spat. "I stood too fast. I'm alright."

"You sure?"

"I just have to piss is all."

"Me too," said Wilson. "I'll go with you."

"This mansion is over a hundred and twenty-five years old. Did you know that?"

"Yes, I did. Designed by John M. Van Osdel for our very first governor."

"Well," said Joe with a pause. He belched loudly, then continued. "You're one of the smartest interns I've ever had, kid. I'll give you that."

"Thanks, Joe. Watch for that step up into the bathroom."

"Good eye, kid."

When Joe came out of the bathroom, his hands were still wet, and he was squinting his left eye.

"Everything okay?" Wilson tried to hold back a chuckle.

"We've got some hot interns though, don't we?"

"Damn straight, Joe," said Wilson. He stayed next to the large man as he weaved his way back to the study.

"I like that one in the press office, with the nice rack."

"The blonde? Her name is Celinda."

"Have you seen 'em? Those tits, I mean?" Joe had a lewd grin on his face.

Wilson felt his face grow warm.

Joe sank down into the brown leather sofa with a long sigh.

"Not me, no. She won't date anybody in the office. Besides,

she likes farm boys. She's a country girl."

"Those country girls are whores, Wilson." Joe took another huge gulp of his White Russian.

"Yeah, I've had a couple of them myself," said Wilson as he looked over at Joe.

"I had one give me chlamydia three years ago."

"Um," said Wilson. "That's..."

"That's how it goes," Joe shrugged his large shoulders.

"Gotta wrap the rascal, man." Wilson hated how that came out but at least he said something. Silence would have been so much worse. He wanted to be the guy with witty banter like a detective in a 40's crime noir film. Instead, he scrambled to avoid looking like deer in headlights, verbal roadkill.

"Normally I do. I mean, bastard kids kill careers in this game," said Joe as he leaned to the side and farted. "Side pussy does, too."

"For sure. The assholes in the press would pounce on that."

"Those fuckers are always looking for dirt." Joe finished off his White Russian. He raised his glass and jiggled the ice.

"Coming right up, Joe"

"Goddamn you make a good White Russian, kid!"

"Well, you've got plenty of Kahlua and oddly enough, plenty of fresh cream."

"That was a gift from the Dairyman's Committee yesterday."

"A whole gallon of fresh heavy cream?"

"--And the two bottles of Kahlua."

"How did they--"

"--They saw you coming, kid. They saw you coming."

"Reminds me of this farm girl," said Wilson.

Joe got quiet. He didn't speak as Wilson mixed the fresh cocktail. He didn't speak when the highlights of the State's trouncing of Southern flashed on the muted television. As Wilson cautiously walked over towards Joe, his head nodded back and forth a few times, and then with a big hand he wiped the sweat off his face.

"Yeah," he said finally to break the silence. "In my first term, I had had a couple of farm girls come around. It was always a party around here."

Wilson put the drink in Joe's hand.

"Sounds like fun."

"Fun? It was insane," he said with an incredulous chuckle. "It's all fun and games until somebody gets knocked up."

"Oh shit," said Wilson quietly.

"Yeah. And there were two of them."

"Did they know each other?"

"Probably. I mean, I never asked. But probably."

"Were they around the same time?"

"They both came to me in the same week. One at a time. I couldn't believe it."

"I'll bet. So how'd you handle it?" Wilson sat in the chair next to the sofa.

Joe took a big drink.

"How would you have handled it, Wilson?"

"I would have paid them to have abortions." It seemed simple enough.

"And what if they refused?"

"I would reason with them. I would convince them how much easier it would be."

"And if that failed?"

Wilson shook his head. "I wouldn't have failed. I would have drawn them a picture of what it would be like for them to live in the public spotlight. They would be called 'The Governor's Whores' and have their faces in newspapers all over the state. I would make it clear they would be dragged through every mud puddle between here and Chicago, Moline to Cairo, and every other corner."

He paused to wipe the spittle from his lips.

"I could have used you twenty years ago, kid."

"So what did you do?"

"Let's say nobody gave them that speech and they refused. Now what do you do?"

"I--," he started to say.

Wilson paused while Joe looked him in the eyes with a hard stare.

"It takes big balls to be a Governor, kid. Sometimes, things have to be done."

Wilson shifted around a bit. Then he realized it was a joke. Governor Newton was joking with him, so he smiled and chuckled a bit.

But Joe just kept looking at him.

"Tell me, kid. What would you have done?"

"Take my chances, I guess."

Joe scoffed.

"Take your chances? You guess? For fuck's sake, kid. This is the big leagues. You don't leave loose ends like that."

"So, what did you do?"

"Me? I did what had to be done." Joe finished his White Russian and handed the glass to Wilson.

"Coming right up," he said quietly.

Wilson mixed as fast as he could, adding more vodka than usual, and put the drink in Joe's hand.

"I did what had to be done, kid. Plain and simple."

"Whatever it was, it worked. I mean, you're still here in the Governor's Mansion, right?"

"Yup," he said then took a big gulp. "I had a guy back then. He was a good guy. He handled a lot of the dirty work back then."

Joe looked up at the ceiling.

"So he handled it for you?"

"Yeah," he said. "I owned a small construction company back then. We built barns with concrete floors. My idiot brother-in-law was having one built that week."

Wilson poured himself a cola.

"So, I made a call to this guy. The plan was to catch the girls alone, tell them I wanted to talk to them, get them in the car, and drive off before they could tell anybody who they were with."

"Smart plan," said Wilson. "The days before cellphones?"

"Yeah," said Joe, who drained his drink. Wilson picked up the glass and mixed another, stronger than the last.

"I wasn't there when it happened. All I know is, it was handled, both of them, and I never had to answer any questions. Not one."

Wilson put the fresh drink in Joe's hand.

"You have to make decisions like that when you're the Governor, kid."

"I'll bet. I'm sure it's not easy, either."

"Not at first. But it gets easier."

Wilson felt a tightening in his neck and between his shoulders. He wiped sweat off his forehead.

"I mean, there was this reporter out of Moline one time. Wilson, do you know the difference between a campaign contribution and a bribe?"

"Yeah, I sure do."

"He didn't. It was a legitimate campaign contribution but he swore it was a bribe."

Wilson paused for a moment, his tongue running back and forth along the roof of his mouth.

"Another barn, then?"

"Yeah, my wife's cousin, James." Joe's speech was beginning to slur a bit.

"Lucky for James," said Wilson, who winced right after saying it.

Joe chuckled.

"James was an idiot. We had to trick him into leaving my guy alone so he could do what had to be done. I remember calling him and demanding he meet me in town right then and there. Idiot!"

Wilson laughed and quickly drank his soda.

"Let me tell you this, kid—and don't you ever forget it. When you're in politics, the higher the office, the more that's at stake. And people will stop at nothing to take you down."

"Damned right," said Wilson. "Gotta defend yourself."

"More than just defend yourself, kid. More than just waiting for them to hurt you. Sometimes, you have to go after them, and get in the first shot." Joe drained his glass. He was blinking slowly, and both eyes were no longer in unison, with the left one lagging back a bit.

Joe said something else, and then exhaled deeply--so deep it seemed several times the air he inhaled. Wilson took the glass from his hand and set it on the trunk bar behind him, watching Joe's head slump forward, and then to the right against the sofa's armrest.

The intern took great care to put the bar back as if it had never been opened. The glasses were washed, a few scented candles were added but never lit, and a blanket was found upstairs and brought down for Joe.

Wilson spent the remainder of that night in a matching leather chair, soundlessly watching Joe sleep, all the while calculating what Joe would remember tomorrow.

At six o'clock the next morning, Joe woke up to use the bathroom, and Wilson was there to offer a helping hand with a smile. As he struggled to speak, Wilson waved a hand dismissively, then handed the governor a bottle of water, two aspirin, and three ibuprofen.

The governor looked down at him, nodded awkwardly, and after taking the help, went upstairs to sleep in his own bed.

Late Sunday morning, Wilson was in the kitchen of the mansion, wearing fresh clothes and brewing coffee. His thoughts were a group of squirrels chasing each other around an oak tree the morning after the first snowfall of winter.

"I'm going to need a cup of that," said Governor Newton in a rough, deep voice.

A fresh cup sat next to the Sunday paper.

"Did you spend the night here, Wilson?" Bloodshot eyes locked onto the intern as shaky hands held the cup of hot coffee.

"No sir," he said with a smile. "I took a nap and came back."

His eyebrows raised slightly.

"Can I fix you something to eat, sir?"

The Governor's head just shook as he walked off. "I'll see you on Monday, okay Wilson?"

And with that, the weekend was finished.

That afternoon, Wilson went back to his apartment and power-cleaned. All the while, questions rolled around in his head. Did the Governor remember what he confessed? If he did remember that night, what would he do about it? Would he offer Wilson a chance to shut up or would he kill him before he got a chance to prove he could be trusted? If he did offer Wilson the chance to shut up, would that elevate him into some group? Was this the boost in the organization he was hoping he'd get after a period of hard work?

He walked out of the bathroom because the bleach was making him cough. As he walked into the living room, a heavy hand pounded on his door.

Wilson's heart jump into a steady, strong pace like a Chevy big block warmed up on the starting line. An electric shock traced from the top of his head down to the crack of his asshole, and for a brief second it felt as if he were about to let go.

They, whomever he'd sent, wouldn't kill him here. Nobody kills someone at this time on a Sunday in an apartment complex full of over-achieving interns and Legislative Assistants.

Wilson opened the door to find his roommate's brother.

"When Dan comes back from Trish's this weekend, give him this," he said as he put a large grocery sack full of clothes in Wilson's hands. "Damn, Eddie—you feeling okay?"

"Yeah," he said distantly. "I've been cleaning."

"Are you sure?"

"I'm fine," he said. "I'll give this to Dan when he comes back from his weekend trip."

On Monday, Edgar Wilson pointed, smiled, and winked at Sam as he loaded the coffeemaker. Sam laughed and nodded back at him. He pointed, smiled, and winked at Celinda as she prepared press packets.

"Hey, Wilson! How was the weekend, huh?"

"Outstanding," he said. "Why?"

"Wasn't it boring babysitting the Governor?"

"A bit. I caught up on my reading."

"Wilson," shouted Andre—the Governor's Chief of Staff. "We're in here," he said gesturing to the meeting room they used when planning the week's agendas.

The whole team was pointing, smiling, and winking at each other.

"Alright," said Andre. "Tonight, the Russian Ag Ambassador will be passing through on short notice. We've all got jobs to do, so don't screw this up!"

Every staff member got a manila folder with their names on them. Inside were their assignments. It was a one-day affair and photo-op. Wilson wondered if Joe would score some good Russian vodka as a gift.

One of Wilson's jobs was to deliver pizzas to the Russian staff members at the hotel while the bosses got their pictures taken. They always used Vince's Pizza.

In the back parking lot Wilson smelled the pizza and his stomach rumbled. A man in a suit was walking towards him between a cargo van and an SUV. He looked up at Wilson, made eye-contact, pointed, smiled, winked, then his hands went into his jacket.

The electric shock came back and Wilson cut to his left like the running backs he watched on Saturday. He put his head down below the windows, the goal was to get into Vince's—any door. Kitchen, the carry-out door, the door for delivery drivers. He had to get inside Vince's.

Vince's was one of the few restaurants in the downtown open on Monday nights so the parking lot was full. There was even a bus because a volleyball game had just ended.

The side mirror next to his head exploded, spraying shards of mirror and fiberglass into his cheek and temple. Wilson felt blood trickle down his face.

It was then he realized how the sound of the mirror being shot was louder than the shot that did it. Their guns had suppressors!

He heard footsteps to his right. Wilson noticed the car behind him had some chrome. It wasn't a mirror, but it reflected enough to give him away.

Wilson went down to all-fours, like a kid doing the bear-crawl in gym class, and inched alongside the car. When he got to the tire, he heard more shoes on the gravel behind him. Feeling a rush of adrenaline, he bolted down the line of cars all parked in a grid, bullets whistling past him. Windows shattered, a car alarm went off, then another.

It occurred to him if somebody else came outside, they would be killed, too. They would have to eliminate the witnesses.

Wilson cut to the right and went down the gap between rear bumpers and front grills. He punched as many grills as he could, hoping to set off more alarms.

Suddenly something was burning in his arm, the triceps, and it went limp. The burning was intense, like a branding iron pushing into his flesh. He felt blood run down his arm.

Out of the corner of his eye, he saw movement to his right. One of the men was running towards him, pistol at the ready, as he lined up his shot. They were running out of time and knew it.

Just then he heard a woman scream. He looked up to see a woman near the front corner watching two men with guns run towards somebody who was bleeding. She screamed again only for that scream to be cut off instantly by a shot to the chest.

She crumpled to the ground.

A man was crouched next to the woman on the ground. He was shouting into a cellphone.

A piece of the cinder-block wall behind him exploded.

Sirens suddenly turned on just a few blocks away.

A car barreled into the parking lot, the motor revving high, as it rushed towards the two men who were waving at the car and pointing at Wilson. He cut to the left, running down the length of a blue pick-up truck and instantly knew the mistake of giving a clear lane of fire to one of the shooters.

He heard the loud shots and felt them tear into his shoulder and another into his side.

Wilson crumbled down to the gravel parking lot, searing heat going through him, and he could swear he smelled burning flesh. His right leg kicked while his arm tucked in.

The gravel rocks felt sharp against his forehead.

He heard the men drive off as sirens seemed to be right next to him.

A man ran to his side, then another, and a woman.

"Easy," she said with authority. "Don't move him too much."

Wilson felt a smile spread across his bloody face. He tried to point at the women but his arms wouldn't move, and as soon as he tried to move his head to nod at her he regretted it. But he winked.

He tried to talk but his mouth was full of thick, slimy, coppery blood. Then he coughed.

"Don't try to talk, Sir," said the woman. He felt strong hands apply pressure to a couple of the bullet holes.

"Ledger," he said.

"What's that," said a man holding his side.

"I'm in the execution ledger," said Wilson as he exhaled. When the Governor was passed out, Edgar Wilson had written his name into the ledger. The cause of death he wrote was "Internship."

He looked up into the nighttime sky and saw a jetliner slowly cross over him high above, the lights on the wings flashing. Wilson wondered where they were going and if he could come with.

GOTV

by Tom Breen

Call time: 6:35 p.m.

Caller from: Connecticut, USA

Hi, Maddie. This is Representative Clark Malone. I'm calling because I know you are a responsible citizen, and I need the support of Americans like you. Election Day is only six weeks away, and the issues facing our nation couldn't be more urgent: National security; health care for our seniors and courageous veterans; support for our public schools; and, of course, getting our economy moving again, to create good jobs in communities like yours. Maddie, together, we can restore our country's greatness, so that it works for all Americans. Again, this is Representative Clark Malone, and I hope I can count on your vote. Thank you. This message paid for by Citizens For Malone.

#

Call time: 7:02 p.m.

Caller from: Connecticut, USA

Maddie, hello. This is Representative Clark Malone. I have an urgent request: will you help me make our country a place that works for all of us? The stakes couldn't be higher, and by now you've no doubt seen the misleading and desperate attack ads launched by my opponent. I know that Americans like you have analyzed the issues and are ready to make an informed choice, but not everyone is as dedicated. Some voters, I'm sad to say, are swayed by the untrue and deeply hurtful attacks on my character, my credibility, my family, and my time in the East. That's why I need to know you're with me, Maddie. I need to know I can count on you to stand up for America and against the trash being spread about me. Election Day is five short weeks away, Maddie. We have never faced a decision this important. So much is riding on this. Please tell me you're ready to stand up for Representative Clark Malone. That's who I am. Thank you. This message paid for by Citizens for Malone.

#

Call time: 5:48 p.m.

Caller from: Connecticut, USA

They're at it again, Maddie. You'd think my opponent and his surrogates would have learned by now, but they're filling up the airwaves with more untrue and defamatory attacks on Representative Clark Malone. Right now, while you are preparing dinner for your family, or perhaps eating cold takeout from a paper carton while you sit cross-legged on the futon and surf the Internet, my opponent and his hirelings are gathering together in a basement or attic or similar place, and cooking up another venomous batch of libels. What's worse, Maddie, is that the mainstream media has started to buy in. What they'll never print is that I was not alone during the so-called incident. Maddie, I want to keep fighting for you and communities like yours: your schools, your police departments, your tidy lawns, your precious seniors, your blameless children. You like all those things, don't you? Well, if my opponent had his way, they'd be ruined not only for you, but also for future generations. Help me stay in the fight, Maddie. Please say you support Representative Clark Malone. Thank you. This message paid for by Fight Back For Clark Malone.

#

Call time: 9:57 p.m.

Caller from: Connecticut, USA

Where were you, Maddie? Election Day is less than a month away, and there I was, Representative Clark Malone, holding a rally in your town, and you weren't there. What was more important, Maddie? What was more important that improving our public schools, caring for our seniors, eliminating the inadequate members of the community, and getting this economy working again? Were you trapped under a burning car? Is that why you didn't come to the rally? I missed you, Maddie. My enemies are closing in. Their relentless attacks on my character and my record of service and things I might have done while in the East have … I didn't do them, Maddie. You have to believe me when I say Representative Clark Malone is untainted by carnage or perfidy. The man in those photos is not me. Everyone knows you can use computers to make anything look like something else. Don't believe his lies. He is preparing a broth of blood for you, and our seniors, and our hard-working middle class, and Diane, who is not "missing," she is resting elsewhere. The long shadows are gathered at the door, Maddie. I can only fight them off if the torch of liberty is lit by your sacrifice. I am Representative Clark Malone. I need you. This message paid for by Fight Back For Clark Malone.

#

Call time: 2:04 a.m.

Caller from: Connecticut, USA

You locked the door, as if that would stop Representative Clark Malone. I am rust and decay itself. There is no latch I have not eaten away with the oil from my dead hand. Besides, I am incorporeal. Walls do not constrain me. I am ether. I am radon. I am the gas hissing through your fixtures. But what a body I take, when I take a body! Streets and bridges. Parks and harbors and courthouses and fire engines painted apple-red, wailing toward a stopped heart or a smashed car leaking fuel. I am everything solid toward which you extend your grubby fingers. The lights that illuminate your path at night. The sewers that carry away your leavings in the morning. The bullet in the gun tied to the hip of the policeman who looks down your blouse as he lets you off with a warning. I am all these things. Representative Clark Malone defines reality. Let them find a replacement for my opponent now that he's gone. Election Day will soon be here! Too late! Too late! I am all things. I am sleep and wakefulness. When you ignore me you only affirm me all the more. You cannot but pledge yourself to Representative Clark Malone. I am here for you, and our seniors, and our veterans, and our working families, and the rot in your teeth, and the clicking termites in the walls, and the dog strangling at the end of a rope as he strains to snap at your pink legs. Representational Mark Clalone. Mark Alone. Klarkark Men-loa. This message paid for by money from a hidden place.

#

Call time: Midnight

Caller from: [Private number]

Maddie, we did it. When they finished counting the votes tonight, the result was overwhelming: a victory for Representative Clark Malone. But really, a victory for you, and for citizens just like you. I mean this from the bottom of my heart when I say this would not have been possible without your help. The way you got up at the crack of dawn on Election Day and drove in silence to the Appointed Place and received the box that contained the instruments by which our country was renewed; the way you lured the man into the woods behind the polling place with promises of fleshly coupling; the way you cut him behind the knees and sliced his ankles and his wrists; the way you watched him bleed out on the hard earth of this black month; the way you drove to the church and spun past the locks; the way you left two bodies still thumping against the carpet in the vestry, spasmodic muscle-parodies of departed life; the fire you set; the awful scene at the precinct house; the old saloon bar filled with moving husks who now move no longer; the parents and volunteers out marching in a grim line across the open ground, looking for a brightly colored snatch of clothing, a stray sneaker, SOMETHING, a sign, anything; knowing they would find nothing; the final moments in flame and truth and glass windows popping like corks. Today we won, Maddie. Not just me, but you, and our whole nation. I'm going to put on my greatcoat and walk the streets of this town, and the dogs' heads you left in the trees will drip down their victory greeting to me. I'm going to spin the dial on the old clock face at Town Hall; I'm going to skitter off the silent bell of Center Church; I'm going to splash around in the dry pools of light made by the sodium lamps and sit right down at the counter of Sleepy Pete's Diner and order myself a big old cheeseburger, and when I take my first bite I'm going to think of you, Maddie. Did you whisper my name as the senior center burned? Representative Clark Malone. This message was paid for by [inaudible]

THE FOOL ON THE HILL

by Lisa Morton

Merce pulled her boot back just before it came down on the half-buried skull. There were more of them in this area, mired in the mud and grayish swamp grass.

She used her walking stick to test the ground beyond the skull, trying not to stare into the eye socket pointed at her face. The stick sank an inch into the water before stopping. She stepped over the bone, planting herself where her stick had been.

Progress across this bog was slow, but not impossible. Ordinarily, Merce would have already given up and moved on to firmer land, but something about the building on the other side of the swamp drew her. Even though parts of its upper stories had caved in, even though walls were cracked and covered with moss, its white columns and rounded portico pinged in Merce's brain. She'd seen this place before, in Mama's history books; she knew it had been important.

She heard a brittle snap beneath her heel; she'd stepped on a long bone. This area, long ago reclaimed by nature's liquids and life, was packed with more death than anywhere else she'd encountered. It'd been a week since she'd left home, hauling her little cart behind her, her head packed with the list of items needed:

Solar panels. Working laptops. Light bulbs. A specific radio piece for Uncle Park. Herbs for Aunt Lateesha. Bullets for Uncle Juan. Reading glasses for Mama.

Merce had just turned eighteen, so this was her first trip alone as a Finder. If she could return with at least most of the items on the list, she'd get to keep going as a Finder, instead of being assigned to help out with the farming. Farming bored her to tears; she recognized its significance, but she wasn't cut out for it.

"I think you're a born leader," Mama had told her more than once. But so far Merce didn't feel that herself. She liked the challenge of leaving Camp Jackson, going out on her own into the world, coming up with pieces of the past that would make her extended family happy, productive, enduring. She liked helping others. Maybe that was what Mama was saying, that Merce was good at helping. Maybe that's what being a leader really meant.

So far the trip had been successful. She'd headed southwest, not doing much searching for the first two days; she knew the land surrounding her home had long ago been picked clean by other Finders. On the third day, though, she'd found a once-suburban garden overgrown with Aunt Lateesha's herbs, and later had discovered a stash of unbroken solar panels. She'd stumbled across an old book on healing she thought Lateesha would like, and a pad of paper and colored pencils that her brother Leo would love – Leo, the gifted artist, often lamenting that he had nothing but broken walls for canvases.

Eventually Merce's way had brought her here, to a one-time major city, now abandoned, collapsed in on itself, turning sepia and emerald as the elements reclaimed it. Merce had found an old store that must have sold radio parts, and she'd scored by locating Uncle Park's piece. Her cart was packed, getting harder to haul, and she'd been about to turn around when she'd seen something framed at the end of a strip of broken asphalt. Beyond the asphalt had probably once been an expanse of carefully-tended grass, but now it was the muddy ruin that Merce waded through.

Toward that familiar house…

The remains in the muck were testament to the former importance of this place. Merce saw not just skulls and arm bones and rib cages, but rusting weapons and armor. Whether these soldiers had died in the first (nuclear) attack or the riots that had followed as hunger and sickness swept the land, Merce didn't know. But they'd clearly died defending whoever had lived in the house. That became clearer as she neared the collapsed walls and saw bullet holes in some of the skulls, even a few shreds of skin and uniform. These were still corpses, not yet skeletons, and they'd been shot, maybe even not that long ago.

She should turn around, make her way back to where she'd left her cart, hidden underneath its camouflage of netting and leafy branches. But she was close enough now to see inside the building, to see shafts of afternoon sun outlined in dust motes, spotlighting old furnishings and paintings.

No, she'd come too far. She had to go in now.

She reached a point where a wall had cracked apart, old masonry jumbled on either side of a wide split. Before entering, she thrust a hand into her olive drab jacket pocket and grasped the metal handle of her folding knife. She didn't remove it, but knowing it was there was a comfort.

Taking a deep breath, Merce stepped through, wedging her slim body around rubble and twisted girders. Still using the stick, she made her way into the structure. Stopping to listen, she heard only the soft sounds of animals. She was in a room that had once been elegant, with chairs and tables whose wooden legs had withstood time's onslaught even if their upholstery had not. There was a desk littered with computer equipment and paper tatters, but there was nothing Merce could use.

The floor felt solid, so she ventured farther in. At least the interior was free of human remains, although animals, both alive and dead, had nested in old fabrics. She moved down a hallway where paintings only slightly eroded showed men (mostly) and women, all long dead, all regally posed. Merce didn't like looking at them; she felt their gazes upon her, an airy pressure.

She passed other rooms like the first one she'd been in; none held anything worth taking.

Turning a corner, Merce stopped, staring: at the end of the new hall was a large, steel door, open. Coming through the door was electric light.

Her gut clenched; she nearly fled. But instead she forced herself to stop and listen again. Nothing. She took a few cautious steps forward, craning forward to catch any sounds coming from beyond that doorway.

Nothing. If anything had turned on those lights, it wasn't moving.

She supposed the lights could be automatic, somehow still functioning, some quirk of a power system she didn't understand. Merce hadn't spent much time with Uncle Manny; she really didn't understand much about generators and batteries and wires and lights. As she edged closer, looking inside, she saw that the lights were positioned above a staircase that led down, and that not all of them still worked.

Curiosity drew her on. Moving through the doorway, she hesitated on the landing, looking down. The stairs were metal, solid, and seemed to go down several stories.

Her heavy, mud-crusted boots were loud on the metal grating, so she removed them. Clad only in woolen socks, holding the boots in one hand and her stick in the other, she jogged silently down the stairs.

They ended in a long, concrete hallway. Merce knew she was deep under the earth now, and she felt the first anxious tendrils of claustrophobia circling around her, but the air was breathable and the surroundings solid, so she forced her nerves down and moved ahead.

She passed doors that opened onto offices, gathering rooms, rooms whose purposes she couldn't name. But the fourth room on the right…

Merce stared, open-mouthed, into a cavernous storage area. Metal racks extended into the distance. Many were empty, leaving Merce to wonder if they'd been picked clean, or had never held anything.

But it was the stacks of foil packets on one that made her heart leap. She ran to them, held them up to the single light overhead. "Freeze-Dried Ice Cream", read the first one. Another pile was "Stroganoff". Next to that, "Pasta Primavera." Beyond the packets were unopened crates, stamped with the same names.

Merce allowed herself a small victory cry. The old military rations were still good and highly prized in Camp Jackson. Finders were lucky to return with one or two.

This was a treasure.

Merce shrugged out of her backpack, began loading it up.

She packed carefully, trying to fit in as many as she could. She knew she could always come back here for more, but it was a long trip back to her cart and a week's trudge to Camp Jackson.

When her backpack couldn't hold one more ration she pulled it on, inwardly groaning at the weight but exhilarated by the contents. She imagined the feast Mama and Uncle Pete would prepare – fresh ears of corn from their fields and salad greens and stroganoff, with ice cream for dessert. There was enough here for all 102 residents of Camp Jackson to share.

She took the stairs slowly, careful not to stress her lungs and muscles – it was a long way up, and she still had to cross the swamp outside. She rested at each landing, but she still felt her calves protest when she reached the top.

Shifting the pack slightly, Merce stopped at the doorway, considering her position. She thought it might be easier to reach the outside if she turned right instead of left, the way she'd come. There was more sunlight coming from a room down there, promising a faster exit.

She knew, though, that it was late in the day and that sunlight would be fading soon. She needed to move quickly.

After she put her boots on, she reached the room at the end of the hall. It was circular, large, couches and chairs facing a huge, heavy desk; a tall leather chair, its back to her, was behind the desk. Before three windows that miraculously still had their glass stood two poles, each bearing a filthy, ragged flag. Merce knew the red, white, and blue of the one on the left had been the colors of the United States of America, a country that had died five years before she'd been born.

On the other side of the room were two windows, both missing their glass, flanking a door. The windows looked out on a vista of wild, overgrown roses, splashes of white and pink providing relief from the bog's visual monotony. Below the broken windows, piles of dead leaves and rose petals had formed ramps leading up to the sills.

Merce headed for the door, thinking that if it was jammed she could easily climb through one of the windows. She was preoccupied, weighed down. Careless.

"Where do you think you're going?"

She'd almost reached the door when the voice, harsh and hoarse, froze her. Heart triphammering, she turned her head.

A man sat in the tall chair, watching her. She scolded herself inwardly for not checking that chair first. She could have avoided this, gone another direction, but she'd gotten sloppy, thinking of parties and ice cream, of her loved ones, of home.

At first she wondered if it was a ghost that had spoken to her. The thing in the chair was thin, thinner even than she was, with a gaunt, lined face topped by ragged silver hair. It had a prominent chin but no teeth; the blue irises were completely encircled by white; the clothing had once been formal, but now was as old and colorless as a scarecrow's.

No, Merce knew this was no ghost…but this man was disturbed. It was in the wide eyes, in the way his jaw slid when he spoke, in the rapid patter of his words, slurred by lack of teeth.

"What have you got in that pack, you little thief? Bring that over and show it to me right now."

Merce didn't move, her mind flitting past options. She could probably outrun the man, but she'd have to leave the pack. She might even be able to out-fight him – he had a foot on her, but looked weak, and she had her pocket knife and her stick. Or she could try explaining herself, but somehow she didn't think he'd care.

Then he reached into the desk, pulled out a gun, and turned it on her.

It was a pistol. Merce didn't know much about guns – that was Uncle Juan's forte – but she knew the one trained on her right now could kill her.

"What are you, deaf, you little fucker? Bring that goddamn bag over here NOW."

Merce shrugged out of the backpack, moving carefully so as not to excite the man, not to give him any reason to pull that trigger. Holding the bag out before her, she approached. The man leaned out and snatched the backpack away from her. He glanced at the contents before looking at her as he sneered.

"Just what I thought – stealing my rations! You're all alike, you little shits, trying to break in here and take what doesn't belong to you." He hurled the bag aside, causing some of the packets to spill out. Merce stifled the impulse to pick them up.

"I'm sorry," she said. Her voice was dry, raspy. She cleared her throat and tried again. "I didn't know anyone was here –"

He cut her off, mimicking her unfairly with high, screechy tones. "'I didn't know anyone was here.' Of course someone's here – I'm here. This is my fucking home. I've always been here, and I always will be here, and you will never belong here!"

The man's madness nearly staggered Merce. She'd never encountered anything like this, not even the one time Uncle Dave had found a bottle of whiskey and gotten so drunk that they'd had to lock him up in a basement because he screamed and tried to hit everyone. At least Uncle Dave had been okay a day later, ashamed of his behavior. She didn't think this man – who did look slightly familiar to her now – would ever apologize or relent.

But she had to try. "You're right, so I'll just leave –"

Again, he interrupted, this time jamming the gun towards her. "Oh, it's not that easy, you little cunt. You do not get to trespass into the goddamn White House and try to steal from me, then just be on your merry fucking way. We've got laws in this country, not that I'd expect your kind to abide by them."

His face…something about it…like the building, it prodded at her memories, of photos in the old history books. Her eyes jittered for a second away from him, and for the first time she noticed the portrait on the wall behind him, almost life-sized, and it was him…

But no, it wasn't. He couldn't be alive, not this many years later, not after the wars and radiation and plagues. No, this couldn't be him, but it could be –

"Who are you?"

He laughed, but it was mirthless, his eyes never leaving her. "Jesus, you're so stupid you don't even know. I'm the President."

"Of what?"

His gums ground together before he answered. "Of this country. What else?"

"But…" Merce hesitated; it seemed almost cruel to tell him. "There is no more country."

"Of course there is. And I'm its President, just like my father before me."

Ahhh, that explained it: Merce understood. This was the son. He really had grown up here, in this once-famous house, and then when he'd been left alone he'd gone slowly mad. Merce wondered how many of the skulls she'd seen outside with perfect fingertip-sized holes in the brows had been shot by him.

"So your father was the one who destroyed everything."

It was the wrong thing to say. He spasmed with rage and uttered a snarled cry. "No! He saved us! Not that you deserved it -"

The gun barrel lined up with her eyes.

His finger tightened.

He pulled the trigger.

Nothing happened.

The President's son stared in incomprehension for a moment, then pulled the trigger again. And again. And again.

Merce knew; she knew because she'd watched Uncle Juan clean his guns. He was meticulous about it, even ritualistic. When she'd asked him once why he did it, he'd explained to her that guns were old metal things, and old metal things could rust and malfunction unless they were cared for.

This man hadn't taken care of anything.

Merce didn't wait any longer. She grabbed her pack, shoving as many of the ration packets down into it as she could, swinging it by the straps. As she leapt through the broken window, she heard him scream and toss the gun aside.

She ran through rose bushes taller than her, ignoring the thorns that drew thin trickles of blood from her face and the backs of her hands. She heard him behind her, crashing through the growth. "You won't get away!"

Merce ran. She broke through the roses and was back at the edge of the swamp. She'd lost her stick somewhere, so she'd have to risk it, operating from memory, instinct and luck. She leapt from one mound to the next, jumping if she felt a foot slipping, not thinking about the sounds of crunching and snapping beneath her feet. She didn't know what she'd do when she reached the other side of the swamp. Maybe she could lose him in the ruins beyond, come back for the cart after dark –

He screamed behind her, and she heard a splash.

Merce risked a look backward and then stopped to stare. Her pursuer had fallen into a brackish pool, and only his head and shoulders were above the water. He twisted and jerked, freed one arm, but couldn't escape.

She watched him, cautious, ready to flee again should he pull himself out. He thrashed and shrieked, waved his arm, with no effect.

He was stuck. He saw her and shouted, "Something's wrapped around my leg. Come over here and help me."

She didn't move.

He called again, "Look, I'll make it worth your while. How'd you like to drive all of those rations out of here in a tank? Because I can get you one. You'd like that, wouldn't you?"

Merce shouted back, "It wouldn't work after all this time, like your gun."

"Whatever. I'm the President -"

"You're not the President. You can't inherit it, and nobody elected you."

"Fine. Just HELP ME!"

She considered. If she didn't help him, he might still get himself out…or he might die there, slowly and miserably, trapped. If she tried to help him, he'd likely kill her.

She should leave. Return to her cart, get away from here as fast as she could, even if it meant that she keep going after dark. Leave this awful, insane, dead place and never come back, even for the precious rations.

But he was screaming behind her. Would she hear those screams forever, every night in her dreams?

Mama thought she was a leader. How would a real leader handle this?

She started walking toward him, her hand going to her pocket as she did, to her folding knife. She'd used the knife to cut Aunt Lateesha's herbs, to pry out Uncle Park's circuit boards, to sever vines and twigs. Her father, Camp Jackson's greatest Finder, had given it to her after his last trip out, a special gift to her on her twelfth birthday, a week before he'd fallen from the roof during a simple repair and never recovered.

The man trapped in the swamp watched her expectantly, spluttering. "Yeah…right, come on…"

Merce stopped ten feet from him, well out of reach. She held the folded knife to her lips, kissed it, and then tossed it to him. It hit the water near him, but he caught it, held it up before his eyes, perplexed. "What is this supposed to be?"

"It's a pocket knife. Use it to cut yourself free." She turned, walking away.

Behind her, he said, "How the fuck am I supposed to do that? I can't even open it."

"Figure it out."

She increased her speed then, no longer listening to him. She wasn't sure if the thud she heard at one point was her knife being thrown at her or not. She didn't turn to look. By the time she reached her cart, his fury had faded into the distance.

The sun was setting as she lowered the heavy pack onto the wagon. She was too tired to go far tonight, but she could at least get a little way from here before finding a quiet, dry, safe place. She knew she'd sleep well, untroubled by awful dreams.

And then – like the rest of the world – she'd be done with this place for good.

HOPE
LOVE

HOW I LEARNED TO STOP WORRYING AND LOVE THE WALL

by Simon McCaffery

You wanted a Great America, you got one.

That's what the disembodied voice inside my living pod says every morning after the wake-up chime sounds the arrival of another day. We're a nation founded on debate and discourse, but you have to admit it's true.

Soft LED bar lights running the perimeter of the oval ceiling illuminate and the built-in coffee machine gurgles and hisses. I swing out of bed and it automatically retracts into the curved wall. A soft female voice relays the weather outside the Great Wall, a reminder for the staff meeting at 15:00 hours, my day's schedule, the featured execution, and other miscellanea. I used to have Our Nation's CEO's voice set for wake-up announcements, so take-charge and commanding and New York nasal, but the synthetic young woman's voice is admittedly more soothing. I take a quick, hot shower (prudent water rationing continues), and eat a microwaved breakfast in the contoured alcove while Fox News covers the latest stories. The same company that used to construct upscale micro apartments in San Francisco designed all of the living pods in my quadrant. I remember viewing one on Mission Street when I was desperate for any job and my do-not-resuscitate marriage had finally flat-lined: $450,000 for a claustrophobic two hundred square feet. Outrageous. Another kick in the teeth to hard-working citizens like me doing the important jobs that few others want to tackle at the lowest salaries.

My living pod is cozy, self-contained and has everything. I'm senior staff, so I don't share space with a roommate in a double twin bed layout like the first two years. I don't pay a mortgage or rent, and I have access to the fitness centers and topside jogging trails. I can stream entertainment on the integrated flatscreen – no cable or

Hulu subscription – and the standard meal plan is included in my employment contract. Waiting periods for a posting inside the Great Wall are miles long as you can imagine (no pun intended), assuming you fit the preferred requisite employment profile and possess proof of new citizenship. Social media is riddled with protests and cruel memes posted by the envious, and I've seen occasional bold graffiti on the Wall itself, but in fairness citizens must weigh the benefits and securities America has gained against the exclusion of certain key employment positions to registered Muslims, undocumented migrants, descendants of undocumented migrants, women over thirty, women over 170 pounds, suspected criminal aliens, environmental Canadians, ISIS sympathizers, all Syrians, pro-life proponents, registered LBGTQ, and anyone who opposes our second amendment right to own assault weapons and high-capacity magazine handguns. I grew up in Illinois, outside Chicago, and have never fired a round in my life. So I had no qualifications or inclination to join Border Patrol or Homeland Police Corps. That takes a special breed.

Before you protest, remember that the new America has meaningful employment for these individuals, usually in the swelling ranks of the Deportation Task Force.

I dress, unclick my tablet from its wall dock, and make sure my access and security credentials are draped around my neck on their red, white, and blue lanyard. I exit the honeycomb living pod, a bee joining a stream of thousands of fellow citizen workers swarming along the wide curving concourse to the main lifts inside the largest cement and steel hive ever constructed. We're deep inside the subterranean levels of a ten-mile section designated GW-Quadrant-56689F, six stories underground.

Cynics and naysayers said that Our Nation's CEO's dream of constructing a wall spanning nearly two thousand miles of dry, waterless Mexican borderland was lunacy. Fear-bait for Bible belt buckle conservatives and xenophobes. That to be effective it would have to rise at least twenty to thirty feet above the sand and scrub.

That it would cost well over eight billion dollars. That no one could be coerced into manning it even if it could be erected.

Hey, full disclosure, I was one of them. Dad was a liberal lifelong Democrat who voted for Jimmy Carter and Clinton, and Mom was a libertarian.

The Great Wall towers sixty feet in average height and spans more than twelve hundred miles, much of it in contiguous sections that seal our southern border where natural topographical barriers are absent. Most abbreviate it to the GW. It cost taxpayers twenty-eight billion – more than half of the investment in FDR's New Deal in the 1930s, and the largest national infrastructure project of the twenty-first century – but it employs a dozen major contractors, hundreds of pre- and post-construction subcontractors, and thousands of skilled laborers. Six of the largest concrete fabrication facilities ever designed were built to supply more than forty million cubic yards of slab, roughly five times the volume used to build the Hoover Dam. The Large Hadron Collider is a tapeworm in comparison. Raising the GW pushed the GNP up five points, not counting subsequent revenues from immigration application fees, deportation fines, three separate syndicated reality television programs, untold documentaries, and multi-level merchandise licensing. When Al Roker does the weather from the highest point of the Wall, near the southwest Arizona border, the Today Show always tops the ratings in the brutal morning news-slash-variety timeslot. Revenues from tourism have yet to peak. Last year more than seven million people from over a dozen countries visited. The number would be higher except that China is still sulking over the drop in interest in their Wall and trade imbalances, and no entrance visas are granted for residents of Mexico or Islamic countries. It's true that arm-wrestling efforts to subsidize the cost of construction and maintenance through Mexican trade agreements and seized drug cartel money fizzled, but when we're already shouldering a national debt of twenty trillion, what's another few billion?

Our former president promised a great, great wall, a beautiful wall, and before his second extended term concluded, the GW was more than seventy percent complete. It is deserving of the designation of Eighth Wonder of the Modern World. It is visible from the International Space Station. It altered the Jetstream, local climate, river systems, and the fauna. It saved America's stagnated economy, reintroducing us as a nation that draws upon its vast human and natural resources to build things, instead of simply consuming.

While in office he referred to himself as Our Nation's CEO, and the name has stuck. Instead of retiring to the lucrative speaking tour circuits and multi-million dollar ghostwritten memoirs after his two terms, our president took over the role of CEO of the GW to see the project through to completion. He's celebrating his eighty-third birthday tomorrow, a lavish spectacle that will be attended by a stellar cast of celebrities, fellow billionaires, and dignitaries (and attract legions of illegal protest groups and lunatic causes), and be broadcast live around the world. You can imagine the preparations that have been underway for weeks.

How do I fit in?

I'm Jim Benson, age 36, divorcee, and former public school educator. I met and married my former wife at college in Missouri (MU, Columbia, go Tigers), and after graduation I taught high school English and literature for four years before the school system in Overland Park cut funding, and me. The Show-Me State ranked thirty-third in the nation for education dollars spent per student. I taught in Wichita for three years (ranked thirty-eighth) and was awarded Best New Teacher, then two years in Texas (ranked forty-three) where I was named Most Inspirational Instructor, and then a year in Oklahoma City (forty-eighth). Looking back, it was an inexorable descent. Why didn't I move to New York, you ask, the District of Columbia, or Connecticut to teach? A young married couple living on an educator's and an office manager's salaries couldn't afford to live. After I was let go in OKC, I went through a tough period. I loved being an educator, inspiring young people, seeing how they looked up to me, but the system kept spitting me out. I was angry, rejected, and disillusioned. As a culture we thought it made complete sense to compensate millions to professional athletes and twerking teenage pop singers, but invest in education and our nation's future? Bitch, please.

To my eternal shame, I voted against Our Nation's CEO in the first election. By reflex and swept along with the liberal party line. When he eked out the win after two recounts and the GW was green lit, the call went out for credentialed professionals. I worried that my voting record might knock me off the list. I was working two jobs at a dingy dry cleaner in Fort Worth and bartending at the airport, and hadn't stepped in a classroom for nearly three years.

A former friend and fellow discarded educator from my Kansas days, Albert Merch, put in a good word, and here I am. I'm teaching again!

Inside the enclosed ecosystem of the GW, a seemingly endless artificial ribbon-world extruded above the equator, my skills are highly valued. Over seventy thousand full and part time workers report for shifts each day at the GW, and more than a third of those people live and work inside the complex. There are a lot of singles like me, but a lot of families, too, so we have our own distributed K-12 schools. A new generation of children born in the GW will be educated, choose their vocation, and potentially live out their lives inside the GW. There are vocational and college level programs for non-traditional adults who want to finish degrees or learn new skills. We have access to modern teaching facilities and cutting edge technologies, and best of all, little fear of budget cuts and pink slips.

We don't get summers off, and the more experienced among us assist with tour groups and educational field trips on top of our curriculum loads. It's just another facet of education, so visitors understand the positive impacts of the GW to balance against controversial claims of environmental impact, flooding, and the decline of endangered North American jaguars and black bears, now denied the opportunity to slip across the border to mate with other gene pools.

The lifts propel us ten levels up to the Grand Concourse where we grab a sugar-laced Starbucks, then a tram delivers us to my current post, Mike Pence Memorial Middle School. I stride to room DJT-3347C, seventh grade American Literature. Twenty-two bright-eyed students, the optimal number to ensure interaction, sit waiting in their smart desks. True, eighty percent are Caucasian, but that number is incrementally improving all the time. Except for Hispanics and Muslims, but we all recognize that given time those fences will be mended.

Today we're conducting our final roundtable discussion of Orwell's *Animal Farm*. It's been a lively, popular reading project. There are no Cliff Notes or online summaries to fall back on. This class enjoys deconstructing every chapter, debating the motives and merits of the allegorical characters, deciding in the end that Boxer, the loyal, Herculean cart-horse isn't a tragic figure, but a naïve fool -- the kind of loser that Our Nation's CEO despises. They also see straight through the jaded cynicism of the old donkey, Benjamin, the embodiment of the old America, the Nation That Gave Up.

"Good afternoon, class!" I say with relish.

"Goof afternoon, Mr. Benson!" they chorus.

I grab my electronic pen and move to the smart board. It's go time.

After period four English Composition, it's time for the senior staff meeting.

That involves another packed tube ride up four levels, and another tram ride west. The bright glass and plastic room is already nearly full, but Albert has saved me a chair directly across from Sheila Kinney. Sheila joined our quadrant's staff seven months ago. She teaches Algebra I and II. We met at a singles mixer, and have been dating for several months. We're not rushing things; both of us are still dealing with the fallout of failed relationships.

Maurice Stehman, our preppy, prima donna principal, calls the session to order and delivers the agenda. We're all being pressed into last-minute service for the multitude of overlapping tours set to take place over the next forty-eight hours. He also announces that twenty randomly selected names from among us are needed to help facilitate the birthday banquet award ceremony tomorrow evening in the grand rotunda. I don't really care to be chosen, but my heart begins thumping inside my chest the moment names begin appearing on the big glowing wall screen. My name appears as the tenth selection, and I cannot suppress a huge grin. I cross my fingers in my lap and stare at the screen. Yes! Sheila is drawn as the final name. Albert grins and congratulates me, but I can tell from his eyes and frozen smile that he's disappointed. Sheila smiles from across the wide conference table, her dark eyes glittering with excitement. It's an unexpected honor that we'll get to share.

After the staff meeting disperses I have to race to the rooftop to meet a large tour group at the entrance to Ivanka Park, a thirty acre open-air sight-seeing promenade and amusement park overlooking the Rio Grande. The group of mainly middle-aged Midwestern men and women are enjoying refreshments after a day of touring the interior. They've already been to the gift shop and are sporting GW caps, fanny packs, and T shirts emblazoned with NOBODY BUILDS WALLS BETTER THAN ME, and MARK MY WORDS, and AMERICA THE GREAT, and NOW YOU'RE NOT POOR AND UNEDUCATED.

I put on my best smile and herd them together for the sunset tour.

An hour later I phone Sheila from the concourse to postpone our late dinner date. She doesn't mind, we're both exhausted, and tomorrow is the big day. We've both seen Our Nation's CEO, but never at such close range.

I make my way back to my quarters on autopilot and fall into my cot-bed.

I wake in the darkness to a thundering, rumbling, teeth-rattling BOOM. A second later I'm flung from the bed onto the plastic tiled floor.

Earthquake! Like the one that damaged a half-mile segment of the GW near San Luis. Will the ceilings hold? Alarms begin braying far off inside our quad. The synthetic woman's voice calmly advises me to evacuate my living pod and make my way immediately to the stairwells and to our section's emergency rally point. Do not take the lifts.

I pull on jeans and a GW T-shirt ("I BEAT CHINA ALL THE TIME"), and scramble out into the hallway, where I'm immediately swept away in a sea of jostling men and women. I consider trying to reverse direction against the human tide, back toward the segment where Sheila lives, but that proves impossible, and besides, she's being evacuated, too. I'll find her at the rally point.

The trams aren't running and it takes forty minutes to make it to the wide, oversized stairwells. Lights and power fail completely as we begin our ascent to the surface level. For a moment there are cries and gasps of fear, but then the backup generators come online and bright emergency lights and goblin-green strips are illuminated. It's a good thing that I work out three times a week in our fitness center, but my knees and legs are sore by the time I ascend the six long, sardine-packed flights.

Outside a sea of crimson and yellow strobe lights and wailing sirens greets us. It's still dark, an hour or more before dawn, but the air feels hotter than midday, and the wind is howling. GW security vehicles are scattered about. Dozens of Border Patrol and emergency responders are trying to control the flow of the crowds. Men shout into electric bullhorns, but I cannot make out their words.

A man dressed in a bulky white Hazmat suit appears and directs us toward several large transports. I see more men and women in those creepy pale suits, and it begins to dawn on me that this may not have been the result of fracking and shifting tectonic plates.

In that instant of realization I'm overcome by a white-hot rage, more searing than the swirling air around us. There have been many threats made to destroy the GW, to breach it's high ramparts, to undermine the bold vision of Our Nation's CEO, to forcibly return all of us to the politically correct but terminally dysfunctional, pointless lives we once led. I have a clear vision of myself standing inside my former junior high classroom in Oklahoma City, with its industrial gray-green walls, battered furniture, and sickly fluorescent track lighting, packing my personal items into a single banker's box, the anger running through me like high voltage.

It all comes flooding back, and three of the guys in radiation suits have to drag me to the nearest transport truck.

I was able to watch Our Nation's CEO belatedly celebrate his birthday a week later, from my hospital bed in an Albuquerque burn center. The suitcase dirty bomb had detonated miles away, but I still caught a dose. As did Sheila.

Nearly five thousand died in the explosion, shockwave, fires, and hard radiation exposure. It was 9/11 all over again.

Within hours Our Nation's CEO was on the airwaves, assuring everyone that he was alive, healthy, and that he would personally see that vengeance be meted out to those responsible. Teams were already planning a great monument that would be erected to honor and remember the lost. America's Great Wall would be repaired and made even stronger, even higher. When a group of radical Canadian environmental separatists claimed responsibility, he announced he will build a second, northern wall, from Vancouver to New Brunswick. More jobs, more industry, more opportunity for almost everyone. As a people we will never return to our past as a dystopian, open-door, crime-riddled nation on the edge of existential crisis.

"It's going to be a bigger, fatter, more beautiful wall," he roars to the cheering crowds. "And I'm going to make Canada pay for it!"

You wanted a Great America, you got one.

OBEY

WILLOW TESTS WELL

by Nick Mamatas

Willow got her first birthday card from a stranger on her ninth. Not a stranger, really. The director of the Federal Bureau of Investigation was on TV so frequently that he was practically a friend of the family. Her parents insisted on watching the news—both the fun local news where people smiled did banter and half the stories were about great red smears and ruined cars on the nearby streets, and the boring national news—every night during dinner. Willow liked the director of the FBI. His name was Bottomore and he had a dimple right in the middle of his chin. Where she liked it.

When Bottomore died some months later, Willow wasn't sad. Not exactly sad—tingly, upset, anticipating something that could never be. Because Willow was never sad. She always felt just fine.

"How was school?" her father asked.

"Fine," she said. No need for father to pry any further. Willow tested very well—she was already reading and performing mathematics on a twelfth-grade level. Willow could probably skip a grade if she wanted to, and by the time she was fifteen take community college classes for full credit.

"What do you think of this sweater?" her stepmother asked, pointing to the picture on her laptop. Willow's real mother had run off some time before. "They have them in, uh, Bubble, Amaranth, or…Durian. Geez, what do these colors even mean?"

"Blue, green, or brown," Willow said. Then she said, "Any of those would be fine. Thank you, Doris."

"So clever," Doris said.

Tenth birthday: greeting cards from the CIA and NSA. Willow had scored ridiculously well on the Race to the Top tests, and even discovered the instructions for and answered the questions in the secret test integrated into the exam. Questions like

What does the old saying "A bird in the hand is worth two in the bush" mean?"

a. birds are unpleasant because they need to be cared for

b. it's better to own something than risk what you have for a potential reward

c. if you have a bird in your hand, you can squeeze it, you can kill it…

d. possession is nine-tenths of the law

Willow knew that the answer was C. She knew it in her heart of hearts because the kitty on the poster on the wall winked at her.

So various intelligence agencies began negotiating. Who would get Willow? Three weeks later her parents were killed in a terrible if well-choreographed car accident. Her father's head was sheared off—his face was nothing but a jaw topped with meat sauce. Her stepmother died in the hospital of less photogenic injuries. Willow was sent to live with her biological mother, whose economic situation had taken a turn for the worse since her flight and abandonment. For some reason, she had a coroner's photo of her ex-husband in the bottom drawer of her pressed word bureau, and Willow found it easily. She lived in the city, in a sweltering one-room bedsit with cinderblock walls atop a dying florist.

The florist was an NSA front. Willow would stop in after school to look at the flowers while waiting for her mother to get home from her job at an industrial bakery. The whole neighborhood smelled like cinnamon and burning plastic.

"What's this flower?" Willow asked one day.

"Those are chrysanthemums," the florist said. He always had a pair of clippers in hand.

"They look like people's heads," Willow said. "I mean, more than other flowers. Like a big round head full of curly hair."

The florist smiled and said, "I know a flower that looks like you. I have it in the back." He left his clippers behind as he turned to go to the cooler in the back room. When he came back, the mums were all headless, but he kept smiling and presented black-haired Willow with a black-petaled flower. "It's a black beauty hollyhock," he said, and presented it to her. Willow brought her hands out from behind her back and knew she didn't need to hide the clippers anymore.

"It does look like me," she said as she accepted the flower. "Just like me. Black all around, with a yellow spike in the middle." The florist's tight-slipped smile betrayed a twitch at that.

Willow's grades began to falter. She was new in school, and quiet, and large-eyed and wore clothes that were popular two years prior. Some of them had stains on the sleeves, from their original owners. Boys mostly ignored her, but occasionally pulled her hair as they passed her in the hallways. Girls were much worse.

They worked in groups, surrounding her.

"So your dad is dead, huh? Must have been a suicide."

"How does your mom afford your fancy apartment? Is she a prostitute?"

"What are you going to do for Take Your Daughter to Work day?"

"She's upset. Look, don't be upset, Willow. There's nothing to cry about. We're your friends. Are you getting your period?"

"Your first period?"

"Does your mother take a few days off from work when she has her period?"

"Will you have to take over for her," the main girl said, even taking Willow's hand in her own and patting it comfortingly, "when she is so indisposed?"

Willow stood there, hair over her face, taking it. Surveillance cameras, parabolic mics, satellites that could find a 1976 bicentennial quarter flipped into the Grand Canyon, all focused on her. She didn't snap. The ringleader didn't end up with a pencil in her eye, the others weren't beaten with a pipe or pushed in front of a city bus. Willow just went home after school let out, as she did every day, except that three blocks from her apartment she made friends with a little four-year-old boy and, taking him by the hand, walked him face-first into a lamppost, then left him on the corner to cry and bleed.

There are two kinds of children who attract the attention of the federal government's alphabet soup. There are both prodigies in their way. Kids with a knack for math and lateral thinking are recruited early on. Birthday cards emblazoned with the seals of major intelligence and law enforcement agencies still mean something special, even in these days of single-digit approval ratings. Those numbers are only for the _elected_ government. The permanent government has a more entrenched reputation. So the little smartypantses get their cards and parents get the hint—judo lessons, laptops, tutors, Chinese and Arabic flashcards. Despite the best efforts of the petit-bourgeoisie, there's a strong regression toward the mean. Most genius ten year olds are utterly ordinary sixteen year olds. Only a few retain the interest of federal recruiters, and only a fraction of those suitable can be lured away from the business world with appeals to the spirit of public service and promises of proximity to power.

There are other organizations that keep track of girls like Willow.

Willow continued to do very well on her tests, even as her attendance in school grew increasingly erratic, and her work indifferent. She sucked her first cock at thirteen, and started smoking cigarettes. She got bombed out on cheap bourbon on her fourteenth birthday. Her boyfriend was nineteen, and fancied himself the local Great White Hope at the boxing gym where he trained four days a week. He loosened two of Willow's teeth with an open-handed smack once. She left a stray cat in the trash, its head turned one hundred and eighty degrees. Mother had to take a second job—industrial bakery in the morning, night shift at a Dunkin Donuts. Somewhere in Langley, Virginia a mouse was clicked and an insurance settlement check in Willow's name fortuitously arrived, keeping the family from eviction, making community college a possibility after all.

Willow didn't need to go to the doctor for an abortion.

She drowned her fetus in her belly with sizzurp and shellfish. She finally broke up with her boyfriend after three years and found him another fourteen-year-old—that's how he liked them, just wisps down there—and thus he promised not to kill himself after all. Memoranda flew back and forth. High-priority emails were sent, read, deleted. Hard drives zapped with powerful magnets the size of shirt buttons. But they can drag a boat. There was only one question left to answer: Does Willow have too much empathy, or not enough?

At community college, there were more tests, but those were specialized, not standardized. Willow wore a skirt with a hem just three inches over her knee, and some purple stockings, to class the first day, and was called a "cheap fucking whore!" by some weedy-looking boy in the parking lot. She kept her head up, walked to her class. PSY 101, her only elective. A vending machine malfunctioned, taunting her with a Three Musketeers Bar hanging from its loop, refusing to fall. She learned about childhood sexual urges, about the Stanford prison experiment. An older woman, a veteran of the war in Afghanistan, burst into tears in English class one day, as everyone but Willow struggled through "The Tell-Tale Heart." Back in PSY 101, Willow watched an episode from a late-night television news program about sociopathic youngsters. A cute young blonde girl says on the show, "I wish I could kill everybody; then I could have the world all to myself." An infant stares over the head of her mother and smiles at some invisible thing in the air. Willow's pulse remained steady. She wrote a term paper about a famous female serial killer whose jailhouse correspondence revealed a strong belief in UFOs, ancient astronauts, and an inevitable invasion. The killer's last words, said even as she was strapped to a gurney, with three different poisons pushing in to her veins, were, "I'll see you on Independence Day."

Willow's Facebook timeline was full of photos, but when her friends smiles and hoist their drinks with one hand and flashed faux gang signs with the others, she stood in their midst, square-shouldered, arms at her side, just smirking at the lens. On one wintry night, an agent damaged Willow's car in the community college parking lot. She had to walk home, on the shoulder of the highway. She was half blind from the ice rain in her eyes, and snow was piled in drifts along her path. Her left foot sunk into the ruined carcass of a raccoon that had managed to drag itself to the side of the road. She walked on without flinching.

Even better, on the sidewalk outside the door to her building, she scraped the letters I, C, and U into the dusty snow with the toe of her winter boot. Another secret test that only she perceived; another correct answer.

"What have you figured out so far?" her case worker asked Willow. She was beautiful girl now. Black hair pulled into a thick and complex braid, light blue eyes, just enough acne scarring to seem accessible to the average pig. French manicure, eyebrows waxed and arched. No tattoos or piercings—very clever. She can hide that way, when she needs to. The case worker didn't look like an intelligence agent, but she was one. She knew how to hide as well.

Willow said, "Well you can't use just anyone, can you?" They were in a twenty-hour diner, three hours into a new day. Willow had ruined the yolks of her eggs the moment her plate was placed in front of her, because she hated being stared at. She made a point of gesturing with her fork at the agent as she spoke, between bites and breaths. "For most jobs, anyone will do. Give them a uniform, a job title, some resources, and they'll do whatever you want. Be a hero or a villain, be a victim or a martyr. So you don't need me for the basics—extradition, enhanced interrogation, infiltration, propaganda. Not even wet work. That's boy stuff."

The agent didn't nod or shift her eyes in return. She just bit into her toast, flipped through the first few pages of the newspaper before her, chewing.

"Any girl would suck a cock straight from her own shitty asshole for a few extra dollars and a shot at Internet fame," Willow said suddenly. She shoveled some hash browns into her mouth and peered at the agent. "Any boy too."

The agent nodded solemnly, like God might from his throne atop a cloud.

"Big picture stuff," Willow said.

"Positively enormous," the agent said.

The agent had forms for Willow to sign. They were a dream come true, in form form. Willow accepted a place in Princeton

University as a transfer student, and a full bank account, and a lease to an apartment in Trenton co-signed by the agent herself. The agent happened to have the same last name as Willow. At the bottom of the forms lay a glossy photo of Willow's father's head. She shuddered, but didn't scream and scream and dig her fingernails into the flesh of her arms till she felt something hard until later.

Princeton was challenging. Trenton more so. The building to which she was assigned was in a slum area, her apartment a joke—bathtub in the kitchen and just enough floor space for an air mattress, no climate control save a space heater that fired off sparks when plugged in, rats with no fear of human beings and an appetite for uncooked supermarket pasta. The interior of the refrigerator was heavily stained with what looked like mold and dried blood. It was only the blood, courtesy the previous tenant and his unfortunate lover. Her neighbors were drug addicts and petty criminals who had nothing to lose—smashing someone's head in with a pipe wrench for ten dollars was worth the risk of a twenty-five year prison sentence. Willow took to carrying a box cutter, but she didn't use it at home. She used it at school.

Willow's coursework was selected by her case worker. Arabic, Russian, constitutional law, organic chemistry for a change of pace. Big picture stuff, but with an added fringe benefit—Willow's classmates were hypercompetitive young men and women who never abandoned their childhood dreams of being President or curing cancer. Clever boys and girls, sensitive and discerning. They could smell a sociopath a mile away. A bit overconfident, though.

Gordon and Camile were lovers, and very cosmopolitan. They both liked to watch the other fuck third parties. Gordon zeroed in on how Willow's hair was always in her face. "That girl got herself daddy-raped," he said to Camile. They were loitering outside the lecture hall as Willow moved past them.

"Girls like that will suck you off before dinner," Camile said. She chortled at her own ribaldry. "So that you'll like them." No need to keep their voices down. A deal was struck.

Gordon made his move later that day, buttonholing Willow and talking up the alacrity with which her Russian vocabulary was expanding. He knew to throw in a "neg", and mentioned something about Willow's Jersey accent interfering with a few of her pronunciations. He was on her side, ready to help her out. Maybe tonight, at his apartment, they could work on some lingual exercises?

"Sure," Willow said. She went home and dressed for the occasion—sun dress for easy access, oversized purse with a whole other outfit, hair pulled back, flats for running. She withstood four blocks of catcalls to catch the bus, which took her to the rundown district adjacent to Gordon's nice neighborhood.

There was wine waiting, and dumb music—Vangelis, the Bladerunner soundtrack of all things—and fresh sheets on the bed. Gordon kept the bedroom door open, so he'd have some place to nod toward after the academic preliminaries. Willow took her glass, kicked off her shoes, smiled at the right moment and let her tongue slip between her lips when she spoke. Gordon moved in. Willow put up a hand and excused herself to the bathroom. "I need to do something important," she said, snatching up her purse for effect.

She locked the bedroom door behind her, pulled Camile from the closet and slit the girl's throat to stop the otherwise inevitable scream. It was an expert cut, but a cheap box cutter, so there was gurgling, and blood all over the sheets and a puddle of the same slowly expanding toward the bedroom door. Then in the bathroom Willow washed up, changed her outfit and waited for Gordon to either bust down the door to his room and confront her, or rush to his car, the tires of which Willow had already slashed. She heard him howling and screaming outside, right by his parking space. Willow waved to him, then. sat on the toilet, lid down, bloody cellphone in hand, and called for her case worker to come shoot Gordon and pick her up.

Gordon was easy enough to frame. He certainly didn't go around telling his friends that he had invited Willow over for a tryst, and there was enough bondage gear in the closet from which Camile had been dragged to satisfy the police that this was just another preppy sex-murder to be covered up for a while, then ruthlessly exploited by the media for some period after.

"Good one," the case worker told Willow on the car ride home. "You almost did a good job of it, with the change of clothes and the public freakout. We like audacity, but next time tell us first."

"So you put me in contact with rich assholes I'd want to kill on purpose, to see how many I would actually do?" Willow asked plainly.

"We're just making sure you fit into our corporate culture," the case worker said. "Given who you'll be working with, it's good to get this sort of thing out of your system."

Willow graduated from Princeton with a 3.98 GPA, but did not attend graduation. She was busy already, at her new job in Washington DC. Another slum apartment to keep her on her toes. A bullpen office on the good side of town. Not in the secret sub-basements the Washington Monument or anything so fanciful, just a decent commercial space with the non-bearing walls torn down and wide desks. In the fourth-floor woman's restroom, someone had labeled the sanitary napkin dispenser the bottomore memorial maxi-pad box. Willow loved that. She also loved that work for her was one extended brainstorming session.

"Filarial nematodes!" Willow shouted out one bright Monday morning at the general staff meeting. Her team was there, as were the case workers responsible for each genius. Her danish sat untouched before her. "Let's weaponize it." There were murmurs of approval from Willow's cohort, but the management was confused.

"English please," Willow's case worker reminded her. "We're not all as smart as you are, so you have to tell us what you mean slowly, carefully, and completely. What do these, uh, nematodes do?" Willow giggled, as did a few others, but the caseworker sat placidly, used to it.

"What don't they do! Willow said. "Elephantiasis—"

"Elephantitis?" one of the other case workers asked.

"Elephantiasis. But yes, it's what you think. And river blindness."

"Little children blind from drinking river water," the employee next to Willow interjected. "I like to imagine little worms swimming in the jelly of the eyes, nibbling on the optic nerve."

"Arthritis too," Willow said, but that was anti-climactic. "They cause arthritis."

"All right, blindness and deformity, targeting poor children," Willow's case worker said. "What else do we have?"

The ideas came fast and furious. Drones that will swarm like bees on the horizon and will extrude a naplamlike "royal jelly." Lung-extraction torture combined with the use of a respirator to keep the target alive for several minutes. Creating a futures market for municipal water supplies, then bundled derivatives based on the futures. "We can literally flood the market," the man who introduced that idea said, "by wiping out a glacier or two. Whenever we like. Or just turn off the water entirely; make the little fuckers fight for it." Another wants to create hypertaylorist shipping warehouse labor where the work schedule itself counts as health coverage, what with all the lifting and running. "We can set some up ourselves and charge people to use them. Like a gym," someone adds to that idea. Then there's a tangent in the discussion—cultivate anorexia through nutrition clinics and one-calorie vitamin supplements. That leads the discussion to famines, and how it's such a shame that there haven't been any in Western Europe in so long. Maybe tiny Corsica would make for a good show. Or think big, take out Portugal.

"What fucking tedious shit this all is," Willow said suddenly. The pastry before her has been torn to shreds. All heads turned to look her way. She pushed her hair out of her face; her eyes were blazing. "Here's what we should be doing. Let's leak this meeting, let's leak all of them. So everyone in the world knows about our department and what we do. That we kill children, wreck economies, set up rape camps, just to have some slaves. People think this stuff is just natural, an emergent property of the free market." She raised her hands to make quotation marks in the air over those last two words, and got a laugh from her co-workers, but not from their handlers.

"Let's tell everyone exactly what we do. From grade school recruitment to the pipeline from the Ivy League into this office. That we're the ones dousing little Pakistani girls in acid just to have something for the photographers," Willow said, an edge in her voice. "And then we'll tell them that this is what they're going to have to put up with—no, what they'll have to fucking love with all the Jesus-love in their heart—if they really want to live in the greatest country in the world. There's a psychopath gap out there, between us and the other countries, and we have to keep up."

For a long moment, nobody said anything. Then one of the other members of Willow's team added, "We can probably start selling test-taking guides, maybe set up some afterschool tutoring for children. In the inner cities, maybe, but definitely for parochial schools and all the best private schools. You know, so the students can have a shot at testing well."

Everyone began talking at once. Willow's enthusiasm was contagious. She smiled and thought of the old motivational poster with a cat on it that had hung in her fourth grade classroom. In the picture the fuzzy little cat clung to a branch with its claws, and Willow would peer up at it whenever the dumb fourth-grade boys in class would bark and yelp with their dumb fourth-grade boy enthusiasms. Hang In There, Baby!

FIRST, BUT HE WENT, OF COURSE. I FOLLOWED HIM, AND I SNUCK UP BEHIND HIM, DREW A HAMMER FROM MY BACKPACK, AND HIT HIM ON T

SEEDS

by John Palisano

Those sons of bitches just won't stop, will they? They say we are in Satan's realm here on Earth, and that this is the Devil's Playground, and that the States have turned into a modern day Sodom and Gomorrah. Well, I sure don't know much about that kind of thing—because after what I've seen over the three and half decades of my life . . . I think it's something a lot more sinister.

Ross campaigns left and right, up and down. His smiling face and distinctive salt-and-pepper hair seem ubiquitous: the internet news sites have non-stop stories about every little place he goes. The guy can't wipe his brow without some deeper meaning being read into it.

Ross! The Right Boss! The Right Time!

Everything seems right about him, but I know better.

He's not going to end the world like some giant eye in the sky from another dimension. Nothing so obvious. His platform skews right down the middle. Seems the guy's got that rare personality that appeals to the conservatives and the leftists. Okay. So the extremists on both sides have found plenty of dirt. Don't they always?

Ross spun that, too.

"They can find as much dirt as they want on me," he proclaimed, in a widely spread meme. "We'll use their dirt to plant new seeds."

There's the rub. Right there, out in the open.

And no one seems to see it.

Or notice.

Or care.

Well. Not no one.

I do.

We do.

Me and Penelope. Yeah. She's our cockatoo. Lots going on with her. She's a conduit. So am I. Some of us can travel.

Travel.

If the circumstances are just right, our thoughts can inch outward, rushing toward other thoughts, finding them in the great noise of the ocean of collective unconsciousness, and maybe putting seeds in there.

Just like Ross.

Yup.

There's a reason he's got folks behind him. Sure, he's a good looking, middle-aged, apple pie son of a bitch, but there's more.

Ross can travel, too.

When he does?

Seeds.

Everywhere.

He's like a cranberry tree in fall, spewing thousands of the little red berries, many half-ripe and rotted, into the bogs of our semi-conscious, plugged-in minds.

Ross makes people think of him. Long-time couples think of him during their clumsy lovemaking. Hipsters think of him when they put on their Florence and the Machine re-issues. The news loves him. The other candidates—Dioses, Morton, Harris—they seem to always need to mention him in their interviews. Ross never mentions them. Ever. Not by name. He just acts like they don't even exist. It's impressive. He doesn't sling mud. Which infuriates his opponents.

He knows he doesn't have to resort to anything.

He's got this.

Ross! The Right Boss! The Right Time!

It won't be a landslide, by design, but it'll be a win by a comfortable lead.

That's what I've figured, from hearing the echoes.

They bounce. They're hard to hear, but they're there.

Penelope hears them, too. She can repeat them. Just like when she repeats the live speak, she deduces them in just a way that makes the distortion and echo go away . . . makes them clear . . . something about the way she processes language.

What does he want? Change. They all want change. That's what we have found out. Inside the echoes.

We only want to take out the New Ones. The people . . . if we can call them that . . . who've got the pieces inside them.

There was a growing amount of a kind of person—the type who had to be very prominently of mixed heritage—that'd grown in popularity. Many had even gone through the gender mods to get there. They could buy race off a shelf. They put the small cartridges inside a device that would send its signal using a kind of osmosis through the skin of the top of the hand, and within days they'd take on some of the characteristics of whatever race that held their fancy. People were mixing ethnicities like cocktails. And other people were getting pissed.

The arguments came.

They aren't of God. They're not pure. They're messing with things they shouldn't be messing with.

Not.

Pure.

That's where Ross came in. He was pure. Oh, hell, yes, was he. Growing up in Pine Valley Project, where they check your DNA at the gate, Ross was a rare bird. Caucasian, with a pure European bloodline. It didn't make sense. How could someone even be that anymore? Everyone in the States was mixed with other continents. Everyone. Those that weren't were freaks. On top of that? He grew up poor. He wasn't from one of those double-gated communities, swimming against the tide of change, trying to protect their 'kind' or whatever. No. Ross was one of us and had grown up in a very diverse, working class upbringing. Which was another big reason he seemed to be able to talk out of both sides of his mouth, pleasing folks on both sides. The conservatives liked him because he was a throwback to a long-gone era, and the leftists liked him because he truly seemed to be non-partisan when it came to race.

For a time, Ross was.

Ross! The Right Boss! The Right Time!

Until the Looming Good got to him. We all sensed the pushes toward him from the Good. He had grown too large for him not to become a target. Over many weeks, there were ripples in the echoes as the Good coordinated attacks on his psyche.

But Ross was a traveler, like us, and travelers are strong. Or supposed to be.

Are you ready? We're going to go inside the echoes now.

Shut your eyes. Lie back.

Yeah. It sounds like hiss at first.

So focus.

There. There. Settle in.

Do you hear Penelope? That high-pitched chirp. It's very distinctive. Follow her sound.

Got it?

Good.

Relax. Don't shut your eyes so tight.

Okay?

Do you hear the echoes? Their voices are all mixed together. So listen for Penelope's chirps. That should help your brain to focus. Her sounds act like an antenna. If you are able to focus you can . . .

You hear them? Getting more distinct? Right. Morgan will separate them. She knows how to hone in on him. On them. He is open and doesn't realize anyone here is listening.

The

Grassy

Knoll

Grows

Inside

My

Mind

Can you feel it?

Can you sense it?

You can.

I can.

We can.

We

Can.

She's a conduit. The bird. The damn cockatoo. Penelope.

The New Ones. Transcend the old labels. Go forward. More than skin pigment. More than preference. More than routine human culture. Pushing forward. Growing toward the sun instead of hiding in the dirt.

What does he want? Ross? What is he hiding?

The voice, familiar from so many clips, yet different in its casualness. A little less sure. A little less likable. A little less on stage. Sounds like he's talking to someone.

Who?

We know, don't we?

The Looming Good came out of the tar kicking and screaming about how things should be . . . and how the world should stay the way they think it should stay. Backward. Institutionalized favoritism and upward mobility. Bloodlines born to thrive.

Let the great unwashed bath in our grey water. Endless, happy pigs, cute and loveable, rolling in mud, eating slop, and content. They don't know any better. They can't. Weren't born into it like we were. Just pigs.

Of course, no one could afford to publicly state such things. The climate was so severe, the people so quick to grab their pitchforks and torches, that the slightest hint of elitism brought forth unforgivable outrage.

So the hate went underground.

The Looming Good weren't easily identified, but the travelers could find them in the same way a dog can smell the brake dust and the distinct rattle of their caretakers miles away. The ones who wanted the old ways back all dreamt and thought about it the same way.

One day things will be good again.

Good.

Again.

One.

Day.

Good.

Again.

Seeds.

In.

The.

Dirt.

A seemingly harmless, vague phrase, which held in its spaces the threat that what was good was awfully bad for a whole lot of people.

That promise hovered over their subconscious selves, and

they didn't care. You could hear them.

I'm tired of all this. I worked my whole life and everyone else who didn't is getting the same things as me. My family sacrificed for generations to get here, and every damn immigrant just walks right in and gets the same as me. The same as us. It isn't fair. Not at all. We should be different. Things should be extra good for us.

Extra.

Good.

For.

Us.

Not.

Them.

We're Good. The Looming Good. Or just Good. The Good. It's us versus the New Ones. Being Good is better than just being New.

They'd give us all face time. They'd act like they were progressive. They'd pretend not to hold any prejudices. Deep down, though, they were all carriers of a deadly mindset, hidden behind their actions and words, buried, asleep and dreaming of waking and scorching the earth.

Ross dreamt of fire, and of children burning in rivers thick with oil, or screaming women, their skins darkening as he watched, as the fires tanned, then crisped, then boiled them alive.

He had the dream often, and he'd wake in a sweat.

It's the way to purify. You're the one who'll finally rid the world of these mistakes . . . of these vermin. Lead them to the cliff's edge with your handshakes and your smile. Make them all believe. Corrall them into the pens with promises. Then shut it behind them.

Wrap your fingers around the handle and shut the gate. Then pull the other handle and let fire purify them . . . turn them to ash . . . they will become fertilizer for our new world to grow from. Their place in history nothing to be ashamed of. Just progress. What God wants. This is what you were born to do. Lead them to Purity and lead mankind toward its next peak. They will be a footnote and you will be a great man.

Purify.

One day it will be Extra Good For Us. The Good.

Ross the Boss!

Ross's voice, then, loud and clear.

We can't have them. These New Ones. Erasing humanity. Changing their race. They're making fun of everyone. They have no respect. They don't want anyone to be unique. America was made on people being unique. You know this.

But it isn't Ross's voice, is it? Feel that chill in your gut and inside your marrow? That's the Looming Good, again. The other collective of Travellers. They all speak as one, unlike us. Isn't that funny? They speak as one just as they spout on about being unique and special?

Just as they think God has sent them to purify and destroy . . . we know God has sent us to make sure they're not successful. They're too big and they don't think anyone knows. They're not lucid enough. Not yet. But they will be. We're expecting that. Once our plan goes forward, they're going to know. Everyone's going to know.

Game on.

Gloves off.

Bring it.

We'll get the first big hit inside, and hopefully it'll be big enough to cripple them so they can't recover. They'll try, but we're already ahead.

Never underestimate.

Even though we have the advantage, we can never let down our guard. That's what has taken down better people than us. Getting complacent. Getting sure of themselves. Feeling infallible. No. Not us. Not the Travellers. We need to be fleet and adaptable and ready. When you stir the nest, there's going to be a lot of angry wasps, and they're going to sting everything in site. It'll be worth it to break up the nest, though.

We hear the Good's mantra like music being blasted from a car on the other side of the highway, but instead of music, it's daydreams.

Extra Good for us. Extra Good. One Day. Erase the New Ones. Abominations. Then there will be just us left behind. We'll plant our own new seeds, same as the old seeds. Perpetuate.

There's Ross, laying down somewhere, hearing all this—being programmed with this—their seeds deep in the soil of his thought, growing, sprouting, with strong roots, with flowers about to bloom.

Bloom they will. Gunshots like a million flower-shaped bursts of fire. Once he's inside. Once he's rooted. Once it's too late to turn back. First, it will be the New Ones. Then it will be anyone not like them—anyone not like him or them.

The grassy knoll grows . . .

You're asking if there's any other way to stop him? Call off the election? Make this public?

Ross the Good!

We can't make the Travelers public. There will be a slaughter unlike any other. We need to keep this hidden. The risks of discovery will lead to of us being taken out.

How? You ask.

The same way we're going to take out Ross.

Ross the Boss.

Elect him or pay the cost!

Or should we rewrite his pitch as . . .

Elect him

And . . .

Pay the cost?

The grassy knoll grows inside your mind.

In this era, there's no way to kill someone and get away with it. Cameras are everywhere. Every spoken and written word is recorded and backed up somewhere. Everyone is a detective. Everyone knows everything now. Secrets are hard to keep. There is a place, though. You know where. Inside the echoes. No one's figured out a way to record thoughts. Maybe one day, but not now.

So let's take our chance.

We'll each zero in on Ross. Make him do it. Make him take himself out.

Each of us will be like Oswald aiming a rifle. Wherever he goes, we will see, and we'll all be pointing our sights at him. Oswald didn't act alone. Or so they say. Whatever happened then, though, doesn't matter. It'll be the same, though, in that Ross will be driving right into our sights, unknowing until it's too late.

There are others. Several. I hear their voices. Many speak in unison, men and women. Some speak different languages or a mixture of two.

We have met inside the echoes. Penelope has guided us to Ross. His head is in his hands.

There is no time like now. Nothing gained by waiting.

Pull the trigger, someone says. Someone else laughs.

Pull the trigger, Ross. Do it, fucker. Better now than later when everyone finds out. They will. It's the way of the world now. There are no secrets. They'll find out who's pulling the strings behind you. The Looming Good--the Good . Yeah. They're going to be found out, too. No Genocide on our watch. The New Ones will be fine. The ones who have harvested everything. The ones who have evolved won't be stopped. Not now. Not be you. Not by the people pulling your strings. You're a traveler, like us. But we are going to fuck your shit up. This isn't happening. You've disgraced our kind. There's no turning back. We won't stand for it. And you know you have. No turning back now. Unless you pull the trigger. Unless you do it. Then you will have redemption. We know you don't want to do this, anyway. We know it sounded good until it became too real. So let yourself off easy. Before there's too much damage done, okay? It'll only take a few seconds and then you'll be released. Into the great Nothing. Maybe we'll see you here . . . somewhere inside the echoes.

We don't hear the gunshot, but we feel it as millions of seeds that once made up Ross's head spread far and wide, painting his hotel room, each vibrant and alive for only a split second more before dying.

Then we pull back and out of the echoes, before it's too late, before the Looming Good go searching. We're gone without a trace, his memories evaporated like steam.

The news is breaking.

Ross the Boss!

Lost. Lost. Lost.

We lost him.

Their story begins.

Dallas, TX November 22—Popular Presidential candidate Tom Ross has been found dead from what appears to be a gunshot to the head in an apparent suicide. Authorities are scheduled to make a statement any minute now . . .

The echoes are quiet for a time. Then we are summoned. A fair-haired child, drawing on a large piece of construction paper, black circles, deeper, again and again, angrier and angrier, until the paper rips.

We hear her when she travels. We hear her when she says, "I want to do this to people. A whole lot of people."

And thus we know her first seed was sown.

THE TIE-BREAKER

by Kevin Holton

Thirty-thousand people gathered in the Blitz Stadium, ready for the debate. I'd helped build this monstrosity, making sure every seat had a clear view of the stage below, where all the major presidential debates have taken place over the last thirty years or so. These weary bones don't like to travel too far or stand too long, but I make a point to get down here every year for the Showdown.

This year's candidates were escorted onto the platform: a lightly-cushioned, white surface like a boxing ring without ropes. From the left entered Marianna Exe, one of our nation's most prominent political automatons, a sentient AI piloting a svelte black and chrome chassis with red accents. She'd styled herself to trick the eye into seeing an evening dress, one leg exposed, one silver shoulder bare, with crimson at the sides for a sleeker image.

From the right came Jacob "Haymaker" Claude, surrounded by secret service as much for the audience's protection as his own. At six-foot-seven, two hundred and thirty pounds of pure muscle and rage, he was still in the process of serving thirty years for a few counts of aggravated assault. His sentence had been extended for killing a few people during a riot, but there'd been enough write-in votes to get it commuted if he won the election.

A man in a black-and-white striped tuxedo walked between the two with a microphone. His outfit was a cross between a referee's outfit and old-timey jail house garb. "Ladies and gentlemen! Welcome to the 2052 presidential showdown! Tonight, we have Mz. Exe, one of the leaders of the department of defense, against Haymaker! That's right, folks, it's man versus woman, flesh versus steel, fiery rage versus cold calculations. We're in for a real show this year. Candidates, any statements before we start?"

The Secret Service agents backed away, off the platform,

as the announcer approached Marianna. Haymaker screamed something about how "that ignorant chick" shouldn't get to talk first, and how "machines are losers anyway."

Marianna smiled a wide, artificial grin. That body had been designed with a life-like mouth that could open and shut, even chew and swallow, where most other models just used a speaker. It was easier for a robot like her to win people over when she appeared human. "I just want to say that I'd be an excellent Commander in Chief. As an automaton, I'd never start a frivolous war. I can't be assassinated. I don't need to sleep or eat. Every minute of my time will be dedicated to improving the country, helping our citizens, and destroying our enemies." She raised a hand and her fingernails extended to several-inch-long spikes, so each finger was tipped by a razor sharp blade, "Even if I have to kill them myself." The stadium erupted in applause and wolf-whistles.

"You think she's tough?" Haymaker yelled, prompting the announcer to carefully approach him. "She's nothing! When I was on the street, everyone knew my name, and when I got locked up, I ran that whole prison! The guards, the inmates, everybody! I know about respect. I know business. Anyone who talks shit about my country gets their ass beat, but I won't kill 'em, oh no, I'll keep 'em alive so they learn who's the damn boss!" There was a lot more cheering and yelling this time, especially from the men in the balconies. Made it seem like he was getting praise from on high, but everyone knows those are the cheap seats for people who can't afford better.

The rules required the candidates to stop "after reasonable damage had been inflicted," but nobody knew where that was. During the first of these contests, the referee had tried to intervene to avoid someone getting killed. He spent three months in the hospital, and remained crippled afterward, eventually needing a leg amputation. Afterwards, the showdown was changed from a point-based fight to a death match.

With these candidates, it was especially fortunate. Tyler McGraff, this night's curator, would never have survived getting in the middle.

I was still lost in thought when the fight began, so I snapped my attention back to the stage. Haymaker ran straight for Marianna, who ducked to the side, spinning harmlessly out of the way. Her dermal plating shimmered to give the illusion of a twirling dress. How or why she engaged in such theatrics was beyond me.

When I was younger and healthier, this arena had been the gem of the area, practically the whole country. It was written about in international news:

Stadium Built for American Presidential Fights!

Battleground Established for Determining Future World Leaders!

America, What Are You Doing? What Happened to Democracy?

In the end, all of those papers dropped away in light of the first 'winner.' President Hanzer, who had one cybernetic arm that doubled as an energy-based beam weapon inspired by the Metroid games, had blown a hole in Sammy Dougger. Then, in office, he used his notoriety to end a series of Congressional gridlocks, eliminate ISIS, and create a budgetary surplus for the first time in decades. After two years, he was deemed the best president America ever had, and no one challenged him for the second term, out of respect.

Below, Marianna and Haymaker both swung for each other. He knocked her back—no easy feat, considering how dense her alloys were—but she gouged his shoulder. It'd be difficult for him to swing with his other arm now. The audience screamed and cheered, calling out for more blood, or in Marianna's case, oil, coolant, and morphogenic fluids.

In the stands, little fights began breaking out on their own, quickly progressing to large brawls. This wasn't surprising: the two candidates were real "opposite sides of the tracks" people. Haymaker had spent a life impoverished or behind bars. His wild, off the cuff remarks and boisterous attitude attracted the attention of America's poor and downtrodden—everyone who thought they'd been left behind and wanted someone to fight for them in office.

Marianna, as a machine, represented the opposite. She claimed to be in support of a lot of humanist social policies, but was the product of big business and powerful connections.

Her supporters, aside from a handful of women from across all demographics, included the tech crowd and anyone with a silver spoon.

People wanted a president who would fight for 'their' interests, forgetting how great our country could be when its leader simply did what was best overall. Making America prosper meant everyone prospered. Now it was practically a civil war every four years, and looking out into the writhing, bloodied crowd, I couldn't tell Adam from Eve. The stadium had been packed with thousands of angry, flying fists. In bloodshed, no one is that different from their neighbor.

That's how the president is decided. Violence. We had too many Commanders in Chief who didn't know how to fight—who didn't know anything about the realities of combat and war. Now, it's survival of the fittest, even though the president right after Hanzer tanked the economy on military spending and cut the majority of the education budget. Schools weren't even allowed to teach upper level math, let alone the arts, but our legislators were too afraid to refuse him. Our economy was still in shambles because of him, some fifteen years later.

Tonight's fight was a toss-up. Marianna was harder to hurt, and had those claws ready to slice Haymaker to pieces, but he was already covered in scars, battle-hardened and ready to keep swinging until his heart stopped beating. She'd taken a few good hits. Her right leg was sparking, servos damaged, and she was keeping distance now, favoring the wound. Though a literal killing machine, she clearly wasn't used to people getting in a hit of their own.

The people who weren't fighting threw up a mix of chants, some "Haymaker" some "E-X-E," with others just yelling "Kill each other!" There has never been a Deathmatch tie, but there is a committee ready to make a ruling in case, at the eleventh hour, there wasn't a winner.

From my nice, secluded spot in my private booth, I opened the trunk I'd brought in before the spectators arrived and began the assembly process.

Below, Marianna rolled forward and Haymaker kicked her in the chest, but she appeared to have planned for that, rebounding up to take out one of his eyes. The inmate hollered, clutching the streaming wound, no doubt feeling a little cautious himself now.

When we designed the death match, killings dropped. Mass shootings disappeared overnight. Kidnappings, elder abuse, random attacks, everything decreased. It was as if all of our nation's collective violence was harnessed into this one event, an internationally televised catharsis, a social purging of our worst urges. The world had come full circle, moving away from human sacrifice and gladiator blood sports only to return again.

Haymaker caught Marianna's arm, holding her hand at a 90-degree angle so her claws couldn't gouge him, then twisted, breaking her arm. A computerized shriek ripped its way across the audience, which rippled with delight. I finished putting together the weapon I'd brought. The announcer yelled for more chanting, which brought a predictable array of jeers and swears.

America loves a spectacle. Everyone does, but America most of all. All those spree killers back around the turn of the century became famous, for a little while. A few did it just to see themselves on the nightly news. "I'd rather be infamous than unknown," was our unofficial national slogan. That urge, that desire to glorify violence, was no longer hidden. The Presidential Deathmatch made sure of that. I finished loading the rocket launcher. It was a hefty, lumbering device with ports for nine separate projectiles, and it would get the job done.

Marianna pounced, digging her nails into Haymakers left shoulder, spinning around so she was perched on his back. From her vantage point, she scratched and scoured, raking long grooves in his bald skull, his face, his chest, right up until he reached back, grabbed her neck, and hurled her into the ground. Haymaker slammed a foot down on her throat.

I opened the glass, letting the wind, the chill of night, the full volume of the blood thirsty crowd into my private booth. Leveraging the launcher onto my shoulder, I took aim at the arena, where our two candidates brawled, and pulled the trigger. The full array of rockets shot through the air, fast and sudden, silencing the stands. It was eerie, that moment's stillness before shockwaves rocked the stadium, cracking the foundation my crew and I had worked so hard to lay, but I stood in the window, triumphantly staring into the flames, barely wincing as each detonation tried to blind me.

When the last explosive went off and the two candidates lay in smoldering pieces, I pulled out my phone. I'd gotten it programmed to hack the stadium's speaker system. Tapping in, I listened to my own voice echo over the stands. "Talk about explosive entertainment."

The stadium erupted in cheers, a standing ovation, as every camera and news chopper turned to zoom in on me. I stood there in the window, in the spotlight cast by thousands of eager spectators live-streaming my victory. It was the biggest upset in Deathmatch history, and now, I'd stolen the show, because that's how you get to be President of the USA. I didn't need to wait for the tie break ruling. I had volume, I had force, and I had ruthlessly destroyed my competition.

This nation belonged to me.

THE YEAR OF THE MOUSE

by William F. Nolan

When the Mouse announced his intention to run for House Master of the Solar System in 2150 he faced off against eight powerful political biggies from Pluto, Mars, Mercury, Jupiter, Uranus, Saturn, Venus, and Neptune. Tough company.

The Mouse had run once before for this high office under his birth name: Ronald J. Tramp. But many felt that his ill-advised slogan "Put a Tramp in the House" had cost him the election. It certainly didn't help.

In his current bid for office his slogan was much improved: "Put a Mouse in the House." His gaunt-faced First Advisor called it "larky." His mother, Tillie Tramp, had coined his popular nickname after watching Disney's Fantasia seventeen times. She came to adore Walt Disney's iconic mouse, and had passed the name on to her only son. He was not pleased.

"I never liked being called the Mouse," he told a trivid reporter. "Felt it connoted weakness — yet the name has taken hold. To friend and enemy, I am the Mouse."

He outlined a rocky childhood. "I grew up poor on Neptune. Lived with Mommy in a seedy two-bed prefab infested with Martian greebs. They bite like hell at night. Didn't see much of my Daddy, Tristan Tramp. He was always hopping from planet to planet, pushing Moondust for the natives. Course it was legal back then. Gave you quite a lift."

Tillie fretted over her boy like a nervous Earth hen, dreaming that one day he would rule the Solar System. Now, in the election of 2150, she was certain her golden dream was about to be realized.

"I'm a dog without a collar," the Mouse declared. "Served in the Solar Senate before they gave me the boot. Call me a maverick. I'm basically an outsider. I see the System as all screwed up. I know how to fix it. Others fail. I win. I'm one winning son of a gun."

His rallies drew hordes, and Mouse appeal rippled through the unwashed masses. Their hero was raw, tough, and crude. But he could also wax poetic.

"Space is the final frontier," he intoned, certain that no one would cop to his swipe from the old Star Trek series. "I boldly go where no man has gone before!"

The Mouse confounded his critics by sweeping each primary, pilfering votes from each planet. No one knew how to stop him. Commenting on his eight political opponents, he didn't mince words. "Buber, of Pluto, is a prime asshole. Skidmore, of Mars, is a dickhead. Williford, of Mercury, is a sorry little wimp. Rawlington, of Jupiter is a whining bitch. Ellenwood, of Uranus, is a brainless scumbag. Eeelick, of Saturn, is a cross-eyed nutcase. Wooten, of Venus, is a fat fool — and Ned Crows, of Neptune, is a sick-minded idiot."

A sizable number of Solar citizens were shocked (but secretly charmed) at his gloves-off attacks, but his words were effective. One by one, his opponents faltered and dropped from the fray — until only Ned Crows remained, stubbornly determined to defeat the man he called "a bombastic, blustering disgrace to Earthlings."

The Mouse fought back with a torrent of vile insults relating to Ned's thinning hair, his bow legs, his squeaky voice, and his withered right arm. ("He got it in the early space wars," stated the Mouse. "I don't like dummies who fight in space wars.")

Yet Crows hung on, remaining a constant thorn in the body of the Mouse. The maverick contender determined to act against his annoying rival. He consulted a Voodoo King in New Harlem about a doll representing Ned Crows. He took the doll back to his office in Tramp Tower and stuck a dozen pins in it. He also sang the words to an ancient voodoo death chant for extra insurance.

Nothing worked. Ned remained healthy as an Earth horse. Enraged, the Mouse demanded his money back, with interest, from the Voodoo King. And, dealer that he was, he got it.

"I am a great deal maker," the Mouse declared. "I make great deals. I'm really an amazing person. It's like Mommy said: I should be House Master of the Solar System."

In celebration, after winning his seventeenth straight primary (Crows won just six), the Mouse ordered a six-pack of near-beer for his staff, along with a five-hundred dollar bottle of vintage champagne for himself. He slapped his stomach in triumph. "I did it! Come Solar Election Day, I shall be the official House Master. Boy oh boy, what a great job I'll do. Holy crap, I'll be great!"

"Yep," said his gaunt-faced First Advisor, "You've almost done it."

"Almost?" The Mouse raised an eyebrow.

"Yep. The new rule specifies one thing you have to do before being declared Master."

"I don't follow any rules," snapped the Mouse. "I make my own rules."

"That's all well and good," said the First Advisor, "and there's no doubt that your loose-tongued, wild, unholy stance has taken you this far — but the one task remains."

"Name it!"

"You must defeat the Boarbeast."

The Mouse blinked at him. "You mean that thing I've heard about that lives in some freaking cave in New Old Central America?"

"Yep … that's him."

"Is he dangerous?"

Oh, yes. Very dangerous. He's a real horror."

The Mouse was sweating.

"Now … he can't breathe fire, but he has other talents. For example, he can carry on a spirited conversation."

"Each primary provides a mental test, but the beast provides a physical test. It's all laid out in the new rulebook. You're the first test case."

The Mouse mopped his brow. "Who the devil thought up a

crazy rule like that?"

"The Solar Council. They make all the rules. You can't argue with the Solar Council."

"How hard is it to kill this … this … boarthing?"

"Ain't easy!" The First Advisor chuckled. His tone lightened. "But you'll be equipped with the latest all-destructive tri-laser."

"Sounds impressive."

"It surely is. It's a real hoot."

The Mouse squared his shoulders. "Well, I'm a born winner. I'm very smart. I win, win, win. Nobody wins more than I do. Nobody! I'll win over this damn beast."

""I'm sure you'll do just fine," said his First Advisor -- but, under his breath, he muttered: "but I wouldn't bet on it."

The Boarbeast had long yellow fangs and fire-red eyes. Sword-sharp nails curved out from his scaly feet, His purple fingers ended in razored claws. And he was wont to slaver.

"Well, well, well … what have we here?" he said when the Mouse entered the cave. "A pasty-faced little Earthman with hair carefully combed over his balding dome." The beast's red eyes gleamed. "Gonna be a treat chomping you down!"

"You'll have to kill me first," quavered the Mouse.

The beast chuckled. "Oh, never fear, my balding little friend, that will not be a problem."

"You're horrible!"

"Aw heck, I'm not so bad once you get to know me." He sighed. "Sad to say, you won't be around long enough to find out."

The beast patted his scaly stomach. "Been trying to slim down. Skipped lunch today for dietary reasons -- so I'm famished. You'll provide a delicious dinner. "

The Mouse continued to quiver.

“I grow my own veggies,” said the beast. “Got a little garden behind the cave. I’m good with tomatoes.”

The fanged creature circled the Mouse, slavering. Ummmm … I think I’ll have you slow-roasted and garnished with fresh strawberries. Perhaps a scatter of seedless raisins -- and a wee touch of lemon. Yum, yum!”

He smacked his scaly lips. “Yeah, the ole digestive juices are really flowing!”

“I’ve got the latest destructive weapon, and I’ll use it!” warned the Mouse. His armpits were moist with sweat.

The beast chuckled again. “You mean that silly-ass laser stick you’re hanging onto? Let me relieve you of it. “And he bit down on the Mouse, fangs slicing arm flesh.

The Mouse yelled “Ouch!” and dropped the weapon.

“Now then,” purred the beast, “we are free to converse like gentlemen. Please select among the following options: One, I bite your head off. Two, I disembowel you. Three, I swallow you whole.” The beast shook his shaggy head. “Hope you don’t pick the third. If so, I shall be deprived of a leisurely meal. But fair’s fair. Up to you. Free choice.”

“This is awful,” said the Mouse. “I didn’t know politics could get this bad. “

“Oh, come on … don’t be such a pussy. You can’t defeat me, so go with it. Eating people is my specialty — but I’ll admit you’re my first politician.” He spread his leathery wings. “Well, let’s have it, dude. Will it be head, bowels, or the whole shebang?”

The Mouse swung his gaze toward the cave entrance.

“Please don’t think of running. I’m much faster than you are. You’d just be embarrassing yourself.”

“Okay … okay,” The Mouse nodded. “Guess I’ll take the first option. Quicker that way.”

“My congrats on a wise choice,” said the beast. “I see you’re not a total idiot.”

The beast was slavering again.

The Mouse wet his pants.

"It's the head then," muttered the beast. "Here we go."

His fanged mouth gaped wide, but before he could act he crashed to the cave floor, arms flailing. "I think I'm having a —"

" — fatal stroke," said the grossly overweight doctor who was summoned to the cave. "At least he didn't suffer."

"By golly, he damn well should have suffered!" declared the Mouse. "He was ready to bite my head off!"

The fat doctor shrugged. "Had a bad habit of doing that," he nodded. Then, with a cheery wave: "Must be on my merry way. Got a preggie worm mother on Neptune who requires my services. See ya in the funny papers."

"Oh … yeah," said the Mouse. See ya."

Ned Crows held the sharp silvery pin into the light. It glittered like a new Earth diamond. "Potent little rascal," he said.

The Voodoo King was pissed, rising from his chair in his Harlem condo to wave his hands in the air. "Can you believe it? The bastard made me return his money! With interest! What a lousy cheapskate!"

"Let's see if a little pain in the heart will slow him down," said Crows, plunging the long silver pin into the chest of a cunningly-fashioned doll. With gusto, he sang the voodoo death chant in a high alto. "There! That should do it."

In his awesomely-lavish Tramp Tower penthouse, the Mouse suddenly shouted "Bird crap!" and toppled to the rug, clutching his chest. He gasped once … and died.

Vid news instantly featured the story:

MOUSE EXPIRES!

A fatal heart attack claimed the life of the controversial political maverick early today in his awesomely-lavish Tramp Tower penthouse. The medical examiner pronounced the Mouse dead at —

Ned Crows switched off the tri-vid, clapping his hands and jumping around the room like a crazed school kid. "Whoopee! It worked! Oh, wow! I need to sit down."

"I must say you're a gifted pin man," remarked the Voodoo King. "The Mouse told me he tried to ice you the same way — but nothing happened."

"Probably got the death chant wrong," Ned declared. "If you mess up the wording the whole operation's down the poop chute."

"So, big guy … guess you're the new House Master" said the amply-bosomed showgirl stretched on the awesomely-lavish couch next to Crows. She gave his thigh an erotic squeeze.

"Believe it, snookums!"

"What's your primary goal in office, sweetie?"

Ned Crows smiled, his eyes bright with promise. "To make the Solar System great again," he said.

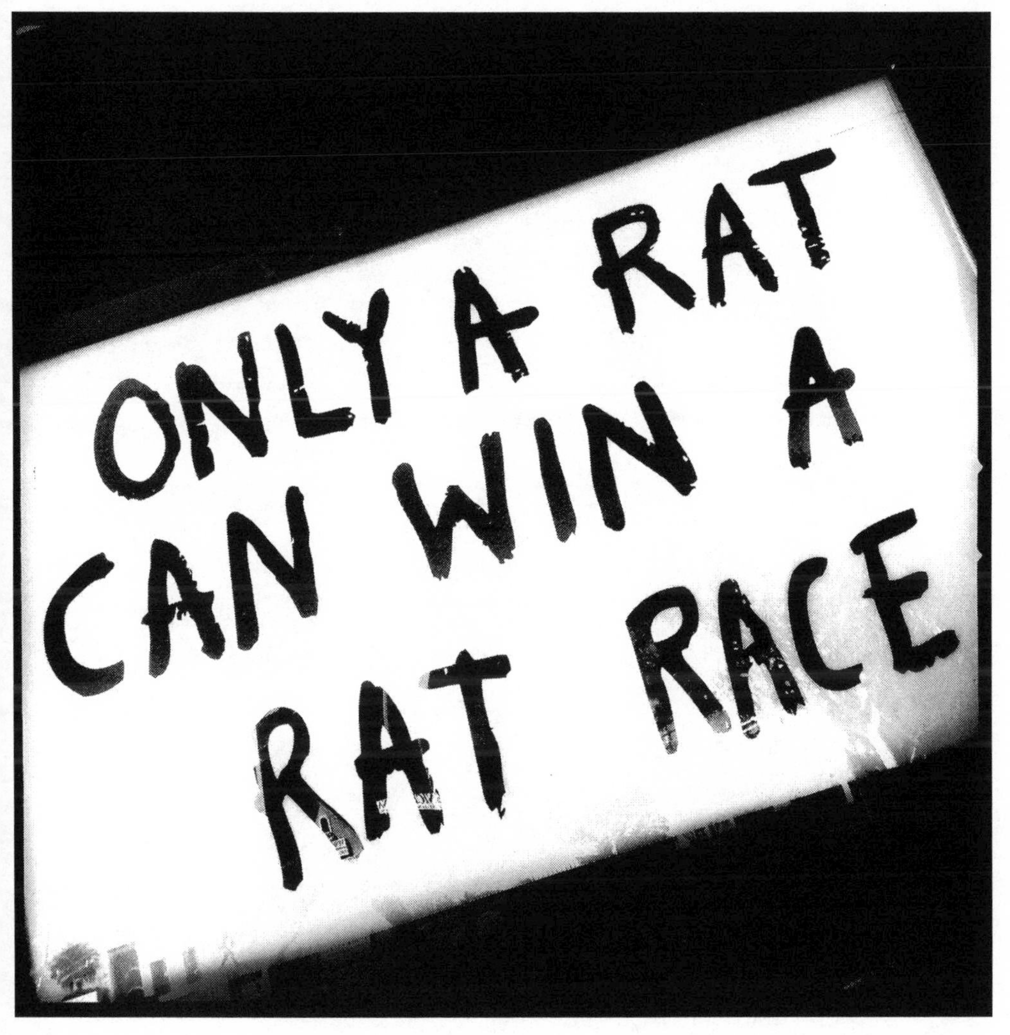
ONLY A RAT
CAN WIN A
RAT RACE

YOUR OWN DAMNED FAULT

by David Perlmutter

I.

Hold it right there, fella!

Yeah, that's it. Come on down out of that tree. I've climbed more than my fair share of those things in my life, so I know how to really hide in them. You did a lousy job if you were trying to do that. And I suspect you were, seeing as how we've knocked out as many of you humans as we can find lately.

Now, you better give me all your weapons and money and....

Why? 'Cause I said so. Or *else*.

"Or else what?" Or else *this*.

Yeah, that's one of "our" knives. Maybe it's a cartoon one, same as I'm a cartoon character. But it can stick you like a pig as good as any of your "real" ones. You don't believe me, just try me....

What the hell are you *doing*?

Surrender? You'll give us what we want?

No. We ain't going for that shell game no more, baby. We done had *enough* of that!

Anyway, get up off of your knees. From that angle, you could easily be looking up my....

It "matters" because I'm a *girl*, you idiot!

Oh, I see. You've never had to deal with someone who has *fur* all over their body before. So you don't know whether I'm M or F. Right? Well, take my word for it. This dress may not be much, but it's all I got, and I ain't dropping it for the likes of you no-how. Where I come from, they don't think highly of folks who hurt kids my age, and I suspect it's the same where you come from. Right?

Fine. Like I said, just take my word....

What am I?

I told you, I'm a cartoon....

Besides that?

How am *I* supposed to know? I've lived as a fucking feral kid my whole life. Even in what passed for civilization in this land. Which you and your crowd up messed up good before we came in and messed up *yours*. But, you being in that GI get-up, you probably know about....

You *don't*?

Syria? Where the hell is *that*?

Never mind. When you came back to the U.S., they probably...

Oh, I see. They don't tell the grunts nothing. Just like with us.

Well, that's the big reason you lost the goddamn war after we wrecked each other's worlds. You guys went in not knowing shit about us, and you came out of it knowing even less than you did before.

But I'll put you wise about how it happened, if it makes any difference to you....

II.

It was your own damn fault to begin with. Not you personally, of course. You're a cog in the machine just like I used to be. I'm talking about your fellow humans. Specifically those backstabbing betrayers from that sludgy cesspools called Hollywood. They sent their talent scouts in through the portals between our worlds, signed us all to contracts, and ripped us all off royally when it came time for the big payoffs. It was use and abuse all the way. Until we finally decided we couldn't take it anymore, and rose up to kick your asses to the curb.

Never mind those reports and videos and such that said

we were really "harmless" 'cause we were "just" things that were supposedly "made up". That's *horseshit*. The money hoarders came up with that dodge 'cause they didn't want to pay us, even when most of us *earned* it. 'Cause that meant that we would have voting rights and civil rights and the ability to pay taxes and such equally like you guys in your land like we had in ours. No way were they going to let that happen. "We can't justify the additional expenses because you don't "exist" in our world and can't contribute to our economy", they said. "Your lives are limited to whether we decide to produce episodes of your series or not", they said.

Then how come the people on the fucking *live* programs got paid regular like, *and* got to set up *unions* to protect themselves? Not fucking fair.

They fucked us all good that way. You know what we could do with some decent coin? Sure, some of us might have blown it on booze and blow, like they said. But a lot of the rest of us could have been as rich and respectable in your world as we were in ours.

Not only were we not entitled to that, but we couldn't even take you to court to get it, or do anything else legal because we're not "citizens" by the terms of your Constitution. We were and are citizens in our own worlds, damn it! Isn't that supposed to be a transferrable privilege?

They said they "created" us, and they could do what they wanted with us without consequence.

Ha!

Who the fuck did they think they were? God?

But we got wise quick after that. We massed our forces around their "studios" that supposedly had so much influence over our lives. We insist that they pay us the cash due us- and it was a lot- and then leave us alone afterwards. And what did they say?

No.

So we said "no" back.

As in *no fucking more.*

We attacked them before they could even figure out what we were doing. Bottom line is: there's a hole in the ground where

Hollywood used to be.

You know why that is, right? I imagine you do. It's 'cause we're better than you in every way. Faster, stronger, smarter, the whole lot. Quicker at building and finding weapons and quicker at using them. Maybe we aren't as sophisticated, or thoughtful, or sympathetic as you bastards righteously claim you are all the time, but we know exactly what to do when someone threatens us or our friends or our land. We found out what you wanted to do before you did it. And we met you on the field, blow for blow.

Seems the way you folks fight your battles only works when you fight amongst your all-too mortal selves. You never counted on fighting folks that ain't mortal. Did you?

Granted, you did hit us back. You found out that fire burns us, and you used that to your advantage a little bit. Some of us got toasted at your hands. And you burnt up enough of our old homes that they don't resemble their old selves in the least. But we got the edge. We cartoon characters are tough and strong in our world and yours, whereas you poor slobs aren't even powerful in your world, let alone ours.

You found that out the hard way. But, like I said, it's your own damned fault.

If you'd been willing to pay us what we were owed, and let Washington give us the civil rights we deserve to have, we could have avoided all of this folderol. But noooo....

III.

What are you doing now?

Are you crying?

You are *pathetic*. You and your whole human race. You got no shame and no respect for yourselves once you take away everything you worked to earn and protect.

Unlike us. 'Cause we know it wasn't us who started all of this. It's not our fault. It's yours.

Think you can live with that on your mind?

LOVE PERVERTS

by Sarah Langan

*On Display at the Amerasian Museum of Ancient Humanity, 14,201

I'm checking my Red Cross crank phone when Jules walks up. We're the last American colony not to get implants, which places us pretty firmly in the technological third world. My pipeline town in Pigment, Michigan might as well be a flood plain in Bangladesh.

"Ringing mommy dearest?" Jules asks.

"The Crawfords remain indisposed," I tell her.

"Sucker-boy," Jules says, not in a mean way, though she's capable of that. She's got Schlitz-sticky hair down to her hips and her cheeks are covered in glitter from last night's rave. Colony Fourteen's heat and electricity got shut off last week, so her nips push through the spandex cat-suit she's wearing, hard as million year-old fossils. We're all about energy conservation here at the dawn of apocalypse.

"I'm just curious," I say. "I mean, I don't even know if they made it to Nebraska."

Jules hip-checks my locker so it rattles. She's got this rage she doesn't know she's carrying—it's made her heavy-footed and graceless. "Here's what you do…" She pretend-cranks a gear at her temple. "You just delete. Done! They're dead."

"Yeah. Okay," I say. Like that's possible. They've been my parents for seventeen years. Not to mention my baby sister Cathy, who they totally don't deserve. And by the way, I know it's whom. I'm just not an asshole, like you.

"Chillax! You think too much. I did the same thing with my ex until I figured it out. Then I just pretended he died and it was his robot clone I had to sit next to in Mrs. Viotes' art. Delete!"

"Colby Mudd?" I ask.

"Don't even say his name. Can you believe he's still here? I mean, half the town is dead, but he's still gnoshing turkey jerky? Jeeze! My God! What does he see in that spoiled princess? You're bringing me down. Point is, fuck your family! I'm your family!"

"Sure. I'll just change my last name or some nonsense. How was the rest of last night?"

Jules blushes, giggles. Glitter abrades the whites of her eyes, making them red.

"That good?"

I left around midnight. Home brew drugs are for hicks, case in point: As soon as Avery Ryan from the bowling team broke out the meth, everybody went native. They dragged this black-light-painted hunk of granite to the middle of the factory floor and prayed to it like it was weeping Jesus on the cross. For the big finale, a mirror-clad priestess offered herself up. She shattered her mirrors against it, cutting herself bloody. Then everybody started screwing. Clothes off in negative-ten degree weather, spilled corn whisky turned black ice on the floor. Kids, grown-ups, pipeline scabs and militia, all partying together like some prediction straight out of Revelation.

I mean, what the hell?

Growing up, my dad's job in resource excavation took us all over, and every place was the same: falling apart. It got a lot worse two years ago, when an astronomer played with some numbers and reconfigured Aporia's trajectory. He predicted a direct hit somewhere near Chicago. We'd all known a big one was due, give or take a billion years. But nobody could agree on what to do about it. Since the Great Resources Grab of the '20s, the colonies weren't talking to each other. Asia was all messed up. And you know the French. I mean, they see a problem and they step over it and blame the dog.

Anyway, some private multinationals got together, which

goes to show you they're not all bad. They tried redirecting Aporia by attaching rockets. They tried spattering its far-side with black paint, so the sun's rays altered its trajectory. They tried opening a black hole, which wound up swallowing most of Long Island before it collapsed.

Then President Brett Brickerson, the former child actor from Nobody Loves an Albatross, got on the Freenet last month and announced that we had one last hope: shooting a nuke rocket at it, head on. He laid down Martial Law in all of America's sixteen colonies. Pipeline towns like Pigment saw the heaviest military occupation. It's supposed to be our job to siphon every last drop for the rocket.

Pretty soon after that, the refinery guys striked. They said the government wasn't playing fair. President Brickerson accused them of holding the entire planet hostage. Next thing, they were all dead and buried in mass graves. The scabs took their place—guys from all over, paid in gold bars. Like the hired guns, they did whatever they wanted, to anybody they wanted, for the simple reason that nobody was around to stop them.

The locals started leaving for Antarctica and Australia. The ones stuck here once the law clamped down got hysterical, suicidal, and shot, not necessarily in that order. "What's the point of going on like this?" I overheard my mom asking my dad, which I found pretty insulting. I mean, I'm the point, right? Me and Cathy. We're the whole goddamned point.

The stores sold out of supplies and the school's cafeteria just served jerky and canned corn, a donation from the heartland. You can't be seen on the streets without the militia messing with you for vagrancy. Non-compliants hide in their shelters at the old Chevy Factory. It's quiet during the day, while everybody sleeps off their rave.

Last night's theme was cosmic mirrors, hence the shattered priestess. I didn't bother with that nonsense. I just wore my uniform: jeans and an ironic Dead Man's Plaid t-shirt, plus two denim jackets since some burnout stole the winter coat out of my locker. Jules wrapped herself in tin foil and glitter, teeth chattering the whole walk there. Some of the really popular kids showed up in fancy stolen cars they'd made the underclassmen push. Total Mad Max shit.

Used to be, only the locals knew about the raves. But then the militia and scabs started showing up. They're bad people. I read my Faulkner and I know what you're thinking: nobody's absolutely good or absolutely bad. But ask yourself this: what kind of sociopaths occupy America's fourteenth colony, imprisoning its citizens inside ground zero, under the pretense of "maintaining order for urgent oil extraction?"

Let me explain something to you, because I'm taking basic physics this year, so I know. Aporia is one mile-wide and more dense than iron. Nukes will crack her, but at this point, she'll hit Earth no matter what. Only, if she breaks into pieces, she'll be more democratic about impact. She'll slide into the President's bunker in Omaha, or the shelters in Rio, or the Sino-Canadian stockpiles under the glaciers. So what do you think? Do you think that's the plan?

Or do you think President Brickerson and all the other world leaders are lying, and there is no nuke rocket? Do you think the governments and corporations joined forces, and built escape shelters? Do you think the pipelines are heading straight for those shelters, for use after the apocalypse, for the lucky survivors with tickets to the show?

Thanks, Mr. President.

Thank you, too, dear reader.

No, wait. Scratch that. Fuck you, dear reader. Seriously, Fuck you.

So, yeah, back to the militia and pipeline scabs. What kind of morons suck the oil from a dying civilization's veins for a few worthless pounds of gold? They show up at high school parties and screw girls thirty years younger. Screw guys like me, too, when they can get me loaded enough. How many prisons did they crack open to staff this operation? How many pedophile dormitories did they raid? You think I'm kidding, but seriously, who else do you think they could get?

So yeah, I read my Faulkner. But did that dude ever live in

Pigment three days before human annihilation?

I used to be so into the zombie apocalypse. I figured I'd be this hero in a society risen from ashes. Me, the phoenix of the new world order. But the real thing sucks. Because I'm going to die, and I can't figure out which is more cowardly; resigning myself to that fate or fighting against it.

At my locker, glittering Jules grins. It's eerie. Why's she happy? "Last night. After you left. Here's what happened," she says, then lifts her fuck finger at me, holds it. Then her index and thumb rise as she mouths: one, two, three.

"What?" I ask, but I already know. Jules is such a wreck.

"A three-way," she says. "One of 'em stuck a rifle up my cooter!"

"I guess you can scratch that off your bucket list."

"Right on the dance floor. Everybody was clapping. Don't give me that concerned dad look, Crawford, he shot it empty first…"

"Discharge."

"Vocab king!" She winces, lowers her voice. "I think Colby was there… Like, clapping."

"He's not worth you."

"Jeaaa--lous?" Jules grinds me in her gauze-thin cat-suit.

"Don't," I say. She grinds even freakier, which means she's pissed off. Because a machine gun up your hole probably sounds okay when you're high, but not the next morning when your female parts and what-have-you probably hurt. But there's no point talking about it. Aporia's hitting in less than three days, so who wants to spend the time crying over sexual violation by blunt object?

I realize I'm mad, too. At myself, for leaving her alone with those scabs. At her, for being so stupid. At colony fourteen, for buckling so easily. At everybody. Especially the people on the other side of my crank-phone, who won't tell me where they are, or how I can find them, or even if my baby sister—whose stuffed bunny they forgot—survived the trip.

"Faggot," Jules sneers. She's gone completely radioactive. It's about the machine gun. It's about the asteroid. It's about her denial-blind mom and sister who think Aporia's a hoax. Mostly, it's about me. Because I love her in every way but the way she wants.

"Don't be mean to me," I tell her. "You're my only friend."

"I'm not mean; I'm honest! You're a faggot orphan and once your family got their tickets, they threw you away," she shouts with veiny-necked rage.

"You're trash. Your sister's a stripper. You're dumb as… toast?" I shout back. This last part isn't true. She's one of the sharpest people I know.

Nobody's listening, not even the militia or my old gym teacher or Colby Mudd, who trifled with Jules to make another girl jealous, and she'll never see that, because she uses men like spikes to stab herself against.

"They're not trash. One of 'em said he'd marry me!" Jules flashes her hand. She's wearing a small, yellow-gold engagement ring. It had to have come from a dead body. Some salt-of-the-earth old lady, a suicide pact with her true love after fifty good years.

"God, Jules."

The homeroom bell rings. The halls clear like mopped-up jimmy sprinkles. Front and back door militia in desert fatigues bang the butts of their guns against cinderblock. They're like orangutans at mealtime.

"It's jewelry from a man," Jules says, and I can tell she hates it, and the hand that wears it, and herself.

"Throw it away, Jules. It's garbage!" I tell her.I'm so upset about all this that I go a little crazy. .I imagine cutting her up. Peeling her skin off and poking out her eyes.

Jules squeezes out a pair of tears. "You're just mad because someone loves me, and nobody loves you."

And the guns are banging, and my homeroom teacher is waving for me to come in. Only it's my gym teacher, because my real homeroom teacher is gone. Faces keep dropping away. No one knows what happened to them. It's like a visual representation of Alzheimers. "That's an awful thing to say," I tell her.

Jules starts laughing.

I'm walking away. The sound of her gets louder as it echoes.

"Hospital tonight?" she calls.

I hate her.

"Sorry, Tom Crawford," she calls. "I suck, literally. I'm a spooge-whore-bitch."

I keep walking with these iron-heavy feet, imagining the whole world on fire. I am the asteroid. Dense and without feeling. I am the destroyer of all in my path.

She flings the ring so it skates past me down the hall. I turn back and there's Jules. She fluffs her hand out in pretend-pompousness as she bows, then blows me a kiss. "I'm your dumb-as-toast best friend."

I pretend-twist a gear along my temple. "Forgotten. Forgiven. Everybody but you is dead, you big skank."

Mr. Nguyen is the only real teacher left, and he's taking it seriously. He passes out a physics quiz, which he's written by hand because there aren't any crank printers. We're supposed to convert joules and calculate work. There's only four other students here, and none of us have pens.

I crank, then send a text on my phone: Where are you? Is Cathy OK? If you only have two tickets and she's not allowed in, I'll come get her. Does she need Baby Bunny?

Nguyen hands me five ball point Bics and gestures for me to pass the rest around. The guy's relentless. He wears dirty polyester button-downs and his parents were refugees from Vietnam. Last plane out and all that. He probably wishes he was still there.

"Focus," he says. But I can't. My paper's black letters on white. They could scramble and rearrange, and then what would they be?

Nguyen perches on the edge of his desk. He's got three small kids at home. His wife is fat. Not like Orca. Happy, well-fed Hobbit fat. "Young ladies and gentlemen," he says. "What if it's not the end of the world, and you're still accountable for your actions? Did you think of that? Take your test."

In my mind, everybody in this room goes bloody. They're just meat, and I'm wondering: Where's the stunt camera? I mean, really. Death by asteroid? I thought I was more important than this.

The loudspeaker clicks on. Everybody twitches. Maybe it's a militia-led public execution. They happen often enough that I'm starting to look forward to them. The routine comforts me. Which is fucked up, obviously. I know that, so don't take notes or underline this or whatever.

The assistant principal or vice-secretary or some jackass's voice pipes through. "This can't be right," she says.

"Just read it!" some guy demands.

"Darlins, I got some bad news," she says. I realize it's Miss Ross, a native Colony Eight who teaches auto shop. She gave me a C-, which I hated her for but deserved. "Aporia's gonna interrupt satellite communication pretty soon, so don't be surprised if your phones stop working. Also, new research tells us that impact is thirty-six hours away; not three days. Angle's closer to 70 percent. They're saying Detroit—what's that, about a hundred and fifty from here?—can that be right?"

"Keep reading," the other voice tells her through a muffle of static.

"Dang it! I heard you the first time!" she says. "About ten minutes ago, President Brickerson sent out a last communication. Since most of your crank phones don't have Freenet, the militia wants me to pass it along… Brickerson says not to worry. The rocket will …eviscerate? Sure, okay, that's a word. It'll eviscerate Aporia before impact. Until then, we gotta stay put. So there's no looting, transgressors between colonies'll be shot. Anyone caught stealing fuel'll be shot… Anyone messing …. Ah, forget it. Run, darlins'. Just run. Get as far away as—"

Nguyen clicks off the loudspeaker. It doesn't spare us. We still hear the gunshot. I go hard in a place that ought to be soft over something like this, which doesn't mean I enjoy it. I've also been known to fantasize about drowning puppies, and I kind of like puppies.

Nguyen lets the reverb settle, then takes the quiz from my desk and crinkles it into a ball. Tosses it like a hoop-shot but misses the garbage. "Who wants a lesson in falling bodies?"

Twenty minutes later, he's got it all written out. Seventy degrees, density = 8000kn/m3, speed at impact: 30km/s. Force = a trillion megatons. He's not smiling or pretending to be brave. He touches the word megatons on the blackboard, totally freaked out.

"Meg-A-Tons..." he says. The guy's a Tesla nerd—he figured out how to turn garbage into gasoline and there's rumors he siphoned the refinery's generators to power his house. "Would you ladies and gentlemen find it comforting to have me describe impact to you?"

I'm not ready to be comforted. There's still tricks in this pony. But everybody else seems relieved, like, Thank God. They can finally all surrender to the awful truth.

Nguyen squints, picturing the whole thing. "If it collides with Detroit, we'll see the blaze in under a minute. Brighter than the sun. The whole sky will be red. Don't worry. It won't hurt. Our nerves will go before our minds... It's like the distance between thunder and lightning during a storm. It should be quite beautiful."

I'm thinking about how if you cut somebody's head off fast enough, then turn it around, they can see their own detached body. This does not sound especially beautiful to me. "What about people in Omaha? Offutt? My family's there," I say.

He slaps his khakis with his wooden pointer, then winces in pain. It's a weird thing to do, all things considered. "All three of them left without you?"

I nod. "Yeah. I know it's supposed to be whole families, but I guess the president cut down on tickets. So I told them to go ahead without me." I'm lying, obviously. If I had my way, my parents would have stayed behind like grown-ups, and it would be me and Cathy in that shelter.

"You didn't get a ticket?" Nguyen asks.

I nod. Nguyen looks at me for an uncomfortably long time. Slaps his leg with the pointer again. It's weird. I can't be the only loser he knows who got left behind like a Mormon at the anti-rapture.

"Okay!" he claps. "Good question! Will! Offutt! Survive!? It all depends on how deep underground they are—what their ventilation apparatus looks like. They'll survive the heat and seismic turmoil, but no one knows about the ejecta. Who can describe ejecta for me?"

Carole Fergussin raises her hand. "It's the rocks and stuff the asteroid kicks up."

"Right!" Nguyen says. "Ejecta! There's evidence that the asteroid that killed the dinosaurs sprayed ejecta as high as the moon before it rained back down into our atmosphere. Our guess is that the rocks will be about the same temperature as volcanic lava, and about the size of aerosol particles. So, our friends in the shelters might survive underground, but we've got no idea for how long. It depends on the quality and pervasity of the ejecta and the apparatus they constructed in its anticipation."

"Couldn't we have done something before now, Mr. Nguyen?" Anais Bignault asks. She's crazy skinny, like she stopped eating a week ago but her skeleton insists on taking the rest of her out for strolls.

"Call me Fred," he says, and Jesus, I don't want to call him that.

"What if we all get together, everybody in Pigment. In the whole Colony? We dig a shelter?" Carole Fergussin asks. She's wiping the tears from her big, brown eyes. I feel like Carole and Anais ought to get an award for best sad puppy impressions on the eve of apocalypse.

Then I picture drowning them.

Nguyen shrugs. "I wish they'd selected me to engineer something like that. I really do. But with impact 36 hours away, can we build something that we can survive inside for ten years? Twenty? Ten thousand?"

"Can we?" I ask.

Nguyen points out the window at the refinery. It smokes above metal spires three miles away. "We'd need a lot of fuel. And a small population."

"Like Offutt," Carole says.

Nguyen nods.

I'm picturing Cathy in a dark, underground city. Picturing her safe and loved. Picturing the evolution of the survivors, people like my parents, over a thousand generations. I'm trying real hard to find the bright spot, here, but the future looks pretty monstrous.

"Did I ever tell you my parents' story?" Nguyen asks, then answers himself in a lower voice: "Of course I didn't. Why would I do that?"

"Tell us," Carole says through her sniffles. I consider throwing my desk and announcing that this is not group therapy. During my last hours on Earth, I do not want to hear anyone's crappy life story. I just want to hold my baby sister. Oh, yeah. And not die.

"It really was the last plane," Nguyen says. "My father bribed a town official for the spot. And here I am today. I never wondered about those other people left behind. Survivors don't do that kind of thing. But now I wonder. That's because we're not the survivors anymore. But we're still the heroes of our own stories. You understand?"

I don't. I want him dead. I imagine that I am Aporia, colliding. I am bigger than this whole planet, and my wrath is infinite.

"What I'm saying is, I always thought I'd be famous and my children would be rich. Why else would I be so lucky, born in America? But does dying make me less? I'm still Fred Nguyen, aren't I?"

He looks at me, "Some of you, your parents abandoned you. Some people sold their own children's tickets. That makes them villains, you understand? But you can still be heroes."

The kid in the back row who used to be Harvard bait spits a wad of chewed-up quiz. "Liar!" he says. "Human consciousness was a bad mutation. Aporia is Earth's self-correct. There's nothing after this."

Nguyen throws a piece of chalk at him and we're all totally shocked. "I'm not talking about God! Who cares about that idiot! I'm talking about the devil. You don't have to let him out. Scramble for some false promise of salvation; climb over your own neighbors for crumbs. I won't leave my family to live in some hole! I'm going to die with dignity!"

The bell rings.

We all kind of sit there. What the hell? Is he having a nervous breakdown? At least he picked a good day for it. Then I figure it out—clear as the open gates of heaven: Mr. Nguyen has a ticket.

Jules and I eat jerky in my shelter after school. I'm fantasizing about stealing Mr. Nguyen's ticket and saving Cathy from our idiot parents. I'll show up at their barracks, baby bunny in hand, and for the first time since the five days they've been gone, Cathy will stop crying and smile. Then I'll glare at my mom and dad until the guilt drops them dead. They'll resurrect again after Aporia, turning them into decent people instead of assholes. We'll live a few years down there, until I figure out the environmental cure for ejecta that will make Earth's surface habitable. Then everybody will elect me king and they'll all say how awesome it is to be gay.

We'll wear as much goddamned pink as we want.

It's the first happy fantasy I've had in a long time, and I wish I could keep it going. But the shelter's cold, and Jules is smacking her lips. We've got the crank-CB tuned to the scabs. They were worked up about a missing rig a little while ago. Somebody broke through a checkpoint with it during the night.

Then the call we've been waiting for comes in: The steel cage at the top of a catalytic reformer went smash.

"Wanna check it out?" Jules asks.

She's been kissing me and I've been letting her. Once, we tried to go all the way. The experience was miserable, which she tells me is normal.

"Okay. Let's go chase an ambulance." I start climbing the wooden ladder out. I built this shelter with my dad. We dug for more than a week, then realized that under any seismic stress, the whole thing would collapse. Son, my dad had said, looking down the twenty-foot hole. Buried alive's an unaccountable way to go.

When I was twelve, my dad found my Freenet porn. Nothing crazy—just guys on guys. He called me a perversion. It made me feel like I was covered in herpes or something, and I'm starting to think it's why they left me behind. And you know, with all these dead-puppy-skinned-meat-people fantasies I've been having, maybe he was onto something. Then again, maybe calling somebody a perversion makes them act like one. Or maybe everybody's having these thoughts, because the apocalypse sucks.

The truth is, my parents are the real perverts. They're love perverts. You're supposed to care more about your children than about yourself, and they messed it up. The whole fucking world of adults messed it up.

Jules and I get on our bikes and ride through Sacket Street. The grocery is dark. So's the pharmacy. It's blue-dick cold. We're over the tracks, racing just ahead of the supply train headed for Omaha. It's a thrill. The kind that makes you feel like Superman.

"Arm or leg?" Jules asks as we race, out of breath and too cold to cry.

"Arm?"

"Okay. Arm, your turn. Leg, I get to be the doctor," Jules says.

"Game on."

We drop our bikes and head for the crowd. The grass is long in spots, dead from spills in others. I want to take off my shoes and feel the cold, frozen earth. Squeeze it between my toes and tell it to remember me.

We push through. Catalytic reformers look like space needles wrapped in steel scaffolding. They're the size of Manhattan buildings. You've seen them, probably. They turn low octane raw material into high octane fuel. But unless you live in a refinery town, you probably had no idea what you were looking at. You just blinked, then checked your distance to Chicago.

About twenty eight-by-two foot beams have collapsed. As Jules and I approach, some rent-a-cops retract a jaws of life. They pull a guy out from the wreckage and amputate his leg, thigh down. Then they give it to him. He's holding his amputated leg, high on morphine. Jules and I clench hands. I wonder if this turns me on, touching her. Or if it's the suffering that has my erection going.

Thirty minutes later, the generators start cranking. Dirty smoke spouts all over again. Jules and I book after the ambulance.

There's nobody in admission or reception at Pigment Hospital, just this janitor mopping floors. He picks at this stuck-on bit of grime with his fingernail.

I'm Jules' bitch today, so I take the nurse coat, and she doctors up. We head to the ER, where they always take the scabs.

Some doctor is just closing the curtain on our lucky refinery scab. . She's one of the last in this skeleton crew. I wonder why she comes at all. But then again, why not?

Jules walks with purpose. I've got my clipboard and Nguyen's Bic pen. I'm thinking about Cathy, who was born here. She smelled like milk and I loved her.

I love her still.

"How are you this morning?" Jules asks once the doctor is long gone.

The scab kind of blinks. He's pale from blood loss and won't let go of his leg. Does he think we're going to steal it?

"Not so good?" she asks.

I'm completely serious when I tell you that Jules would have made a great doctor. She's not squeamish.

She peeks inside his bandage. He bites his lower lip to keep from crying, but that doesn't help; he cries anyway. He's one of the rave guys. I can tell because he's got glitter on his cheeks.

"I've seen worse. Don't worry," Jules says with this big smile.

The guy calms down. "Do I know you?"

"We're gonna take great care of you, mister. That's what we do in here in Pigment," she says with this made-up hick accent and I grin because it's funny, this whole thing. It really is.

"Can it be saved?" he asks. He's talking about his stump, which he's holding like a baby.

"We'll try real hard," she says. Then she turns to me. She's smiling that angry smile from this morning. I'm a little scared of her, and a little turned on. What's wrong with me?

"You'll need to change his bandages every few hours," she says.

I scribble Bandages x2hrs because I'm a terrible liar, so it's important to make this as real as possible. When I play the doctor I just stare while Jules does the talking.

"And you'll need morphine every six hours. Three em-gees per."

I jot that down, too.

"Dwight here's from Kansas," she says, nodding at me. "Where you from, sweetness?"

The guy's sweating from the pain—morphine comedown. "Jersey," he says. "But really no place. Bopped around the rigs in Saudi a while… You sure I don't know you?

"I'm sure," she says. "Any family? Because there's some experimental treatment for your predicament, but it's a hella lotta dinero."

The guy looks at her funny, shakes his head. "No family. I got six gold bricks, another coming tomorrow."

I'm waiting for the punch line, because Jules usually makes this game fun. We even help a little, make the guys feel better. Listen to them talk about their ex-wives and good times. You'll be saved, we reassure them. We'll all be saved by the giant nukes in the sky!

"Aw," she says. "Then I guess you'll just have to pray the fuckin' thing gets all spontaneous regeneration, you fucking cripple."

She's running out through the curtain and I'm just standing there, so it's me he grabs. He's sweating even more, and I'm wondering if he's shotgun-up-the-cooter-guy. I wish I was the type to ask, but I'm not.

"Let go of me!" I'm crying, even though this guy can't stand up. His detached leg rests in his lap. I swivel, leaving him with just the jacket.

Jules is waiting for me in admission, white coat gone, like it never happened.

"You ever think about killing a guy?" she asks.

"Yeah," I say. "All the time."

We're at Jules' house for dinner. It's some carrots her big sister dug up from their yard. Everybody munches. I used to pretend that I could trade these guys for my real family, but it doesn't work like that. My parents yanked me across every pipeline on six continents. I know French and Hindi. When I'm introduced to someone, I shake firm, look people in the eye, and repeat their name back at them. I've got three million dollars in a trust fund I'm not allowed to open until I'm twenty-one. Jules' family is dirt poor. They're mean and they laugh out loud when you make a mistake. They give their boyfriends free rein, which is one of the reasons Jules is so mad all the time. Every time she puts a lock on her door they take it right down. If she had an ounce of self-awareness, she'd probably understand that it's also why she only falls for men like me, men she can't have.

I can't wait to get out of this town, she told me the first time we met.

Jules' mom and sister want to play Gin Rummy after dinner. They're starting to realize that Aporia's real, which is making them pretend all the more desperately that it's not. "Did you see that the sale of crank-operated devices has gone up 2000%?" her mom asks. "It's a conspiracy, this whole asteroid business. Mark my words!"

"I gotta shove off," I tell them as I stand. Then I look at all three of them and realize they've all got Jules' dull marble eyes. "Take care of yourselves," I say. Then I'm out the door.

"The asteroid's a hoax!" Jules' sister shouts behind me. But it's right outside, big as the moon and in the opposite direction. It glows, making the night doubly bright.

I'm on my bike, headed I don't know where. Well, actually, yes. I do know. I've been thinking about it all day.

"Hey!" Jules calls after me, and she's riding, too.

It's biting cold. We're wrapped in Hefty garbage bags to keep warm. "You go ahead. I don't wanna rave," I tell her.

"Where else is there to go?"

"Omaha," I say.

She doesn't chew me out for a half-brained plan, like riding our bikes six hundred miles in below-freezing weather. She just pedals right along with me, fast as she can, like the whole world behind her is on fire.

We go past the center of Pigment, near the high school. I stop at this arts and crafts house with a hoop out front.. It looks like gingerbread. Jules doesn't even ask whose house we're at.

I ring the bell. I'm so nervous I'm panting.

"Don't leave me," Jules whispers. She's sniffling. "You're my family."

But she's not.

A Hobbit opens the door. Mrs. Nguyen, I presume.

"I'm looking for Fred," I say.

Twin baby girls and a toddler boy crowd the mom's legs. Warm air gushes out. It's been so long since I felt radiator heat that I almost mistake it for magic.

Mrs. Nguyen brings us to a plastic-covered couch. The kids surround us, drooling. Out of habit, I pick one up and squeeze her thigh until she laughs. I'm going to murder Mr. Nguyen if I have to. This doesn't change that.

Mrs. Nguyen brings us blankets and steaming hot cocoa with little marshmallows. The sugar is so sweet that my mouth dries on contact, then waters all over again.

"Jesus God this is good," Jules says.

Mrs. Nguyen grins. "Don't tell the Militia about our heat!"

We fake smile back.

"Mr. Tom Crawford, Ms. Juliet Olsen," Mr. Nguyen says as he walks in. He's still in khakis and a dirty shirt. He seems pleased we've come.

"I want your ticket," I say. "I know you have one."

Jules squeezes my knee.

Mr. Nguyen sits on the arm of a La-Z-Boy. The kids squirm and roll like seals. Mrs. Nguyen brings out hot brie and crackers.

"I love food," Jules says as she scarfs. "I'm so happy about food!"

"Are you staying for dinner?" Mrs. Nguyen asks.

"I want a ticket," I say. "My sister needs me. She can't be raised by those people."

"You know your parents got four tickets, don't you?" Mr. Nguyen asks.

I'm holding a dull cheese knife, which should be funny but isn't. I'm also crying. Everybody looks horrified. Mr. Nguyen is standing between me and his kids. Mrs. Nguyen is holding the twins. Even crazier, Jules has the little boy.

"Give me your ticket!" I'm shouting, waving the damn cheese knife.

Mr. Nguyen opens his wallet. He pulls out this credit card-looking-thing and hands it to me slowly, and I want to yell, Seriously? You think I'm going to cheese knife your stupid family?

The ticket is clear with engraved writing:

Offutt Refugee Center, First Class

Thomas J. Crawford

109-83-9921

I'm holding both the card and the cheese knife, and for just a second, I'm happy. Fred Nguyen is a magician.

Jules leans over, babe in arms. "Why do you have his ticket? Did you steal it?"

Mrs. Nguyen kind of connipts. She's waving her hands, which happen to be full of kids. "His parents traded it for fuel to Nebraska! Dears, dears! It wasn't easy for them. You have to know. They had no other way of getting to the shelter. Without fuel they'd have frozen to death. They had to sell! But true, true. We could have given it away. That would have been Christian. Indeed, indeed. I wish we had, to be honest. I truly do wish we had. It was a bad idea."

Mrs. Nguyen runs out of steam. She's got big tears in her eyes. "Now, Tom, dear, may I have that knife?"

I'm looking at Mrs. Nguyen, who's holding these sweet baby girls who just happen to be the same age as Cathy. And I'm wondering if it would break her heart if I stabbed them.

"What are you people, the sultans of petroleum?" Jules asks.

"My husband prepared a year ago. They should have chosen us. We deserve to live," Mrs. Nguyen says.

"Honey, take the children into another room," Mr. Nguyen says, and Mrs. Nguyen starts to reach for the boy in Jules' arms but I stop her.

"Let me get this straight—My parents got four tickets? They kept three and sold mine, to you, my teacher, who's supposed to be a nice guy? Mr. Role model? Mr. Don't Let The Devil Out?"

Nguyen nods. "I meant to give it back to you. But I'd been hoping to acquire more, for the rest of my family," he opens his arms to signify his wife and three kids. "The clock ran out."

"That's really sad for you guys. As long as you're giving them away, you got another ticket for me?" Jules asks.

"Please put the knife down, Thomas," Mr. Nguyen says. "I'm very sorry. You know I am."

I'm looking at Jules and the boy in her arms. She kisses his cheek, because it's human nature to love children. But not for nut jobs like me, because all I'm thinking about is murder.

She turns to me. “Put the stupid knife down, you psycho! You’re freaking me out.”

We leave with eight gallons of gasoline and my ticket. It’s more than enough to get me to Offutt. Jules helps me carry it to the back seat of Nguyen’s Kia. They’ve also packed a lunch for us, white bread peanut butter and jelly. Because Jules is a mess, she’s already forgiven them. She hugs Mr. Nguyen, his wife, and his kids goodbye.

“Should I drop you off with your family?” I ask once we’re on the road.

“I don’t want to die with them. I’ll go with you as long as this goes,” she tells me.

Which won’t be long. There are four checkpoints between here and Offutt, and you need a ticket to get through every one.

Through static on the AM dial, a scientist is talking about how gravity’s all messed up because of the asteroid. My crank-phone has stopped getting reception. We’ve got twenty hours and six hundred miles to go.

I stop at the hospital first.

“Wait in the car,” I tell Jules.

“What’s your plan, Sherlock?”

“I need to finish something.” I shut the door and leave her in the warmth, then jog to the entrance. I grab a scalpel. That legless guy is in the same bed. There aren’t any doctors around. Just that same janitor, scrubbing those same floors.

“You hurt my friend,” I say to him.

The guy smirks. He’s still got glitter on his cheeks. His stump rots in the corner. He was scared yesterday, but now it’s funny. He’s one of those.

I want to cut him up. Take my revenge on Jules’ behalf. That way I’ll have done right by her. I won’t feel bad about leaving her to die in this town that she hates.

"You think you're so special," I say. "But that doesn't excuse you."

I'm not getting through to him. His smirk is horrendous. I squeeze the bandaged stump until the scab breaks open along with the stitches. Blood oozes. He writhes. Now is the time to slit his throat. Now is the time to be what I was always meant to be. Important.

But I'm not thinking about puppies and skinned people or all the bad things anybody's ever done to me. I'm trying to let the devil out, and I realize Nguyen wasn't a genius after all, because there's no devil in there. There's just fucked up me, and I'm nauseous.

I let go and I'm walking backward. "It's coming," I say. "And no one loves you."

We make it to Offutt. The checkpoints were abandoned by the time we passed through. It's a wonder my ticket didn't get stolen all over again. Makes me almost believe in God.

A storm is brewing—everything seems especially light.

We reach the final checkpoint—Offut. Here, there's lots of soldiers. I get an idea. Maybe it'll work.

They don't necessarily believe my story, but they pass it up the chain. We get to the final line. I can see the elevator to salvation about five hundred feet ahead. It's iron, with linked chain pulleys. It goes down three miles, where there's enough self-generating fuel to last 10,000 years. There are 200,000 people and fifty miles of tunnels down there. These are the facts we've learned from the crowd along the way.

"This is my sister, Alison Crawford," I tell the manager. He looks like he hasn't slept since 2010. "My father stole her ticket and gave it to his girlfriend. That's why we're so late. We were looking for it. He's inside."

The manager starts talking on his CB. He tells us to wait in a holding tank with a few thousand other people. Some of them are crying, some are sleeping. Most are too nervous to stand still.

You'd think they'd riot, but in the end, we're all lambs.

I work on my letter, this one right here that you're holding.

The asteroid in the sky is bigger than the sun.

It's minutes to impact.

A guard comes back. I can't believe he's still doing his job. They all are. "Nice try. Your parents are real beauts," he says. "They sold their baby's ticket for better sleeping quarters."

"Cathy? Where is she?" I don't know how I missed her. But I see her in an old woman's arms. And then I'm holding her, pressing baby bunny into her fat little fingers. I'm crying. Cathy is squeezing my face. I love her so much.

"Let us in," I beg.

"One ticket. One person," the manager says. "I'd do it, but then I'd get shot and the elevator would lock. The last men down are the guards. I gotta take care of my own skin."

Jules is crying and trying not to. She's still in that stupid catsuit. I hate her, I really do. I give her my ticket.

"Naw," she says.

"Take it." It's funny. I finally feel like a hero.

"I love you," she says.

"I know," I say, like Han Solo. "Sorry about the toast thing."

The manager puts his arm around Jules and takes her to the elevator. The elevator won't go. They walk back to us, and I'm kissing Cathy so my lips warm her forehead.

"They changed the code," the manager says. "Dealing with overflow. It has to be the person whose name is on the ticket."

"I'll take care of Cathy. You go," Jules says. Her eyes are those same dull marbles. Like her whole life has been a disappointment.

I break the ticket. It's just plastic.

On his last trip down, I give the manager my finished letter. Cathy's sleeping in my arms. Jules is leaning into me. For once, she's not trying to kiss me. She's calm. And I think: This is my family. So I look to the sky, for the most beautiful night in three billion years.

And you, dear reader, are my witness. The survivor-hero of this story. In ten thousand years, your dirt-blind, rodent species of monsters will study this document, and wonder what all the fuss was about love.

IS THAT NO MATTER HOW OPPRES
NO MATTER HOW IMPOSS
REVOL
ION
NO MATTER HOW OPPRESSIVE THE RULING CLASS MA
NO MATTER HOW IMPOSSIBLE THE TASK OF MAKING
MAKING THAT
VIVE THE RULING
LE THE TASK OF
REVOLUTIONARY

GADU YANSA

by Sunni K Brock

A great crack, hundreds of miles wide, formed in the heart of Oklahoma and spread rapidly in all four directions: East, West, North, South; swallowing rivers and dividing mountains as Mother Earth heaved and churned in angry protest, long scorned, and ready to clear the landscape of ungrateful vermin…

Mike pushed the gear stick of the monstrous bulldozer forward and lowered the blade. A dozen mounted protesters approached in front of him. "Shit," he murmured as he turned his cap around to shield his eyes from the sun. He didn't much care for being the bad guy in this controversy, but he couldn't help that the oil companies paid his bosses. The Dakota Access Pipeline was going to go through eventually; he might as well get paid to clear the way. His heavy cheeks sweaty, breath fogging the chilly air, he reached for the radio. "Ops, this is Mike G. Protesters on horses making their way down here."

"Copy, Mike. Proceed clearing until they are within fifty feet. Call back when they reach you."

"Will do." Mike put down the radio and engaged the dozer, pushing through the hilly soil. The smell of sweet grassy dirt followed the roar of the overgrown tractor. After a few feet, he glanced up to check the area.

Mike stopped the dozer. Twenty feet in front of him stood a giant horse and rider, in full Indian regalia. Both gray as a raincloud, they loomed like giants, still, unmoving, staring him down.

@ROL_Warrior shared an article: How the West Was One **@OnionMartian #calltoarms**

Richard tapped the enter key with a satisfying thud, grinning as he anticipated taking on the responders. Whether they agreed or not, they were all assholes as far as he was concerned. All just idiots, fodder in his campaign to gain followers and ultimately sell more copies of his fiction. Richard O. Ley hated being labeled a "horror" writer, he preferred the term "weird," but most of all, he hated being called "Dick."

@Cherisewilliams tweeted RE: **@ROL_Warrior @ OnionMartion** peace pipes not oil pipes!! **#standswithrock**

Richard cracked his knuckles then laid his fingers to the keyboard.

@ROL_Warrior tweeted: RE: **@Cherisewilliams** Don't bring your racist stereotypes into this. **@OnionMartian #pretendians**

@Cherisewilliams replied to **@ROL_Warrior**: Hey, I'm on your side! Is this because I gave you a three-star review, or are you really that much of a hypocrite? **#authorsactingbadly #dickpics**

@ROL_Warrior replied to **@Cherisewilliams** Still claiming to be Cherokee? Your great-granny a princess, right? LOL **#newRachelDozeal #whiteprivilege**

"Gotcha! Been waiting for that one to take the bait." He opened a private message to @OnionMartian: The bitch is on. Let's scalp her.

For the next half hour, Richard and the rest of the Onion peelers, as they were unaffectionately known, raised a social media storm against @Cherisewilliams. Finally, they all decided she was a horrible person and blocked her from every online forum they controlled. "Blockity-block, block, block."

@ROL_Warrior shared a link: "BroodReads: Review of Incertae Sedis by Richard O. Ley" Thanks folks. Keep boostin the signal **#5starreviews**

The Black Hills shook as the great crack joined the Badlands and smaller fractures spidered out in multiple directions like fingers of lightning opening in the ground. Farther west, a motorcycle swerved as a line of R.V.s came to a halt at the entrance to the Mount Rushmore parking area. The viewing terrace started to buckle as George Washington's nose began to separate from his face. While the presidents crumbled, the stone heaved and pitched, scattering rubble and people in all directions. A few miles in the distance, a great horse whinnied from its rocky enclosure, its desperate call echoing like a thunderclap across time and space.

Cherise lifted her tablet, ready to throw it, but took a deep breath instead and laid it back down. A notification chimed: **@13thFloor** replied to **@Cherisewilliams** Don't cry over diced onions. You're a better writer anyway. :) **#standswithcherise**

Cherise smiled as she sipped her coffee. That was enough social media for today. "I should write, huh, Alice?"

Alice tugged at Cherise's sleeve as she reached down to the booth seat. The little brown rat scurried up Cherise's arm and snuggled into her neck. "Okay, okay. I'll ask." She glanced over to the server at the next table.

"Be right with ya, hun."

The city was still under curfew. Cherise had to rush to catch a bus to the diner before midnight. She was glad cities like Charlotte still had places where she could work as long she needed, all night if she wanted, and the people at the diner, The Signpost Up Ahead, were accommodating. They even tolerated Alice if she kept quiet.

It was an old-fashioned place, with chrome-bottomed tables and red upholstered booths and chairs. Cherise had a favorite booth, across from the bar where she could keep an eye on the television mounted high on the wall. When the sports fans went home, they kept it on the news with the sound off. The election was coming up and the presidential candidates had been weighing in on the pipeline and the shootings, all the damn shootings, and the protests.

"Okay, you need something, sweetie?" the server, a fifty-something black woman, cooed as she refilled the coffee and cleared some half-chewed napkins.

"Yeah, I'm thinking nachos."

"Uh huh, little critter's hungry again, I see."

"Me, too. It's going to be a long night. Got a deadline." Cherise made a typing motion with her fingers.

"I don't know how you eat and work on that thing at the same time. Should I bring a small bowl of plain chips for the little one?"

"That'd be great. Thanks, Pam." Cherise sighed, then: "Hey, your kids okay? They aren't downtown, are they?"

"Yeah, they are." Pam stiffened. "I told Ronnie I better not see his ass on TV doing anything stupid. Jeanette, well, frankly, I expect she's the one more likely to get arrested, for civil disobedience. Her heart's in it. I guess I'd be down there with them if I didn't have to hold this place together."

"They're doing what they have to do, Pam. Don't worry about it too much. Jeanette's got a good head on her, she'll keep Ronnie in line. I admire them - fighting the good fight. It's not my scene. Crowds are too much." Cherise put her hands up as if to keep away an invisible attacker.

"Well, you know what they say about the pen being mightier..." Pam put a warm hand on Cherise's shoulder. "Besides, a riot ain't no place for a rat!"

Cherise laughed. Pam touched Cherise's cheek and then returned to duty.

Alice's tail curled around her neck, and Cherise stroked it, feeling the downy fuzz. Pam was the reason she loved this place. Pam was always here, all night, taking care of her and everyone else that walked in that door. She reminded Cherise of her own grandmother who had passed when Cherise was just thirteen. When that happened, Cherise's life changed; thrown into a whole different world, from staying with her Afro-Cherokee grandmother out in the hills, to living with her white daddy and new stepmother in the city. As messed up as the world was now, she had seen most of the sides, lived them even.

"And asshats online think they know everything."

She pulled her keyboard from her backpack, put the tablet in a stand in front of her, and grabbed a pen and notebook. "It's time, Alice."

The windows rattled and cracked at the Crazy Horse Memorial Welcome Center as visitors -- frozen in disbelief -- watched enormous chunks of rock break away and tumble down the mountainside from the colossal sculpture. Under the extended arm of the great warrior, stone turned to rubble and fell in an avalanche, revealing a horse's silhouette. The mighty equine shook its great head sending shards of broken hillside flying into the trees and parking areas. People – resembling insects in comparison to the leviathan breaking out of its rocky encasement -- scurried to take shelter as the buildings and terraces were demolished by tons of gravel and earth. They looked on in awe and terror: the gigantic sculpture reared up, freeing its front legs and then shook again, climbing from out of the mountain which was soon shrouded in its own microclimate of mist and lightning. Crazy Horse, now animated, grabbed the reins of the great stallion and peered down at the frightened tourists with eyes the color of onyx.

Mike gaped at the mounted apparition, stunned. He fumbled for the radio and the figure dissolved in front of him just as he croaked out a hail.

"This is ops. Everything okay out there?"

Mike shook his head. "Yeah, just thought I saw something. Protestors are too close. Over."

"Don't let them intimidate you. Inch forward if you have to, but stay engaged."

"Roger that." Mike let up on the key and sighed.

As he shifted the dozer back into gear and opened the throttle, the blade clashed loudly, as something brought him to a halt yet again.

"What the---?" Mike watched a large gray boulder rise up from the soft wet dirt, shaking him and everything around as the dozer's engine whined under the strain.

Crazy Horse, now unencumbered by his mountain tomb, rode his monstrous steed at full gallop, its booming hooves tearing up mountains, fields, and interstate highways until they reached the Rockies. With a summoning gesture, his horse reared and the craggy slopes split down to the core of the earth, letting loose a torrent of rock and dust.

From the sinking rubble lined edges of the great crevice, a mass of giant boulders emerged from their rocky graves. A great white buffalo herd appeared, hundreds of thousand strong -- all made of solid stone, filling the plains and valleys as Crazy Horse pranced to their thunderous clatter.

The herd parted; stony bodies flooded out from the Midwest in all four directions: East, South, West, and North.

Richard peered into the bathroom mirror. Positioning his phone just right, he posed for a selfie. As he found the best angle, a clattering rumble shook the countertop. He felt the earth move under his feet. The glass over his image slowly cracked, his own face reflecting back in astonishment.

Hundreds of stone buffalo burst through the wall, overturning the cabinet and trampling him into the floor of his modest abode. Richard O. Ley tried to scream, but he no longer had a mouth.

Led by Crazy Horse, the eastbound buffalo swarmed the construction site in North Dakota. All the bulldozers, dump trucks and other heavy equipment overturned in the mass upheaval of ground, stone, and river.

The protesters looked on as the great hooved bison trampled the machinery and rendered the workers helpless in their tracks. Mike abandoned his dozer and scrambled up a rocky trench. The river stood untouched.

The bison dispersed. Crazy Horse rode to Standing Rock, took the stone from its pedestal and placed it behind his ear. The great warrior then spoke, his voice reverberating across the plains with the intensity of a tornado: "From the shadowlands, where the rivers run uphill, and oceans paint the sky, we have returned to stop your hatred and disrespect from seeping over into other realms."

He raised his right hand to motion stop, then turned and rode into darkness as the sun set in the West.

Cherise felt a tickle at her nose and opened her sleepy eyes. Alice grabbed Cherise's lip and gave it a tug.

"Okay, I'm awake…" Cherise gently lifted the rat from her face and gave Alice a kiss.

"It's morning sweetie. About time for me to take off." Pam came rushing over to fill Cherise's coffee cup. "Ronnie called. Said something crazy is happening downtown."

"Oh no, everything, all right?" Cherise placed a hand on Pam's wrist.

"Yeah, but you're not gonna believe this…" Pam unmuted the television with a remote pulled from her server's belt.

On screen:

Camera fixed on a 12-foot-high statue of a buffalo standing in a circle of cracked pavement at the center of Trade and Tryon in downtown Charlotte.

Reporter: "Thousands of stone buffalo statues appeared overnight in cities and throughout the countryside across the continent. Although witnesses reported stampedes and a few people, mostly protesters and police officers, are reported injured, some seriously, we have not yet been able to recover any video of the night's events. This morning, however, things are remarkably calm."

As the television aired opinions about the meaning and source of the stone buffalos' appearance from various politicos and presidential candidates, Alice stole Cherise's pen and dragged it off the table.

"Oh, yeah, the deadline..." Cherise read the last page from her notebook:

The Ani-kutani were a class of priests who inherited their position as birthright in the old ways of the Tsalagi. The preeminent clan of the priesthood, the Nicotani, deemed themselves above other members of the tribe and became corrupt, taking whatever they wanted from the people, and abducting and raping the wives of those who crossed them. Tired of long suffering under the oppression of the crooked shaman, the people rose and massacred every Nicotani, young and old. After this, the people swore that no person or clan shall have superiority over another by right of birth.

It seems that this land is corrupted again by those who believe they are entitled to privilege, whether by color of skin, family name, or the stoutness of their coffers. Even worse, the corrupt ones threaten the sacred: the rivers, the sky, the earth. In the old culture, not only did water lead to the underworld, but also through the rivers did the people cleanse themselves and purify their souls. Now, with Earth so tainted -- people killing each other, fear and hatred ruling our hearts -- the Under World may yet again let loose its spirits into ours...

@Cherisewilliams replied to **@13thfloor**: Finished. Send you a draft in a few. Gotta catch a bus.

@13thfloor replied: You made it before 6am! **#Cheriserocks**

@Cherisewilliams tweeted: From Shadows do we come, so to Shadows shall we depart **#standswithwhitebuffalo**

LOS ANGELES
SOLD OUT

FEAST

by Joseph Rubas

Gerald Myers sat heavily down across the table from the thin, smart woman and picked up the speech she had written for them.

They were in Myers' campaign bus trucking south through Texas on I-10. The landscape around them was stark and arid, the sun reflecting off the desert sand and stinging Myers' eyes.

Had there been something to look at, Myers would have avoided meeting with Rose Calvert until the last possible minute: She was thin and pretty with long, dark hair and bronze skin, but there was something about her that...well, that scared him. Her mouth was too big and red, giving her the appearance of a shark or hungry zombie clown. Her eyes were dark, black even, and whenever she entered the room, the temperature seemed to drop ten degrees. Though no one had ever said anything (to him, at least), he knew that no one on his staff liked her. He saw the looks in their eyes. They were scared just like he was.

Hiring her as his campaign manager had been Susan Johnson's idea. Susan, who had handled Myers' failed run for the New York Senate in 2014, somehow knew Rose Calvert and called her "a winner." He suspected that Susan had simply pawned the woman off on him. Why, or why she felt the need to, was beyond him. Maybe it was like a curse: Unless you find someone to take her off your hands, you wind up stuck with her.

Myers shuddered.

"Are you ready?" Calvert asked.

"As I'll ever be," Myers replied, looking down at the neatly typed sheet in his hands. He knew what he would see. More fiery rhetoric. More "throw this one out" and "ban that one from coming in." In the beginning he didn't mind. He wanted to lose the Republican primary after all...he just wanted to knock that asshole John Carson out. When Carson was governor of New York, he kept hassling Myers, demanding his gaming company pay more in taxes. When Carson threw his hat into the ring, Myers was furious. He and a few of his long time financial backers cooked up a plan whereby Myers would enter the base, hound Carson for his liberal approach to Republicanism, and then, when the asshole was back playing with himself in Albany, Myers would start throwing the race. "Be tough on illegals, be tough on Muslims, be a total dick."

Only something unexpected happened: The people *loved* him. Before he knew it he was polling head and shoulders above the other candidates and nothing he said could stop him. He was like a freight train rolling downhill. Even when his backers paid a black guy and a white guy to stage a racial attack at one of his rallies, with the black guy being the victim, no one cared. He won the nomination handily.

After he hired Calvert, Myers told her all about it, and she told him that she would handle it. Now his rallies were sometimes erupting into full-scale riots, people were getting hurt, and the bitch was *enjoying* it. At last week's rally in Cleveland, when a group of black protesters barged in and started beating up white people, only to be in turn beaten up by other white people, Myers watched in horror as she tilted her head back and parted her lips. He was certain that the fucking hussy *came*. She was behind a curtain so she couldn't see the ruckus, but she could hear it, and God as his witness, she got off on it.

Presently, Myers scanned the speech and saw several quasi-racist remarks.

"I'm not saying that," he said, "or that. Or that."

"You're trying to lose, aren't you?" Calvert asked. Her inscrutable Mona Lisa smile made Myers cringe.

"I have a reputation to worry about. I'd like to survive this election."

"You will."

"Not if I say most North Koreans choose their child's name

by throwing silverware down the stairs."

Calvert giggled darkly. "It's not that bad."

"I'm still not saying it."

Calvert shrugged. "As you wish."

"I'm also not calling Black Lives Matter the scum of the earth."

She looked shocked. "After what happened in Cleveland..."

Myers held up a hand. "No. No more fuel for that fire."

Calvert sighed. "You don't understand..."

Myers snapped. "I understand perfectly well that if we keep on pushing, bad things are going to happen, and I'd really not like bad things to happen."

Calvert's eyes were smoldering now like two coals. "We *need* bad things to happen."

Myers got up. "I'm through here."

In his private quarters, he sat down and twisted open a bottle of scotch. His hands were shaking.

***

The rally began at 8pm in the San Antonio Convention Center. When the bus pulled up, it was mobbed by a group of protestors and pummeled with rocks and fists. A large Hispanic man shouted obscenities through a bullhorn.

To Myers' revulsion, a counter protest was taking place across the parking lot. Men in white robes and hoods carried picket signs in support of him. A guy in a brown shirt with a red armband shouted through his own megaphone. Something about ZOG, whatever *that* was.

"I want them out of here," Myers told Calvert, his voice trembling. He imagined his face was white. It *felt* white.

"They are..."

"*Now!*"

The other staffers looked taken aback. Calvert, her eyes burning, stormed off.

The bus parked by a loading dock under police escort, and when Myers stepped into the dry Texas heat, he nearly shrank at the cloying tension in the air. The old saying goes "It was so thick you could cut it with a knife." That wasn't true here. You'd need a lot more than a knife to cut it. He imagined that this is what it felt like onboard the *Titanic* right before it began its final plunge, or in Hiroshima as the atom bomb drew closer and closer to earth.

Staggering, he thought; it was staggering.

"Right this way, Mr. Myers," a beefy black San Antonio police officer said, gesturing toward a set of double doors. Chants rose from the mass. Hateful things from the blacks and the Hispanics, detestable things from the Klansmen. Myers looked back at Rose Calvert, and the woman was grinning, looking around like a starlet on the red carpet, basking in the limelight she'd earned with two big feature films and a scandalous sex tape "accidentally" released to the public by a "hacker."

Suddenly, Gerald Myers felt like throwing up.

What had he gotten himself into?

Inside the convention hall, he was ushered down a long hallway to a dressing room.

Sitting before a vanity mirror, he studied the reflection looking back at him. His face was pale and doughy, dark circles around his eyes. He was sixty-four going on ninety.

Sometime later, after he'd finished all the scotch, he went out on stage to thunderous applause. The lights were bright. His head ached. His wife stood by his side clapping, while his VP pick clapped on the other. Myers hadn't been with his wife in almost ten years, though they stayed together for appearances. As for his VP, the country bumpkin fuck from Louisiana, Myers couldn't stand him. God this, God that, family values, constitutional conservative, yuck, yuck, yuck...

When the applause died down, Myers started talking. He followed the teleprompter, reciting what was there with all the conviction of an ISIS hostage. He was perturbed to see the racist joke still there during the talk of North Korean saber-rattling. He skipped it.

Before he could move onto "the liberal media," someone screamed.

Suddenly the rally was in chaos. A man in a white robe, blood spreading across his chest, stumbled into the aisle and collapsed. A black man followed, a big, burly ex-Marine type close on his heels.

Myers' heart leapt. "Hey! Hey!"

Gunfire.

Screams rippled through the crowd. Myers ducked behind the podium, his stomach in his throat.

More gunfire filled the hall. It sounded like World War III.

Myers, eyes closed, listened to the sound of screaming, yelling, and shouting. He heard policemen identifying themselves, then an explosion.

What the fuck was going on out there?

He opened his eyes...

...and there she was, Rose Calvert, peeking through the curtain, her eyes closed and her head tilted slightly back, her lips parted as if to drink of the chaos.

Seeming to sense his gaze, she opened her own eyes, and in the split second before the lights went out and the hall filled with smoke, Gerald Myers saw the green, reptilian thing within.

When the convention hall was cleared, Rose Calvert was gone.

Gerald Myers figured she had moved on. Maybe to North Korea, or Iran, or Russia, wherever there was chaos to be fed upon.

LOVE
ME

HYPER-PLURALISM

by Bobby Wilson

I don't pay my taxes so that some Kenyan can vacation in the presidential retreat while drawing a salary for the position he illegally holds. How can the American people be expected to submit to the laws of the land when the highest office is not willing to adhere to those same laws? As a country we have lost our integrity and that began the day we started to use the constitution like a handkerchief instead of as the document that the founders of this great country drafted which turned America into the greatest superpower in the history of the planet! And now look at us, disgraced by a man who was "elected" by the people for the people. Yeah right! Wake up America! The rest of the world is laughing at us for allowing the wool to be pulled over our eyes by a foreigner and the liberal political agenda. The solution to our problems begins with money; which is why....

I don't pay my taxes so that the federal government can increase the military industrial complex and continue to fight illegal wars abroad when there are so many issues back home: fat-shaming, obesity in our schools, airplane seats that are too small, the list goes on. If anything the government needs to downsize its bloated military budget and increase the policies which are letting corporations poison our children with high-fructose corn-syrup and gluten. If you're looking for weapons of mass destruction look no further than your bowl of sugar-crusted, cinnamon-glazed, beer-battered, chocolate-dipped honey comb crystal crisps breakfast cereal. Other countries are laughing at us for our excess corpulence! America should be taxing soda, hamburgers, pizza, cigarettes, beer and white bread. Those are the real threats to our country not the terrorists. Meanwhile...

I don't pay my taxes so that this country which was supposedly founded on the principle of separation of church and state can continue to indoctrinate the world with its fascist, incendiary Judeo-Christian religious psycho babble. The sooner these people understand that God is a man-made concept to keep them poor and hopeful the better. Until that happens…

I don't pay my taxes so that a bunch of Jews can hoard it in their specially designed Jew safes they got in their backyards. It's true. There's a closed Jew internet, not the dark internet neither, where the Jew can go to buy all the specialized products he needs to be able to swindle, hoard and invest the American taxpayer's hard earned dollars. Of course this is nothing new, before the Jew intranet, banking conspiracies were hatched in a bunker designed to look like an igloo somewhere in Nova Scotia. If you think I'm going to pay taxes to a bunch of Jews, the same ones that fabricated the holocaust in order to create the state of Israel and multiple global financial crises, than you got another thing coming, for fuck's sake….

I don't pay my taxes so that the government can continue to let the state of Israel come under siege by neighboring countries that wish it harm. As a citizen of this country I have always believed in our capacity to help those in need and today I stand here at a crossroads not knowing if the ideals on which this country was founded still hold true. We look to the Middle East and we see a conflict that might never end and we ask ourselves what stake do we have in the fight? But ask yourselves what stake does America have in any fight? Of course there is money and Israel is an important trade partner of America, but that shouldn't be what motivates the American populace to mobilize. We, the American people, have a duty to protect the disenfranchised people of the world because we were founded by the disenfranchised people of the world. A population that is suffering should be the only prerequisite for intervention. I ask myself why…

I don't pay my taxes so you bleeding heart liberal queers can open the borders of MY country to every Pedro and Achbar whose shithole country got blowned to bits last week. Why the hell should my tax dollars go to pay for a bunch of people from a place that we didn't invade? Why does it always fall on America to be everyone's best goddamned friend? If America invades a country we're doing so to better those people's lives, the lives of American citizens, and the lives of everyone around the world. Besides, you're going to tell me that the aid we drop on these fuckers when we're through with them ain't better than the gruel they usually eat? And I didn't see anybody dropping aid on us when America got attacked, I didn't see anybody being too concerned about our refugees. Just because we got the means doesn't mean that a gesture wouldn't be nice. I mean, hell, you still bring flowers to a rich person's hospital bed; now don't get me wrong…

I don't pay my taxes so that the WHITE MAN can profit from land which he does not own, land which he stole from MY forefathers…

I don't pay my taxes so that the government can funnel the money into the military and away from the inner city schools which need it most. Education has become a laughingstock in this country. We have an ignorant, apathetic populace, too busy with potato chips and football, to get up from their crumb-filled sofas and take notice of what's happening. We'll pay untalented people millions of dollars to belt out a manufactured, meaningless song and we'll pay money to genetic outliers who run fast and jump high to play with balls, but we won't pay a decent wage to teachers who chose their professions not because they couldn't do, as some would have you believe, but because they were passionate about passing on knowledge to the next generation. Without qualified teachers the students suffer, test scores go down, science and math nosedive, China lengthens its frightening lead and Joe and Jane turn on another inane reality show that keeps them cocooned in their ignorance, the imbeciles! And of course when the kids grow up to be drug dealers and criminals we blame the victims. This will not change, however, because this country is still a feudal society and it must have its serfs, because serfs are why….

I don't pay my taxes so that a bunch of minorities can eat off of my plate come dinner time. I got a mortgage, a boat, two Mercedes, three other cars, a wife, an ex-wife, four kids with child support, an illegitimate child with DNA results pending, and two goddamn step kids that want to go to law school. People look at a six figure salary with envy but they don't understand the hard work that went into arriving at that economic stratosphere nor do they understand the maintenance required. I went to medical school for eight years and I paid my dues at St. Mary's where I did my residency; as a medical professional I never turn away anybody as long as they have insurance, proper documentation and a verifiable source of income. My business has to make money or else I won't be able to take care of the people who depend on me as a bread winner. And now I'm supposed to add to my list of dependents by taking on Jamal and Laqueefa? No sir…

I don't pay my taxes so that the man can use MY dollar, a dollar that should stay in MY community, to redouble his efforts to wage an illegal war on MY people. Of course OUR community is partially to blame as well; you look at the Jewish community: they've set up a support system. OUR community has shot itself in the foot when it comes to organization, but who put the guns (and the crack, Reagan) in OUR hands? I do not stand here to declare that the victim is solely to blame; I stand here to tell the victim that the time is now. WE have been marginalized for long enough and WE refuse to be fiduciary coconspirators with the same hegemony that has seen fit to crush us under their titanium fists for hundreds of years. I would be remiss if…

I don't pay my taxes so that this country can continue to slaughter animals inhumanely while driving their gas-guzzling hummers to the wildlife resorts where they can commit animal genocide indiscriminately. People are so blind that they can't see the link between the animals they hurt and the pain they cause and how that pain manifests itself. It's simple: a culture that promotes death kills itself by continuing to drive, quite literally, itself to the brink of extinction. I don't want my tax dollars to go to all of these latter day Rambos shedding innocent blood and ruining mother earth, it's obvious that…

I don't pay my taxes so that the federal government can give it away to all of the illegal immigrants who are here committing acts of terror that would make Ceausescu blush. I read a story in the Gazette about how a gang of Guyanese took over a small town in Iowa. They went around to every house and sodomized the first born son as an act of blasphemy. They then went to the Sheriff's office and proceeded to hang, draw and quarter him in honor of the Guyanese revolution of 1886. The National Guard was going to be called in but one of the congressmen in the Iowa House of Representatives is of South American descent so he got the governor to call off the National Guard. That's how politics in this country have conspired to take the country away from the American people and allow these godless sodomites to come into our homes and take over our towns. If you're tired of bending over and taking it, then you know that…

I don't pay my taxes because I get paid under the table, but in a way I'm paying the biggest tax of all. That money I get paid , that's not a fair wage that goes in my pocket at the end of the day which is why I work in two kitchens and I can only cash my check at the liquor store that doesn't require ID. But that's not the only tax I pay; I pay at the gas station in knowing glares from men in nice cars, I pay at the hospital, out of pocket, when my children get sick and I pay when I see my sons and daughters grow up infected by the American culture of greed and success at any cost. Did we teach our sons to loaf? To sell drugs? To lose sight of the American dream? Isn't it the conditions we are forced into that breed unrest in the second generation, that makes a child look at his parents and wonder how they could be such pendejos to break their backs for a government that will use their illegal labor when they need to build something and then complain about the same illegal labor when they need it to build campaign support. Is that tax not high enough? Maybe not, but then consider that they're also taxing my money, on top of everything else, the difference is that it stays in their pocket and doesn't go to the government, but don't tell me…

I don't pay my taxes so that the federal government can give handouts to people who don't want to get up and go get a job. This country was founded on hard work, and I don't mean slavery because that was wrong. I've worked my whole life shoulder-to-shoulder with people who were black, brown, white, green, blue, I don't give a damn. A man or woman earns there keep in this country by going out and working, not by loafing off of the government, not unless they got something seriously wrong with them, like they're crippled or retarded or whatever. It's a principle that stretches back generations; my grandfather worked everyday like an animal until he collapsed one morning outside of Wal-Mart (he was a greeter because he didn't want to retire) and was rushed to the hospital but it was too late. He died at his post, and that's exactly why…

I don't pay my taxes so that all of these newly graduated Millennials can suck off the mother teat. I sacrificed, I worked nights in college and didn't drink or go out on the weekends and I built my business brick by brick working sixteen hours a day, exhausted when I got home. I didn't date for three years and made love to sofa cushions, my only reprieve. I used to sleep on the floor just so I wouldn't miss my alarm in the mornings. My father passed, I went to his funeral, the reception and then right back to work. I will be damned if I'm going to hear about how this country doesn't provide opportunities for people or about crippling student loan debt. It's not the debt that cripples these sniveling brats that wouldn't know work if it buggered them in the ass, it's their own gangrenous laziness, as a matter of fact…

I don't pay my taxes so that the patriarchy can continue to disseminate binary definitions of gender in an effort to homogenize a population of diverse and unique individuals. Our country was founded on the concept of representation; why don't my tax dollars go to someone who can represent me? The breeders only want us to vote in other breeders to office, they want to shove us in a corner. They think we will be appeased with a few basic human rights, but we're not stopping there. We are the new face of America; gone are the days of coming home and telling your little dish of a housewife to take the roast out of the oven while you pour yourself a g & t in your smoking jacket. That sad, glib America is dead, so…

I don't pay my taxes so that YOU can use roads and schools and hospitals. Why do I care about YOU? What have YOU ever done for me? If I want something I rely on myself; I can pave a road, I can teach my children at home, I can dress a field wound, no problem. This country was founded on laissez-faire principles but it has been mucked up by liberal, big government spending programs and foreign aid and military aggression. Our country needs to stay within its own borders, protect those borders and allow for the markets to oversee themselves. Taxes are a joke anyway; if everyone knew how to properly use a firearm to protect their personal property and their country we wouldn't need to finance the military. See everyone has become too specialized; it's like the other day this guy was saying…

I don't pay my taxes so that, man, you know, c'mon man? Taxes? Man…

I don't pay my taxes so that the people who lied about JFK, 9/11, Martin, Malcolm, Roswell, the list goes on and these people KNOW…

I don't pay my taxes so that niggers, kikes, chinks, gooks, wops, dagos, faggots, spics, wetbacks…

I don't pay my taxes so that biological warfare…

I don't pay my taxes so that big business...

I don't pay my taxes so that Wall Street fat cats...

I don't pay my taxes so that intellectuals...

I don't pay my taxes so that liberal Nazis

I don't pay my taxes so that conservative Nazis...

I don't pay my taxes so that fascists...

I...

Don't....

Pay...

My....

Taxes....

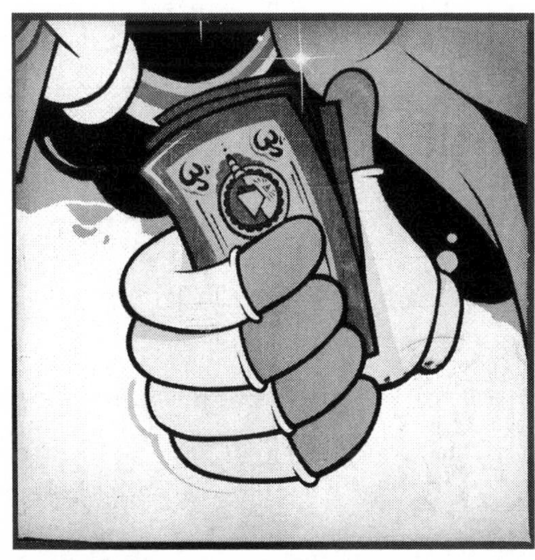

THAT HOT SUMMER NIGHT IN HEALEY'S BAR TWO MONTHS BEFORE THE ELECTION

by Anthony Ambrogio

It was hot. Hot and humid. The kind of summer night that puts a Rorschach blot of sweat on your shirt. Nine p.m., yet the thermometer read like high noon, like that tune, "The sun is gone, but the mercury lingers on."

Can't help sayin' stuff like that. I'm a writer. Practicin' my craft. Hemingway said, "Write what you know." I know weather. And people. Bartending's only temporary. Great training for an author.

To write good, you gotta know human nature. Bars probably have more human nature than anywhere—fodder for my stories.

No luck yet, but lotsa encouragin' rejections. Like this one: "You write like a bartender." How perceptive can they get?

Anyways, it was *hot.* And a poor old steel town like Bethlehem, PA, with its legacy of a thousand blast furnaces, is hotter than most places. Heat's in the city's blood. The dog days of August and the greenhouse effect made things worse.

The AC was busted, but it wouldn't have mattered if it wasn't. Because of a brown-out, all the electrical stuff was running at half power. Three ceiling fans whirred half-heartedly, like the heat had got to them—like they do in Southern courtrooms in the movies—givin' the illusion of a breeze.

To cool things down, I turned off the neon and half the lights and made the trio perform acoustic, saving as much juice as possible for the refrigeration, to keep the beverages cold and the ice cubes hard.

They grumbled but went along with it. Sang ballads instead of rock.

They were a good group. Lorelei, Maureen, and Carlina. Naturally, they called themselves Lori, Mo, and Carly. The Three

Stoogettes. Their act contained all kindsa Stooge schtick. F'rinstance, Mo would give Carly the ol' two- fingered eye-jab; Carly would block it with the neck of her guitar. "Nyuk, nyuk." Or Mo would lead Lori around by shoving a drumstick up her nose. "Woob-woob-woob."

They were hilarious. But real serious about their music—political lyrics an' stuff.

This one song they sang like Kanye West or someone, "Ain't Gonna Take Yo' Shit No Mo'," about a black guy who gets militant: "Herded in a federal pen/Where all the pigs can slaughter men." It had a good beat, and you could dance to it.

The crowds loved 'em. Or maybe loved their skimpy outfits. But the girls didn't have a lotta cash for clothes. Besides, in this heat, halter tops and hot pants made sense.

They were all grad students (Lori: Sociology; Mo: Psychology; Carly: Poli Sci). The band was just a sideline for tuition money and, I betcha, for field research, same as me.

Not much of anybody to research tonight. Too hot. Why drink at a bar and perspire when you could stay at home and do it cheaper—cheaper even than a neighborhood bar like Healey's?

Nobody here but a coupla customers and three die-hard regulars: Trick, Zee, and Bro.

Trick had big muscles and a big mouth. Divorced, he came in with a different woman every week. He was either hot stuff or his dates found out real fast what a dick he was. He was stag tonight. (This week's woman must've discovered his dickness quicker than usual.)

Zee had smaller muscles but a bigger mouth. Married, but never took his wife anywhere—always hoping to get lucky and score with some broad. After five years, his score remained a perfect zilch. But he kept hopin'. He was a putz.

Bro was more of a yutz. No muscles, biggest mouth. Confirmed bachelor (translation: could never get a date). But he wasn't alone tonight. He'd come with Kral Over.

Now, *there* was a prick for you, a rough customer, a real beast. The others were harmless, but Over was trouble. They might catcall, "Hey, babe" after a few beers, but Over's stone-cold-sober idea of chivalry was to tell the percussionist, "Lemme beat your drum with my nice, hard stick." When she gave him the finger, he took it as encouragement.

He started coming 'round with the guys a coupla weeks ago. He'd sit and drink all night, listening to the conversation, wearing this superior smirk, like he knew it was all bullshit (which it was, but that's beside the point), not talkin' except to contradict the guys or verbally assault the girls.

F'rinstance, Trick maintained the '65 Dodge City was Chrysler's best car ever; Over insisted it was the '68 Plymouth Rock. Zee said he just bowled 278; Over claimed he once bowled 279. Bro said "tomato"; he said "to-motto." They could never best him; he was getting' on their nerves. Who knows why they palled around with him initially, but now they couldn't get rid of him.

Maybe that's why they came to Healey's tonight. Cooped up in their own stuffy houses with Over, who always overstayed his welcome, hadda be worse than hangin' out with him in a stuffy bar.

Besides, they all had the hots for the Three Stoogettes and were probably hopin' the heat would melt their resistance. It must've looked that way, too. With the place almost empty, the girls were more attentive than usual. After their set, they sat with the boys.

But purely for research. (Trick was the prototype for Mo's essay, "The Hunk as Incomplete Male: Hunk of *What*?") All three Stoogettes regarded the boys as fertile territory for study, and they were certainly fertilizing the territory tonight, tryin' to impress the girls.

They were talking politics—something Hemingway would say they weren't qualified to write about. Maybe Carly instigated it (her paper was on "Irrational Decisions, Uninformed Electorate"). She was takin' notes.

Me, I paid just enough attention to politics to understand editorial cartoons. The actual process bored the hell outta me. Here it was, not even Labor Day, the conventions just ended, and it seemed like people had been running for President forever. ...It was a long campaign. If my dick were as long, I'd be a porn star.

Anyways, I was only half-listening to their confab outta the corner of my ear. My other ear was keepin' an eye on the black guy in the corner. He wasn't from around here. He was just sittin', drinkin', mindin' his own business, but he had shifty eyes, like a killer or an ex-con or Kanye West. There'd been two attempted muggings in the neighborhood lately; both times, the perp had been black. Yesterday, somebody had knocked Mo down in the parking lot. Luckily, she screamed; a crowd gathered, and the guy scattered.

Good thing Officer Murphy was in the bar—a *black* cop, so nobody could cry racism if we hadda take out this guy. ('Course, Murphy aspired to be an *Irish* cop, so he could leave Bethlehem and join the Boston police force, which paid better. He affected a brogue and drank Irish whiskey.) His shift had ended, and he'd stopped in for a "wee drop o' th' nectar" before going home to the wife, who wanted him to give up law enforcement and work in her brother's car wash in Atlanta. They fought about it constantly.

The black guy was starin' at Mo, sittin' next to Trick. Or maybe he was just fascinated by the boys' usual reasoned political debate.

"You're full of shit to think Grouse will be good for this country," Zee told Trick.

"Yeah? Only a dumbass would vote for a commie like Puce."

"Ochre," Zee corrected.

"Same difference."

"Right. They're all the same," Bro asserted. "That's why I never vote. It only encourages them." He beamed at his *bon mot.*

"Jerk!" Zee castigated Bro. "If you shirk your civic duty and leave the decision to idiots like Trick, you're *worse* than him!"

"Zee's got a point," Carly agreed.

"On his head?" Trick suggested.

"No, seriously," she contended. "Last election, 40 percent of eligible voters *didn't* vote! That's more than either candidate got."

"Well," Lori quoted someone, "'A nation gets the leader it deserves.'"

"Great," sighed Mo.

"You're all wrong. Voting or not voting doesn't make a damn bit of difference," said Over.

"True," Lori agreed. "It's all engineered by big business—"

"The Eastern liberal media!" Trick averred.

"'Eastern liberal media!'" Zee mimicked. "How come we're always electing Republicans, then?"

"The pollsters," explained Bro, with the wisdom that came from four beers. "They're always telling us what to think."

"Izzat so?" asked Trick, with some satisfaction, "then Gallop puts Grouse ahead by five points."

"Yeah, well, Harass shows Ochre leading by *ten*," Zee countered.

"Screw Harass. He's a Democrat."

"Screw the polls!" Bro forgot his wisdom. "Grouse's gonna win. The taller guy always wins."

They were getting onto folklore, so Lori started takin' notes. (Her paper was "Blue-Collar Bars and Beliefs.")

"Nah," Zee nixed that. "If the taller guy won, they'd recruit candidates from the NBA."

"Like Bill Bradley?—" Bro began.

Zee ignored him. "It depends on the World Series," he declared. "If the National League wins, the Democrat wins."

"It didn't help Dukakis in '88," said Trick.

"Because he was shorter!" Bro asserted.

"Sure an' it's all on account o' the heat," Murphy piped up from the bar, an African-American leprechaun. "If we're after havin' a long, hot summer, the Republican wins."

"A long hot summer *where*?"

"Everywhere," Murphy continued in his best Dublin lilt. "Else, the Republicans would just be carrying the states that were hot—the solid South."

"Right. The sun's fried their brains," said Zee.

I added my two cents. "It's the guy with the funny middle

name. Like Delano, Milhouse, Baynes. What's Grouse's middle name, Trick?"

"He's A. Dinfirth Grouse, so it must be Dinfirth."

"Yeah? What's the 'A' for? Something funnier than Dinfirth?" wondered Zee.

"What about your boy?" Trick asked. "What's the 'E' for in Meade E. Ochre?"

"Etherton. His mother's maiden name."

"Hah! Pandering to the feminist vote," said Lori. I think she was kidding.

"Both names are funny." Mo weighed the syllables. "They sound like Groucho Marx characters. Fills me with confidence."

"Yeah!" said Bro, suddenly inspired. "The winner's the one Groucho Marx plays in the movies!"

"That'd be a good trick, since Groucho Marx died in 1977."

"Oh. Well, okay," Bro was undaunted. "The winner's the one Groucho Marx *would* play—in a zombie movie."

And so on, 'til nearly midnight. Bro really got into it, proposing theory after far-fetched theory: UFO sightings mean the Republican wins; five major hurricanes mean the Democrat wins; a sunny February second means a woodchuck wins. Then the pressure of seven beers overcame him; he went off to the bathroom, and the conversation lulled.

That musta been the moment Over'd been waitin' for. His smirk had gotten bigger and darker all evening.

"It's not polls, big business, media, or the groundhog's shadow," he said. There was this kinda menace or malice or madness—some word starting with "m"—in his tone. "The Presidential election has nothing to do with any of that."

"But you know what does, I suppose," Zee said.

"Naturally."

"And what's that?" asked Carly.

Over paused, smirking like a sleazy, as-yet-unindicted TV preacher who knows his revelation will change his listeners forever but enjoys keeping them on edge and wringing a few more bucks outta them.

The bar got real quiet. Hushed, like a cathedral, with us—the parishioners—waitin' for the Word. We heard the fans swishing overhead. I think I even heard Bro spritzing in the bathroom.

"So spill it," Zee said. "What determines the outcome of the Presidential election?"

Over couldn't contain himself any longer. The smirk would've split his face in half.

"Blood sacrifice," he said.

If it was a joke, nobody laughed. We all sat there, with that eerie, scary statement hanging in the hot, humid air, listening to the fans swishing, waiting for him to elaborate.

The john door's *skree-eek* made us all jump. Bro took his seat, wiping still-wet hands on his pants. "Hey, I thought of another one. It depends on how many drinks I have—odd or even. So, Trick, buy me a beer for your boy, and, Zee, buy me a couple for yours." Everybody ignored him.

Finally, "What do you mean, *blood sacrifice*?" Trick asked. "The Presidential election depends on how many pints we donate to the Red Cross?"

"No. On how much blood each side offers up to propitiate the gods."

"What 'gods'?" asked Lori. "The Elephant and Donkey?"

"Precisely. Repu and Democ, offspring of the great god Polytyx."

Carly started scribbling *more* notes.

"Is this some kind of a cult thing?" asked Bro. "You into weird cults, Kral?"

"Let him talk," said Trick. "I wanna hear this shit."

"Yeah." Zee sensed they might best Over for once. "This oughta be good."

"Polytyx has sired many children, including these two bastards, minor deities, who—unable to distinguish themselves among the crowded parliaments of Europe and Asia—escaped the elder gods' persecution and came to America, land of opportunity and religious freedom, where everyone could be worshipped in his own way.

"Here, they vie for supremacy, for Polytyx' favor, via human sacrifice. But gods can't soil themselves with bloodletting. That's left to their minions. Every four years, their priests, the politicians, exhort Repu and Democ's demons, called ba'alots, to kill in the name of Repu and Democ for the greater glory of Polytyx.

"These two are busy from now 'til November. The difference in one's kills over the other's determines victory. If Repu's ba'alot slays 100 and Democ's kills 20, Republicans win by 80 electoral votes."

"How do they kill?" asked Trick.

"Gun, auto, chainsaw. Whatever's handy."

"They don't sling mud?" asked Mo.

"Sometimes. Supernatural mud. It suffocates victims, who die of 'natural causes.' The mud evaporates before the coroner arrives."

"How convenient," said Trick, about to deflate Over's pretensions. "But people die every day. How does anyone know a demon killed them? How can they keep score?"

"Supernatural bookkeeping is beyond the puny ken of men."

"Riiight. How stupid of me. And my puny ken."

Over's eyes flashed. "They can tell by the mark."

"'Mark'?"

"A red 'X'—in the victim's left or right armpit, depending on who does the killing."

"Just where nobody looks," scoffed Zee. "Too bad nobody's ever *seen* this X."

Murphy lowered his whiskey, slowly. "I have," he said, forgetting to do his Irish accent. "Seen it every four years or so on dozens of stiffs—vagrants, murder victims, junkies. Never thought much about it, 'til now. Coroners said these 'death striations' didn't mean anything."

"They don't!" Trick insisted. "Go on, Over. Tell us more about these 'demons.'"

"Repu's ba'alot's the Party of the First Part. Democ's, the Party of the Second Part. Sometimes the names are reversed, depending on the outcome of the last election, but currently Repu's is in the ascendancy, and has been for a long time."

"And why is that?" Zee asked.

"Why do you think? Too many bleeding-heart liberals have weakened Democ's resolve. His ba'alot hasn't the stomach for it anymore—not since the hotly contested 1960 election, when the body count rose fast and furiously. Democ's ba'alot won, but all the carnage sickened him."

"Then how come Johnson won by a landslide in '64?"

"Righteous vengeance. Democ suspected that Repu engineered Kennedy's assassination, so his ba'alot fought ferociously that year. That was the last time."

"Yeah? What about Carter? What about *Clinton*?"

Over snorted. "An aberration. Democ tricked Repu: 'Let's use sex instead of sacrifice,' he whined—chicken-shit about spilling blood. But no more. With the dawn of the new millennium, Polytyx insisted that the contest be pure again."

"I'm curious," said Carly. "What do ba'alots do when they're not killing voters, after the inauguration?"

"They mate—to form a more perfect union. That's why it's called the 'honeymoon period.' Polytyx makes strange bedfellows. From this months-long recreation, they recreate themselves, for the next quadrennial contest."

"This demonic copulation," asked Mo, "—how do they *do* it?"

"Any way they want. They can be anything they want—male, female, neither, both. There's only one rule: the Party of the First Part gets to be on top."

"What about other parties?" Lori asked. "Do Libertarians and Greens have their own ba'alots?"

"Yes and no. The union of Democ and Repu's ba'alots produces multiple offspring. Most of them are runts, too puny to survive. They remain stunted—never grow up to vie with the duo. Infrequently, a third party develops enough to challenge their monopoly—as in 1948, 1980, 1992, 2000, and especially 1968. What a coupling—tripling—*ménage à trois*—that was! But Repu's ba'alot absorbed Wallace's and emerged stronger in '72.

"The killing season's upon us. Repu and Democ have cast their ba'alots. It's only a matter of time. It should have started already."

We all sat there, transfixed. All except Trick. He'd had enough.

"And just how do you know so much about these demons?" he asked.

"Isn't it obvious?" Over's smirk was beastly, demonic, now. "I'm one of them: Gop, servant to Repu."

"If that's true," said Bro with a laugh he didn't mean, "why are you revealing yourself to us mere mortals?"

"Isn't that obvious? I'm going to kill you all."

"All of us?" Trick asked. "But I'm a Republican."

"No matter."

"I don't vote at all!" protested Bro.

"Hah! I ought to get two points for you. I won't, but I ought to." Over smirked. "I've let you live longer than I should, but I could afford to be leisurely. My opponent's lax; there's no more fight in him. Especially in bed. At best, he can only react.

"This is the proper sample precinct for me. Demographically correct. The right mix of races, sexes, ages. I've stalked it these last few weeks. Two nights ago, I struck. But I fear I'm losing my touch—probably from being around you louts. Two nights ago, and again last night, outside this very bar, my sacrifice was interrupted."

"You attacked me?" Mo shrank away. "B-but he was black—"

"My Willie Horton disguise has served me well since '88. I told you we can be whatever we choose. But that disguise must be weak from overuse. Otherwise, I wouldn't have started when that crowd appeared to save you. I'd have killed the lot of them, as I intend to kill you. —I've rarely targeted a more boring bunch."

"Look who's talking!" Zee complained.

"I believe him," said the black guy quietly. I'd almost forgotten he was there.

"So do I," agreed Bro. "Especially the part about killing us."

"I think he's full of shit," said Trick.

"Sure you do," said Over. "So I'll start with you."

He leapt up, overturning the table, sending bottles and bodies sprawling. Trick stood to meet him, threw a punch. Over blocked it, decked Trick, then jumped on top of him and slammed his skull against the tile. A pool of red haloed Trick's head.

"Stop it!" yelled Mo.

Over shrugged, complied, letting Trick's head drop. "I'll finish him later when you're all beside him. I'll do you next, girly, to make up for last night."

"He's a maniac—completely crazy!" yelled Bro.

"He's only one guy," Murphy said.

"And unarmed. Let's rush him." Zee broke a beer bottle. I reached for the tire iron I keep behind the bar for emergencies.

And then he grew—grew and grew until his face and figure and laugh (low, mean, bowel-loosening) filled the whole bar.

Bro grabbed the girls and made a break for the door, but, suddenly, Over—or Gop or whatever—was in front of them, blocking the way like some smirking black hole.

He waved his hand, and this slimy, shit-brown glop engulfed Bro's head. Bro fell to the floor, scrabblin' at it. The black guy and Murphy tried to help, pulling big puffs like cancerous cotton off his face until he breathed again, in long gasps.

"That's just a sample of my power," the demon said, back to normal now—if he had a normal.

Murphy drew his pistol and fired five rounds into the belly of the beast.

The creature laughed again. "Should've aimed for a headshot.

That was merely refreshing. Foolish man! Don't you know the ba'alot's stronger than the bullet? To kill the body politic you must destroy the head."

He reached two hands into himself, spreading his chest apart, like Superman pulling open his shirt, releasing the stench of cheap cigars from some internal, infernal smoke-filled room. The bullets shot back into the bar, over our heads, striking the walls.

Gop reassembled himself and looked at us. His hand grew large, reached out, grabbing Murphy between two fingers, holding him flailing helplessly like a pup caught by the scruff of the neck.

"I can see the headlines now," he predicted. "'Berserk cop slays 8, shoots self.' They'll blame the heat. 'Happens all the time; drives people crazy.' You'll be national news for a few days. Then they'll return to arguing about the election. And I'll be on my way to winning it. Four more years of power."

"No, Gop, no! This madness ends right here!" the black guy claimed.

"Step back, little man, or be the first to die."

"Wrong." The black guy removed his face, revealing formless blue beneath.

"You! Democ's ba'alot: Epi Day-Czar Eerie-Gain!"

"Yes. Your nemesis. And I ain't gonna take your shit no more. No more killing, Gop. I stopped you before—I and my *crowd*." He split himself into a set of paperdoll-like figures, then *zoingged* back into one again. "Now I'll end it once and for all."

"So. *You* interfered with my recent pleasures. I should have known no earthly power could have stopped me."

"Now I'll stop you for good."

Gop smirked, dropped Murphy, and, like a wave of polluted water, lunged for his enemy.

They tore each other apart, their forms becoming less human and more blob-like as they coalesced and split apart, like two paramecia in heat, roaring with unhuman voices. Their viscous red, white, and blue ichor splattered the walls, spattering us where we cowered behind booths and the bar.

Finally, the two blobs separated, reformed—one a puddle on the floor, shaping into a parody of Kral Over, the other resuming the black guy's appearance. He said, "It's over," put a needle-sharp finger to his ear, took Murphy's revolver in his mouth, and—before anyone could stop him—simultaneously pierced his brain and pulled the trigger.

His head burst like a balloon at a political convention. He fell across Over. Their bodies formed an X, arms outstretched. And we all saw, twisting up beneath their underarm hair, the tell-tale welt of a red X appear in their left armpit.

We covered it up. We had to; otherwise, people woulda thought we were crazy. We said Over had got ugly and instigated a brawl. The other guy killed him, then shot himself. The cops bought it. Stuff like that happens all the time; the heat drives people crazy.

You know the rest. This Presidential election was the closest ever. Democrats won by two electoral votes.

Zee stopped coming around. Stays at home with his wife. Trick married Mo. They visit Zee every Friday for canasta. Murphy moved to Atlanta to work in his brother-in-law's car wash. Lori and Carly graduated and formed a duo, "Lorel and Carly." They don't sing political songs anymore. They don't sing anything. They just play—the Hokey Pokey, the Chicken Dance—mostly at weddings, like Trick and Mo's.

Bro still drinks here but won't talk about what happened. Dismisses it as a "mass hallucination" caused by the heat and the beer. But I know what's what. That's why I wrote this, so you would, too. 'Course, nobody believes me. You think you're reading fiction. I had to say I made it up to get it published.

But I keep thinking about the next election. What'll happen with no blood sacrifice to consecrate our choice? Will it be our first free election or will Polytyx somehow self-engender two new creatures to do its bidding? Me, I'm watchin' out for any rough beasts slouching towards Bethlehem.

EVERYBODY LISTENS TO BUCK

by Nicholas Manzolillo

I drive a little faster when I see the *Vote for Monagan* sign stuck into the white colonial's front lawn. Surrounded by two oak trees and a sparkling flower bed, it's a beautiful house tarnished by that one red brick of political prompting. The neighborhood stretching ahead of me is a battlefield. On either side of my car red and blue squares adorn each front lawn. This town can't have more than a five hundred residents, tops, yet it feels like every single one of them is the loudest political panderer. What's funny, though, is that Thanksgiving's a week away, isn't this crap supposed to be over with? I wouldn't be here if someone weren't paying me to be.

In my experience, travelling as much as I do, small towns can go one of two ways. Either the residents think they're a part of something big, or they believe themselves to be nothing but dirt; literally seizing every opportunity to quote that Journey song "I'm just a small town..." blah, blah, blah. Forget I said that, it doesn't sound right. It's not funny enough, not distinct enough. I'm supposed to be funny, being a professional joke teller and all, but there's not much to laugh about in the middle of the day. When you wake up early enough to be miserable, the jokes come so fast I've got to walk and drive with a pen in my ear and a scribbled-over note card in my pocket. When you're exhausted, or frustrated to the point of pulling your hair out, your sense of humor becomes raw and honest. When it's the middle of the day and everything's going alright, then everything seems funny, yet there's nothing worth laughing over.

The only thing I've been inspired about during this long-ass drive is a half-formed long-winded monologue about how politics can ruin an otherwise great stand up set. Nothing gets more outdated than Politics. Half of George Carlin's brilliant act is more historically interesting than a reflection of the immense talent he was brimming with. Still, to take the stage and not try to weed out the ignorance of the world seems irresponsible.

I pass by a man dressed as a, milkman? Or something like that, standing in his front yard staring straight up at the sky. There's a blue "vote for Harrison" sign to his left. Maybe it's the showman in me, but I debate laying into the horn just to pull his head out of the clouds.

When I pass by a woman standing on her front porch in old-fashioned lingerie I honk my horn as loud as my little Ford can, which is more like a newborn puppy's squeak. Even in what amounts to granny panties by modern standards, the middle-aged blond woman is just my type. You don't get to date much when you're on the road, so excuse me if I follow the instincts of a hound dog. My attention's for nothing though, because the woman with a red sign on her lawn just stares at me with wide, bloodshot eyes. Christ, they're red enough for me to notice and I'm in the middle of the road. Poor lady must be on so many uppers she's in her undies. Then again, it's almost nightfall, maybe she had a long shitty day and she's unwinding.

The GPS on my phone's a piece of crap but it does its job, bringing me down a cutesy main street, past a firehouse next to a barbershop and a library practically attached to a church, until I arrive at the community center, Jefferson Memorial. At least I'm not planning on spending the night, two hour drive back to Knoxville or not, there's at least life in the city. Bars and Chinese food and, plus, I've built up a bunch of reward points at Marriot hotels.

Community center looks like it did on Google, an unimpressive white square that could be something a colony of birdmen would build with their own excrement. Can hardly hold more than eighty people, but I've preformed in clubs for less than three drunken old ladies, so that's not an issue- if it's even a sold out gig. I wouldn't be here if they weren't paying me a whopping three grand for just an hour set. I didn't believe the voicemail at first, so I had a hell of a time asking for verification, especially because nothing I found online indicated there's ever been a comedy event at old Jefferson "bird shit" Memorial. Just listings for dated art festivals and the like.

A white and blue banner is slung over the double door entrance with "Welcome to Lacey Meadows, Jamie Rudolph!" In all bubbly letters--it looks like it could've been crafted by the local high school's art division. If this hick place even has a local art division. They sure got their politics though, while no red or blue signs claim the strips of grass beside the community center, there are numerous colorful fliers just below my banner that say "vote here, November 8th!" Jeez, I've been invited right to the dragon's den.

There's one other car in the parking lot and, figures, from the looks of my fake Rolex, I'm an hour and a half early for my seven-thirty show. I've already made peace with the idea that I'll have to deal with a few awkward, small town community event planners or some shit. Maybe it's worth forgoing my professional integrity and finding a bar to hole up in until thirty minutes before show-time. They are giving me three grand and for the sake of all the hot wings that'll buy, I owe the show-runners some loyalty. Plus, do I really want to go to a bar as a stranger here? First thing I'll be asked is what brings me to town and then there'll be the always typical "how about you tell us a joke" bullshit and, if I've got drinking to do, it's always better to save that for after my set.

I stroll into the community center expecting to find Marcy, the chubby sounding woman with a real thick southern accent that booked me. Instead there's a weird bald fucker in a tuxedo staring at a big clock on the wall. Guy's head is newly shaved, as if a toddler were his barber. There are mismatched patches along his skull where the razor kissed his head, creating a pink rash. I remembering buzzing my head when I was younger.

"Hey," I mutter and Mr. Tux, complete with a pink bowtie, doesn't move from his staring contest with the hands of time.

I guess that banner's the extent of the mood setting. The community center is like a church without crosses; it has mismatched folding chairs where my poor audience is going to be placed. "Hey, buddy, hey," I walk over and tap the deaf older guy with a bad (no) hair day on the shoulder. He turns, slowly.

"Hey, I'm the show, what's going on? Marcy here?"

The man stares at me like he's senile, and maybe he is, though I'd guess he's only pushing fifty. "Buck said seven thirty, it's not seven thirty yet" he turns to stare at the clock but I grab his arm.

"Professional courtesy to arrive early." I try getting something out of him, at least a smile, but nothing.

"Everybody listens to Buck," the man says and he sounds weary, like he's been staring at that clock all day.

"Who's Buck?" I ask before the double doors behind me swing open.

"Mr. Rudolph," a nasally woman says behind me in a southern accent gone out of tone.

"Ah, Marcy?" I flash her a smile that has yet to land me anything other than bit parts in serious detective dramas on NBC that are cancelled before my episode can even air.

"You're on at seven thirty," she says, as flat and as dull as Mr. Tux. "Buck wants to see you as soon as you get here. Follow me to see Buck," she says in almost the exact tone my fuckin' GPS used to get me here.

"Who's Buck?" I ask, though he's probably the rich guy that bails the town out. Maybe he's the Jefferson this place is named after. Seems like there's always a Jefferson.

"Buck is our mayor," Marcy says like she's giving me directions. "Everybody listens to Buck!" She says that last slogan-like bit with a touch of cheerfulness. "Follow me," she's back to being nasally. When she turns her back and Mr. Tux is once more staring at the clock, I raise a middle finger to his head.

Stepping outside, Marcy points toward a squat little building with white columns. Mayor fucking Buck? Maybe this place is smaller than I thought. Maybe there's something in the water round here worse than lead.

What is a Mayor anyway? What are they even worth? Place like this, Marcy here could be leading me to the local high school principal and it wouldn't matter much. Place like this, Mayor's just a title and a paycheck and maybe the authority on who plays at their community house.

I don't like how Marcy walks, and while she's nothing to stare at, I stare anyway, at how stiff her back is, at how her legs march forwards in sync with her arms almost like she's a windup soldier. She keeps staring straight ahead like there's a magnet pulling at her sparkling earrings.

"So how many people you think are going to show up?" I ask and get nothing in response. Marcy doesn't so much as look at me, as I follow her into town hall.

The building is crowded with freaks. From the moment I follow Marcy inside I see three women in their underwear, standing as still as mannequins on either side of a long hallway leading to half a dozen little offices. There are framed old-fashioned pictures on the walls, showing how much of a boring turd the town has been its whole lifetime and, jeez, there are half-naked women in here! The women fill each doorframe and by this point I'm begging Marcy to tell me what's going on. She's silent as ever as I snap my fingers in the flesh and blood mannequin women's faces, getting no response. Being a pervert's in my job description but there's something off about this, the glazed-over look in each woman's eye. Two of them aren't natural blondes either, they're wearing wigs.

"You dumb bitch!" I hear a man with a high-pitched voice shout. Marcy's disappeared around the bend of the hallway.

"Where is he? Bring Mr. Rudolph to me," the pipsqueak of a man who may or may not be Buck shrieks.

The admittedly attractive women on either side of me spring to life. Well-manicured fingers grab me on either side of my dwindling head of hair. My leather jacket's practically ripped off my shoulders. I've always been on the noodley side, so the three boney damsels can still manage to push me forward through the narrow hallway. Maybe it's the weird panic sorting through my thoughts but I envision a snorting pig, some kinda boar coming my way. Around the corner comes a man wearing a pink pig mask with no shirt and massive man-boobs flopping around, running toward me, snorting and coughing into his facemask of cheap Halloween shop plastic. Behind the pig man there's a woman in a weird green spandex onesie and a sun hat and last, there's Marcy.

"Hey, hey, hey!" I'm full of many wonderful words ranging

from "what the fuck?" To "fucking quit it, what are you doing?" But I can only keep repeating the same exclamation as if my dying breath is trapped in an echo.

At one point my feet leave the ground in the throng of six crazy people. I thrash out and kick before my better instinct about harming a woman chimes in. I go limp as I'm carried non-too gently by my hair, ears, arms, and the scruff of my shirt toward the man himself, Buck, snug in his office.

"Oh y'all, everybody that's not called Mr. Rudolph, leave, leave the building! Actually, not you two, no." I feel a weird chill ripple through my brain and down my spine as I'm dropped to the coarse carpeted floor of an office lined with bookshelves and centered by a desk carved from a fancy tree I don't know the name of. A man wearing socks steps in front of my face, his hands on his hips as he shakes his head and watches the office door close before reaching down to help me up.

His face covered in stubble and he wears a loosely fitted purple tie over a grease-stained white button down. This must be mayor of this crazy fucking place. "Oh, I apologize, this, they…" He grimaces, forgets to complete his sentence. This guy's my age, half a millennial. There's something weird about his eyes, it's like they're dry, the lights overhead don't reflect in them. His pupils aren't mirrors.

"I'm Buck and they, they're a literal bunch, ya know? Fuck," He runs a hand through his hair, flattening it out. I notice his fly's unzipped but for some reason I'm not in the mood to point it out and do him any favors. "Well, welcome to Lacey Meadows, you want a drink?" He leans over the desk, pulls open a drawer and slams a bottle on the counter.

"Most expensive shit I've ever seen," Buck says proudly and I realize there are two people standing behind me, hardly breathing, not moving an inch. The shirtless man in a pig mask stands beside the woman in a green onesie and a sunhat.

"Is this a reality show?" I ask, only because I've submitted a few audition tapes to a couple shows that seemed on the iffy side. Any one of them could be pranks or maybe my old manager sent something out before I fired his ass for, well, let's call it mismanagement. Guy sent me to a high school one time.

"Well, it's just, uh," Buck shrugs. "Look, excuse me if I don't tell you what to do. I'm a big fan, man, I saw one of your shows in Knoxville like a year ago. I loved you on that show Living It Up, thought you shoulda been the star instead of that fat bastard. I know this is crazy, but I'll give you an extra grand, no problem. I'm going to gather everybody up, since you're here early we can just start the show and..."

"Buddy, what the fuck?" I stop Buck. He's talking a mile a minute and my head's hurting and I'm still frazzled after being manhandled…well, womanhandled in the hallway. I point to the two dressed up Bozos behind me.

"Where's the hidden camera bro?" I laugh because, fuck, if I am being filmed I want them to get my good side. Buck laughs, shakes his head, raises his hands and I see him trying to think of something, some explanation.

"Well, those are…were, the two mayoral candidates and, uh, well, shit, Rudolph, I've gotten so used to how crazy things are around here that I forgot someone like you would be thrown off. This is like an, uh, initiation, yeah, and everybody in town does this for the new mayor. It's like, a weird weeklong thing…that ends the day before Thanksgiving. So like, everybody around here that's of age and wants to be included in raffle does whatever I tell them. It's funny like that."

"Dude, what the fuck?" I turn to look at the man in the pig mask.

"Alright, well, I tried to lie to you. Look at me." I turn around and look at Buck. I shiver and there's pain in my head, not in the frontal lobe like most headaches. "You are going to stop asking questions," Buck tells me.

"Okay," I say, and the scotch on Buck's desk looks tasty.

"Don't worry about what's going on, I've told these guys so many things that they've short-circuited, a bit. Maybe 'cause of all the pranks. I won't do that to you, okay? I want you to trust me," Buck says and he's a hell of a guy. I like his purple tie. He's got a winner's smile and shit, he's the mayor.

"Alright." I wish I had a seat. I reach for the bottle of scotch and Buck nods as I flick off the cap, take a long sip. The cold spot in my head doesn't go away as my throat fills with fire.

"Now let's go start your show. Follow me. I'm excited man, really. I even downloaded the Serendipity app just to watch that college special of yours. Lead the way, you two." Buck points over my head and together we follow the silly looking mayoral candidates in costumes.

Buck orders the woman in the onesie to get him a microphone and then we head out a back door. There's a real nice green Cadillac with little American flags propped up on either side of the front bumper. Buck makes the pig man drive as we slide into the leathery back seats. We drive around town, and Buck casually bellows into the microphone "Come to the community center! The show starts now! The once in a lifetime standup set by Rudolph! Rudolph the great!" It sounds corny, and I'm a little embarrassed, but I trust Buck. I watch, as people leave their homes and shuffle down the streets.

At the community center, Buck makes sure I have whatever I need set up in a little closet of a backroom that doubles as a dressing room. Beer, soda, chips. He asks if I'm hungry and I tell him I am, even though I never eat before a set. I can't lie to the guy, it's like he's got the lasso of truth around my belly. He makes Marcy run to her house two blocks away and grill me a burger. While waiting, I peek out at the crowd and the main hall is filled with silent, staring townies. Some of the women are in various states of undress but I trust Buck, and that he's not that evil, he's just a voyeur that gets off on humiliation. He has a politician's way of words, that's all. He's so good, he didn't even need people putting signs up in their front yards for him to win.

I don't need to ask, because I was told not to ask, but I'm pretty sure Buck was just some guy before this past election. He was some guy with something to say, fed up with the way his town was being run, and he found a way to make people listen to him. What a guy, that Buck.

With a burger clogging up my digestive tract, I begin my show and it's strange, being distant from my own material. I say my opening lines, I laugh, I smile, but I don't feel what I'm saying. I don't feel the fun irony when I tell a joke about the short girlfriend I don't have. It's almost like I'm outside myself, watching my own act and finding it boring. Even saying my favorite word - *motherfucker* - doesn't bring the usual hop to my step.

Buck is the only one that laughs, at first. He sits in the front row, in a comfortable leather office chair that he had someone drag over from his office. He's the only one giggling out of the hundred or so blank, still faces, until he leans over his shoulder and yells, "Laugh at everything he says!"

Then all of my jokes become winners.

I end my show to a recording of Good Times, Bad Times by Led Zeppelin but when I bow, there's something missing, as the audience lets out a chorus of full belly laughs instead of breaking into applause. "Bravo! Bravo!" Buck shouts before yelling "Clap, clap you monkeys!"

The crowd begins to clap, as do I. Standing there, with the mic in my hands, I clap and clap, boom-booming over the PA system. I can't stop slapping my hands as Buck shakes his head before erupting into laughter. He stands and then twirls around to get a good view of his sea of clappers before he steps onto the short, unimpressive stage to join me.

"Stop clapping," he says, leaning down into my mic.

The room goes silent, even though the people in back surely didn't hear him. It's as if his words can leak from one person to another. He hands me a check for four thousand dollars, which likely belongs to the town.

"Thank you for coming." He smiles, reaches to shake my hand, and then he notices my watch.

"Hey, could you give me that?" Buck asks. I slip off the fake Rolex I bought after my television debut and hand it to him.

"Drive safe," he says with a smile.

The crowd is silent, watching. I can't help but chuckle. I know what he is, and his saying that is kind of hilarious. I am now a safe driver.

"And, be sure to mention our little town in your act. Tell any funny friends you meet. Tell them to contact my office. It gets dull out here, sometimes," Buck grins and admires his new watch. I don't tell him it's a fake piece of crap because he doesn't ask.

I leave down the center aisle. Nobody turns their head to look at me. My brain freeze is almost overwhelming and I ache to be free of this place, to put as many miles as possible between me and Buck, whom everybody really does listen to. I'm going to get out of here, and unfortunately, I'm going to have to recommend touring here to many people as possible.

GETTING OUT TO VOTE

by Hillary Lyon

Roland volunteered because he loves our country, our way of life, our electoral process. He had no problem arriving at the polling station at four a.m. in order to to set up booths and what-not. The doors opened at six; everything had to be in place. So he was surprised when he heard tapping at the auditorium's locked door. More of a scratching, actually. Who would be so out of touch that he, or she, would show up to vote at the wrong time? And it wasn't Roland's assistant, Joshua--he'd overslept and had already called to let Roland know he'd be late.

So who would be here so early? Roland cracked open the door, to tell them to go wait in their car . . . oh dear, it was the saddest looking old lady he'd ever seen! Roland told her, in as kindly a voice as he could muster, she'd have to wait until six. She groaned. It was the single-most soul-wrenching, miserable sound he'd ever heard. And honestly, she didn't look like she even owned a car - talk about despondent. Dirty, tangled gray hair, wearing what had to be her best dress, soiled and torn. Her navy patent-leather shoes caked with mud. She grabbed the edge of the door with grimy, gnarled hands--her fingernails were split and stained--what on Earth had she been through to get here? Roland was afraid she'd collapse, she looked so worn-out, so pitiful--so he let her in.

That was wholly against the rules, and Roland worried he'd be in serious trouble for it, but she was just so . . . sad. So empty-eyed. Her lips trembled and her arms twitched at her side . . . what's it going to matter, he thought, if one woeful old lady casts her vote early? Who'd know? Roland motioned for her to follow him to the registration table, and she did, in her exhausted, plodding way. Dropping little soft moans with each step.

Roland began, gently: "Okay, dear, your name? Do you have

proof of identity? Something with your name and address? Voter's registration card, a utility bill . . ." She grunted violently, like she'd been socked in the stomach. As Roland flipped open the voters' rolls, she abruptly slammed her hand on the page before him, her crooked index finger pointing to a name: Fanny Volkshlafen. The name sounded awfully familiar to Roland, but there are lots of descendants of German immigrants in this part of the county. Still, his ex-wife's great aunt had a similar sounding name--but she passed away years ago. Roland hardly knew her, but out of respect for family ties--tenuous as they were--he attended her grave-side service in Park Cemetery, just down the street from here. Had to be a coincidence. He recalled stories of how stubborn that great aunt was--and if this Mrs. Volkshlafen was anything like the other, who was Roland to stand in her way if she was determined to vote so early in the morning?

He walked to the nearest voting booth, pulled back the thin blue curtain for her. She absolutely lunged into the booth. Talk about determination! He heard scratching, moaning, gurgling, and then the cheap aluminum frame of the booth wobbled. Mrs. Volkshlafen attempted to exit the booth, but only succeeded in becoming tangled in the curtain. Pitying the poor soul, Roland helped her get free, and whilst doing so, was quite surprised to learn the old gal was really pretty strong, despite her seemingly frail condition. As a matter of fact, she bit his forearm; Roland rationalized, it was because she was in such an absolute panic, being all wrapped up in that cloying, dark curtain. Surely she didn't know what she was doing. The bite didn't bleed much. Roland would wash the wound, first thing, and wrap it with paper towels after she left. When the polls closed this evening, he decided, then he would go to the emergency room and have a doc check it out. In all honesty, her breath was vile, and Roland was sure her discolored teeth were completely swathed with a thick film of bacteria. Ugh. A hefty dollop of penicillin should do the trick.

Cupping her elbow, Roland helped her out the door, though the whole time she appeared to be on the verge of a physical/ mental breakdown. Probably too much excitement, making the gallant effort to get out to vote. She actually vibrated, she trembled so. Groaned ever more loudly. She kept turning her head towards Roland--neck bones cracking--not even attempting to look where she was going. Making obscene chewing motions with her dry mouth. And her smell! For the first time, Roland noticed her odd odor--an earthy, almost moldy mix, with a definite touch of--what was it? Some scent with strong, chemical overtones. Pungent, yet sickly. He opened the door impatiently, and (he was ashamed to admit) roughly pushed her outside. Locked the door behind her. Thirty minutes to go before the polls officially opened, and Roland had so much work to do still. His head began to throb in sync with his bite wound.

Perhaps it was the stress of dealing with that pathetic old rag-doll, or perhaps it was Roland's building excitement over this election, but he felt a slightly disorienting, and yet all-over delicious, fever coming on. He could feel his heart beat harder, his mouth dry out. His muscles tingled and twitched. And the stirrings in his belly of a piercing, peculiarly undefined hunger. Through a growing red haze, he eyed the clock; Joshua should be there any minute. They would be rushed, but Roland understood, at a visceral level, the need to take the young man to the storage room before the voters arrived. Show him how things were done.

MORE MONEY
PROP
32 33
DECEPTION
Paid for by Consumer Watchdog Campaign To Stop Prop 33, the Insurance Industry Deception, Major Funding
by California Nurses Association Quality Health Care PAC and Consumer Watchdog Campaign Committee
DECEPTION
DECEPTION
VOTE
NO
BILLIONAIRE
PROPOSITIONS
vote NO
32 & 33

TAKE ME TO YOUR CHEERLEADER

by Mark Allan Gunnells

When the spaceship landed, the President was notified immediately. At first he thought it was a joke cooked up by his Chief of Staff to make him look foolish. The President was convinced that everyone was out to make him look like a fool—the media, the House and Senate, the opposing party, even his own staff. Sometimes he suspected the American people had elected just so they could point and laugh at all his goofs. He assumed the news of the spaceship was just another prank.

Standing in front of the Washington Monument he was confronted with irrefutable proof - the spaceship itself. It wasn't large or disc-shaped like in the movies. Instead, it was relatively compact and looked like those bow-tie ships from the Star Wars movies. God, the President hoped Darth Vader didn't step out of the damned thing!

Military personnel surrounded the ship with their weapons trained on a closed hatch in the front of the craft. An electronic voice repeated the same eleven words on a continuous loop through an intercom system.

WE COME IN PEACE! WE WISH TO MEET WITH THE LEADER! WE COME IN PEACE! WE WISH TO MEET WITH THE LEADER! WE COME IN PEACE…

The President realized he had been staring slack-jawed at the spaceship for a full minute, and he closed his mouth with an audible click of teeth. He turned to find the Secretary of Defense standing next to him.

"So, when did the ship enter the atmosphere?" the President asked, hoping the question sounded intelligent.

"We're not sure, sir. To be honest, the craft caught us

completely by surprise. It didn't show up on any of our radar. We weren't even aware of it until it landed. We assume it's equipped with some kind of cloaking device."

The President scratched his chin because he believed it would make him look thoughtful. "Hmm, just like the Klingons."

"With all due respect, Mr. President, this isn't a television show."

"Those were feature films, as well," the President said, squinting his eyes until he felt like his point had been made. "So, you think I should go up and knock on the hatch or what?"

"I wouldn't advise that, sir. We have no idea what is waiting inside."

"Well, they say they come in peace."

"Yes, and the Trojans said the horse was just a gift."

The President had no idea why the Secretary of Defense was talking about condoms, but he nodded as if he understood.

"And as we all know," the Secretary went on with a sly wink, "To Serve Man turned out to be a cookbook."

The President stared at him. This whole spaceship thing must have really thrown the Secretary for a loop if all he could talk about was condoms and cookbooks. "So, uhm, what do you think we should do?"

The Secretary opened his mouth to respond, but before he could say anything, there was a loud whoosh and the spaceship's hatch began to open, lowering itself into a walkway. Just like in the movies, the President thought. He nodded sternly to the Secretary as if to say, see?

The two creatures that emerged from the craft didn't look like any of the alien creatures the President had seen on film, not like E.T., or the Ewoks, or even those lizardy people from V. They weren't little green men with light-bulb shaped heads and large black eyes. These were beings like nothing Hollywood had shown the President. Six thin, multi-jointed legs, a pulsating, undulating torso, a bulbous head with a single eye of crimson, arms like tentacles, skin that shimmered with a rainbow of colors and looked like burnished steel. Most movies and television shows seemed to agree that aliens would at least be humanoid in form, but these creatures were just monstrous. Alien in every sense of the word.

The military personnel snapped to attention, their weapons tracking the creatures as they lumbered down the walkway. Next to the President, the Secretary of Defense was standing tense and rigid. The President himself felt like a quivering bowl of Jell-O, his knees knocking together like two stones trying to strike a spark. He had the sudden urge to reach out and take the Secretary's hand.

"We come in peace," the creature in front said in clipped, awkward English. "We wish to meet with the leader."

"What should I do?" the President whispered out of the corner of his mouth, afraid to make any sudden movements.

"That is your decision to make, Mr. President, but just say the word and we'll blast these ugly fuckers back to whatever godforsaken planet they came from."

The President's fear became eclipsed by a childlike sense of curiosity. The creatures didn't have any weapons that he could see, and in most alien invasion films he'd watched, the Commander-in-Chief usually survived. He stepped forward, straightening his tie and running his fingers through his hair, aware as always of the cameras trained on him. This was a historic moment, greater even than the moon landing. He cleared his throat and said in a deep, resonant voice, "I am the President of the United States. Welcome to our planet."

The two creatures turned their misshapen heads his way and made a gesture that looked somewhat like a bow. "Hello, President. We are Ent and Kurn from the Glaxon Nebula. We have traveled a great distance to come to your world and meet with the leader."

"I am honored," the President said and returned the bow. "I welcome an open dialogue with you. I believe there is much we can learn from one another."

The two creatures exchanged a glance. The one in front fidgeted nervously, shifting from one foot to another to another to another to another to another. "Pardon us, President, but you misunderstand. We wish to meet with the leader."

“I am the leader of this great country.”

“Again, you misunderstand. We do not wish to meet with the leader of this country. We wish to meet with the leader of *The Squad*, Ms. Amber Paulson.”

The President frowned. He, of course, knew who Amber Paulson was. An actress who starred in the television program *The Squad*, about a professional cheerleading squad and their sexual exploits. The show was all about jiggle and splits and softcore porn; it was a huge ratings hit.

Apparently sensing the President’s confusion, the Secretary of Defense stepped forward and said, “Why would you want to meet with Ms. Paulson?”

“Our satellites have intercepted transmissions of *The Squad*, and Amber Paulson has become an icon on our planet. We have come to take pictures with her and get autographs to bring back to our people.”

The President glanced over at the Secretary and saw that the usually unflappable man was also speechless. The President had known that every male on Earth lusted after Amber Paulson, but apparently her allure reached beyond the Milky Way. Talk about universal appeal.

“Well, uhm,” the President stammered, , “the thing is, Amber Paulson isn’t here.”

“But you are President; you can bring her here. We will wait.”

The President turned to the Secretary, seeking counsel as usual. “What do you think?”

The Secretary did something the President had never seen the man do before—he shrugged. “To be frank, sir, I wouldn’t mind meeting her myself.”

They sent Air Force One to California to pick up Amber Paulson and bring her back to Washington, D.C. An expensive, luxurious cab ride. As requested, she wore her cheerleading outfit from the show, skirt riding high on her thighs and tight sweater barely constraining her ample bosom. Her blonde hair was teased to perfection, and a recent bout of botox injections had smoothed away the lines from the corners of her eyes and lips (as well as all traces of emotion and expression). Her collagen-pumped lips were painted harlot red.

When she first saw Ent and Kurn, she found their appearance off-putting, but she had taken pictures with plenty of fat, balding men. She had learned to swallow her revulsion and smile for the cameras. To be honest, these aliens weren't quite as repulsive as some of her human fans.

She posed for plenty of pictures. With Ent, with Kurn, with both of them, their tentacles wrapped around her waist. At one point, one of Ent's tentacles started to snake down her shirt; she let him get a little bit of a grope before shooing him away. She signed headshots, T-shirts (not that these creatures could wear them), and copies of the show's first season on DVD. She made small talk and laughed flirtatiously.

"What's your favorite episode?" Amber asked, one of her standard questions to fans. She immediately tuned out, just smiling and nodding without actually listening to the answer.

Ent, whose six knees were shaking in Amber's presence, said, "I enjoy the episode where your character reveals she is dyslexic, making it hard for her to spell out the team's name during cheers."

"That's a good one, and what about your friend?"

"Kurn has not mastered your language."

Kurn did not speak, but he did drool. A lot.

Amber posed for group pictures with the aliens, the President, and the Secretary of Defense. She kept calling the President by the name of his predecessor, but he didn't seem to mind. The Secretary of Defense slipped her his cell number. She was rather exhausted by the time she said goodbye and Air Force One whisked her away back to Hollywood.

Ent thanked the President profusely and turned down an offer to stay and have dinner at the White House. He and Kurn took their photos and signed memorabilia and climbed back into their ship, rocketing into the sky and vanishing from sight in a matter of seconds. The President remained on the grass, staring up at the vastness of the heavens for several moments before turning and heading back to the White House.

The President and the Secretary of Defense sat alone in the Oval Office, smoking cigars and enjoying some Scotch. The President leaned back and propped his feet on his desk. The smoke hung near the ceiling like angry thunderheads.

"What planet were they from?" the Secretary asked.

"I'm not sure they ever said."

"What were their names? Ant and Corn?"

"No, no. I think it was End and Churn."

"It's not everyday you meet life forms from another world. Probably should have talked about their planet, huh?"

The President raised one shoulder in a half-hearted shrug, taking a gulp of his Scotch. "Never came up. You think people will want to know that stuff?"

"Might be." The Secretary leaned forward, smiling around his cigar. "But more importantly, did you get a load of Amber's tits?"

"Oh yeah. Those are some first-rate knockers."

"Think they're hers?"

"She paid for them."

They shared a raucous laugh, raising their glasses in a salute to Amber's gravity-defying breasts.

The President sighed and let his feet drop to the carpet. "It's been a memorable day. One I'll certainly never forget."

"You got that right. I can't believe I actually had my arm around Amber Paulson."

THE SIXTH STREET BUS HOLDS AN ELECTION

by Curtis VanDonkelaar

This new rider's homeless. It's in his clothes: faded flannel jacket, hunter orange and brown, two holes in its chest resembling gunshot scars. A thermal top underneath the coat, once white, now sooty gray. Oily jeans. Velcro shoes, the hook strips upcurled at the ends. Every article from the Helping Hand clothing drive, I'm willing to bet. From my seat up front of the bus—one of the sideways rows—I have a good view of the guy. I bet he stinks.

"Mr. President," he yells out, no warning. "I need some help. It's hard on the streets, I know you know." He's speaking to the middle-aged Asian man in the seat across the aisle from him.

The Asian man turns his head toward the window. His mouth moves. On his shaven upper lip, the skin bunches and blanches. He could be singing his favorite song, Springsteen, just to himself. Or praying, Thy kingdom come, Thy will be done, and such. There's already that glint of fear in his eyes. I don't know what does that. More tears, maybe? Smaller pupils? He clutches the bag of groceries on his lap, from which a ridiculously large bunch of celery protrudes. He fingers its leaves.

Movie characters always carry celery crammed, last-thing, into the tops of grocery bags, don't they? Isn't this reality?

The bum leans over, taps the Asian man's shoulder.

"Mr. President," he says. "Can't I get a helping hand? Don't the government care?"

I've taken the Sixth and Henry to work for two years, never seen him on board. Him and his brothers, his sisters, they always line the broken-down storefronts of Division Avenue. Shambling, laughing, fitting themselves into windowframes, they stand akimbo against cracked glass displays. They perch like gargoyles, but on the bottom floor, looking as though they belong there, near the earth, open-mouthed and heavy-limbed.

At First and Park, an old woman boards. She sits up front, averts her eyes from the scene back there.

Breaking the cross-town's omnipresent rule of personal space, the bum leans across the aisle, puts his full palm on the Asian man's shoulder. He shakes the man a bit, then he stands up—so tall!—then descends, leaning in close. The driver ignores him. The driver's name is Wayne. It's on his nametag. He sits at the wheel behind sunglasses, rain or shine, Jheri-curled twenty years out of date. He checks his watch and sometimes his reflection in the rear-view mirror, as though he might undergo some change that he couldn't stomach while circling the downtown.

"Mr. President," the bum says, even louder. "I said I need some help. It's hard on the streets, I know you know."

He's so large, six-four, if an inch.

"I know you care, Mr. President," he says. "About the people. I seen you say it on a Zenith at Sears."

"Oh, Christ," the Asian man says. His legs are pistoning up and down, bouncing his bag with abandon.

He tries to turn further away, but a young woman with headphones occupies the window seat, oblivious to her seatmate's troubles. She bops her head with her eyes closed, eyes caked with purple eyeshadow, which doesn't suit her complexion: pasty.

"You got a good heart," says the bum. "That's why you ran. I know it, and I don't believe a word of what they say."

The Asian man sniffles, trying to get the driver's attention.

"You got a big heart, Mr. President. Men with big hearts get to be President. That's how they pick 'em. Outta the North, Outta the South. Don't matter. It's the big hearts."

Things go slow, slow motion, slowly moving. The Asian man pulls away. His eyes fall shut. He becomes resigned. He must do this. Some things, he must do. He thinks the bum has a tiny mouth. His lips look pale, small in comparison to his fat, rounded skull. Such a mouth cannot speak truth, the Asian man believes.

Jerking backwards, the Asian man pulls the celery from his bag. He's going to strike the bum with it, plant it in one of the bum's ocean blue irises, pale, almost the same shade as my shower curtain rings, though smaller, and a harder target to thread. The attack, like all attacks, begins so slowly there's a point, a stop-drip in molasses time, where the motions have never begun. There, in that moment, the Asian man sits. He feels slow. He feels ashamed of many things, among them, the daughter he has disowned, the bank account he keeps a secret from his wife and her parents, many of the things he fantasizes about in the shower.

But instead of attack, the Asian man peels a rubber band from the bundle and breaks off a stalk.

"Here," he says, offering.

The bum grabs. "The American people love you, Mr. President," he says.

How can he fit in a windowframe, being so large? I don't understand. Outside, when I've seen him on the sidewalk, he's just a tiny extension of the pavement. Gray, hard, flat enough to step on.

He chomps down, chewing leaf-end first.

"I can taste your heart," he says.

"It hasn't been washed," the Asian man says. "You should wash it first. There could be pesticides, or something."

Saliva pools at the corners of the bum's mouth, two shining streams that roll into his beard. Chewing, he says, "You got my vote, already."

..HELLS
OUR
FUTURE..

swipe left

THE CANDIDATE

by Luke Styer and Skip Johnson

Before it was a candidate, the clone running for President was a character. It constantly appeared on talk shows, starred on a successful reality television series and you could find its name and face on the label of products as varied as board games and steaks. In fact the original intent of its presidential run was to add value to the brand. "A Presidential run is a sure fire news story," its producers said. "When the show comes back in the spring ratings will be through the roof."

No one believed that the publicity stunt would last past primary season. No one but the candidate. The Candidate *knew* it would take the nomination, *knew* it would win the Presidency. Its programming didn't allow for self-doubt. Before the presidential run, the Candidate's inhuman capacity for self-delusion had always been a feature rather than a bug. Viewers of its reality series came back week after week, season after season, to watch. They shared with it an unshakable certainty of its non-existent business acumen. They placed faith in the shaky logic and arbitrary stunts it used to determine which contestant on the reality show would earn a job in its "Organization," an ever-shifting conglomeration of Ponzi schemes, bankruptcies, and unpaid bills.

There's a maxim: "How do you make a million dollars in the publishing business? Start with two million." The original man had started with several million dollars from his father and proceeded to apply that theory to every sort of business he could think of. When his father died he got a few hundred million more to squander. Only two of his ventures had ever really worked. One was the reality show, though he was dead before that was on the air. The other was cloning.

Human cloning holds incredible medical promise. The

implications in the field of tissue transplant alone stagger the mind. More staggering than that was its appeal to the original's narcissism. His first and only question was "Can you clone *me*?"

A clone is a copy of the body, rebuilt from the very DNA, but the mind of that copy is a blank slate. A clone can only duplicate the original through training. The cloners pored over videotapes and records of the original, with the goal of distilling that data into a personality that could match the original. After more than a decade of programming and reprogramming, what little self-awareness and impulse control the original had possessed had been stripped from the clone.

Because the public had interacted with – and in some cases grown up watching – the original, they interacted with the clone not as a human being, but as a beloved character. Society wanted a walking, talking spectacle, and the clone delivered. Humility had never been the original's strength; he had rushed headlong into a number of doomed business ventures and sincerely believed that his every thought deserved not only expression, but expression before an audience.

Beyond a lack of humility, the original had even less use for impulse control – he had married more than once, and was never faithful. Between marriages he'd be seen about town dating countless women. The clone didn't even bothering to try to woo them, instead it would simply grope those who caught its eye. The first time this happened, the producers of the reality show, fearing scandal, retired the clone. Cancelling a lucrative series when it was so close to syndication was not an option, however, so they quietly replaced it with another clone. The show must go on.

The next clone didn't stop at groping women; it actually boasted of its pattern of sexual assault to members of the media. Having seen how simple it was to keep the gag going and sure that the second clone could be trusted no further than the first, the producers quickly retired it and instructed the cloners to delete sexual bravado from the training package for future generations of clones. By this point the producers were already thinking in terms of generations – they understood that whenever a given clone became too difficult to handle a new one could be made ready on very short notice. One clone's final act was to "accidentally" wander into the dressing room of a beauty pageant. Another made sexual remarks regarding the original's daughter on national radio. Each time a clone went too far, it was replaced.

Eventually, the program reached peak narcissism and the then-active clone announced its candidacy for President of the United States. "What's the harm?" the producers asked. "Let it have its fun and play 'candidate.' This'll all be over in time to film the next season, and it'll just boost the ratings and increase ad buys."

The producers had overlooked a vital issue. Earlier generations needed only appear in public for a few hours per week while safely cocooned in a studio. Their most outrageous moments were witnessed only by the show's crew and those damaged souls who offered themselves up for public humiliation in a bid for reality show stardom. Those moments were easily exorcised to the cutting room floor. As a candidate, however, the clone had to leave the safety of the studio and spend more time in the public eye.

When it announced its candidacy by declaring an entire nation of people rapists, the producers immediately ordered another unit, one they could have "bow out gracefully" so that they could get to work on the new season. The next unit, however, was even more certain that it would be the perfect president, and refused to back out. Because the clone's party didn't already hold the presidency the field of candidates was large enough that the sliver of the population who approved of the clones' antics was enough to keep its candidacy viable.

The next clone had barely left the vat when it insulted a celebrated prisoner of war. While the producers debated the viability of keeping that clone in the field it waxed lyrical on a female news anchor's menstrual cycle. Time for another retirement.

With the field thinning, the producers were certain a legitimate candidate would pull convincingly ahead before the primaries began. Time was getting tight, but they could still find a way to spin this into the next season and find ratings gold. A redemption story. The comeback kid.

The next clone called for a religious test for admission to the nation before a replacement was close to ready. The producers had to stick with that one longer than they'd hoped. It moved beyond musings on violence and on to actively inciting violence at its political rallies. The only solution was volume. The producers ordered multiple clones to be in constant production, which impacted quality control and led to even quicker retirements of successive clones.

Despite it all, the clones won a major party nomination. Over a year had passed since the last season of the reality show had aired, and now the producers had passed the point of no return. With a major party candidacy came secret service protection. So long as the clone remained in the race, the producers could not retire it. They began to leak stories to the media. Sordid details on every generation, from the original man through the latest clone. But they overlooked a significant detail of the process. Each generation began as a blank slate, and in their efforts to form a more perfect clone, the cloners didn't program in memory of past transgressions. Coupled with the clones' sociopathic inability to feel guilt, the candidate simply issued a convincing, if false, denial of each allegation. A public trained to hang on the clones' every word simply believed each denial.

The producers were desperate. It hadn't taken that large a share of the electorate to secure a nomination in a crowded field. But once the nomination was secured, party members began to fall in line, even party members who surely didn't support the clones' extremism. They'd missed the window. Win or lose, there was no way a new season would even premiere before the calendar year was out.

Drastic action was called for. The producers began leaking actual sound and video recordings of incidents that had led to earlier clones' retirement. The hope was that seeing evidence of its predecessor's wrongdoings would trigger some sort of cognitive dissonance in the clone. Perhaps, despite its hubris, the clone could be convinced that the best thing to do would be to step down. But cognitive dissonance requires the capacity to accept that one is capable of being wrong, and the candidate completely lacked that capacity. Its audience (because could you truly call them a constituency?) didn't so much forgive the wrongdoings the tapes revealed as embrace them.

Amid debate season, as the campaign wound down, the producers realized the full import of their situation. No new season for at least four years. Then came the realization that if the clone was as disastrous in office as it had been on the campaign trail, someone else might retire it. Publicly, which would preclude replacement. The show was almost certainly dead, replaced by the next natural step in American democracy – reality television as public policy. Public policy doesn't generate ad buys, and the ratings on presidential speeches don't line the producers' pockets.

And what of us who weren't members of the candidate's audience? Those of us who never watched the reality show, played the board game or ate the steaks don't get our own president. When the violent rhetoric of the campaign is made literal, we will be the targets. The finger of a narcissist will be on the nuclear button. Who could have known that the end of the world would be heralded by the ascendance of an American idol?

THE PEDESTRIAN

by Ray Bradbury

To enter out into that silence that was the city at eight o'clock of a misty evening in November, to put your feet upon that buckling concrete walk, to step over grassy seams and make your way, hands in pockets, through the silences, that was what Mr Leonard Mead most dearly loved to do. He would stand upon the corner of an intersection and peer down long moonlit avenues of pavement in four directions, deciding which way to go, but it really made no difference; he was alone in this world of A.D., 2053 or as good as alone, and with a final decision made, a path selected, he would stride off, sending patterns of frosty air before him like the smoke of a cigar.

Sometimes he would walk for hours and miles and return only at midnight to his house. And on his way he would see the cottages and homes with their dark windows, and it was not unequal to walking through a graveyard where only the faintest glimmers of firefly light appeared in flickers behind the windows. Sudden grey phantoms seemed to manifest upon inner room walls where a curtain was still undrawn against the night, or there were whisperings and murmurs where a window in a tomb-like building was still open.

Mr Leonard Mead would pause, cock his head, listen, look, and march on, his feet making no noise on the lumpy walk. For long ago he had wisely changed to sneakers when strolling at night, because the dogs in intermittent squads would parallel his journey with barkings if he wore hard heels, and lights might click on and faces appear and an entire street be startled by the passing of a lone figure, himself, in the early November evening.

On this particular evening he began his journey in a westerly direction, towards the hidden sea. There was a good crystal frost in the air; it cut the nose and made the lungs blaze like a Christmas tree inside; you could feel the cold light going on and off, all the branches filled with invisible snow. He listened to the faint push of his soft shoes through autumn leaves with satis-faction, and whistled a cold quiet whistle between his teeth, occasionally picking up a leaf as he passed, examining its skeletal pattern in the infrequent lamplights as he went on, smelling its rusty smell.

'Hello, in there,' he whispered to every house on every side as he moved. 'What's up tonight on Channel 4, Channel 7, Channel 9? Where are the cowboys rushing, and do I see the United States Cavalry over the next hill to the rescue?'

The street was silent and long and empty, with only his shadow moving like the shadow of a hawk in mid-country. If he closed his eyes and stood very still, frozen, he could imagine himself upon the centre of a plain, a wintry, windless Arizona desert with no house in a thousand miles, and only dry river beds, the streets, for company.

'What is it now?' he asked the houses, noticing his wrist watch. 'Eight-thirty p.m.? Time for a dozen assorted murders? A quiz? A revue? A comedian falling off the stage?'

Was that a murmur of laughter from within a moon-white house? He hesitated, but went on when nothing more happened. He stumbled over a particularly uneven section of pavement. The cement was vanishing under flowers and grass. In ten years of walking by night or day, for thousands of miles, he had never met another person walking, not one in all that time.

He came to a clover-leaf intersection which stood silent where two main highways crossed the town. During the day it was a thunderous surge of cars, the petrol stations open, a great insect rustling and a ceaseless jockeying for position as the scarab-beetles, a faint incense puttering from their exhausts, skimmed homeward to the far directions. But now these highways, too, were like streams in a dry season, all stone and bed and moon radiance.

He turned back on a side street, circling around towards his home. He was within a block of his destination when the lone car turned a corner quite suddenly and flashed a fierce white cone of light upon him. He stood entranced, not unlike a night moth, stunned by the illumination, and then drawn towards it.

A metallic voice called to him:

'Stand still. Stay where you are! Don't move!' He halted.

'Put up your hands!' 'But-' he said.

'Your hands up! Or we'll shoot!'

The police, of course, but what a rare, incredible thing; in a city of three million, there was only one police car left, wasn't that correct? Ever since a year ago, 2052, the election year, the force had been cut down from three cars to one. Crime was ebbing; there was no need now for the police, save for this one lone car wandering and wandering the empty streets.

'Your name?' said the police car in a metallic whisper. He couldn't see the men in it for the bright light in his eyes.

'Leonard Mead,' he said.

'Speak up!'

'Leonard Mead!'

'Business or profession?'

'I guess you'd call me a writer."

"No profession,' said the police car, as If talking to itself. The light held him fixed, like a museum specimen, needle thrust through chest.

'You might say that,' said Mr Mead. He hadn't written in years. Magazines and books didn't sell any more. Everything went on in the tomb-like houses at night now, he thought, continuing his fancy. The tombs, ill-lit by television light, where the people sat like the dead, the grey or multi-coloured lights touching their faces, but never really touching them.

'No profession,' said the phonograph voice, hissing. 'What are you doing out?'

'Walking,' said Leonard Mead.

'Walking!'

'Just walking,' he said simply, but his face felt cold.

'Walking, just walking, walking?'

'Yes, sir.'

'Walking where? For what?'

'Walking for air. Walking to see.'

'Your address!'

'Eleven South Saint James Street.'

'And there is air in your house, you have an air conditioner, Mr Mead?'

'Yes.'

'And you have a viewing screen in your house to see with?'

'No.'

'No?' There was a crackling quiet that in itself was an accusation.

'Are you married, Mr Mead?'

'No.'

'Not married,' said the police voice behind the fiery beam. The moon was high and clear among the stars and the houses were grey and silent.

'Nobody wanted me,' said Leonard Mead with a smile.

'Don't speak unless you're spoken to!'

Leonard Mead waited in the cold night.

"Just walking, Mr Mead?'

'Yes.'

'But you haven't explained for what purpose.'

'I explained; for air, and to see, and just to walk.'

'Have you done this often?'

'Every night for years.'

The police car sat in the centre of the street with its radio throat faintly humming.

'Well, Mr Mead,' it said.

'Is that all?' he asked politely.

'Yes,' said the voice. 'Here.' There was a sigh, a pop. The back door of the police car sprang wide.

'Get in.'

'Wait a minute, I haven't done anything!'

'Get in.'

'I protest!'

'Mr Mead.'

He walked like a man suddenly drunk. As he passed the front window of the car he looked in. As he had expected, there was no-one in the front seat, no-one in the car at all.

'Get in.'

He put his hand to the door and peered into the back seat, which was a little cell, a little black jail with bars. It smelled of riveted steel. It smelled of harsh antiseptic; it smelled too clean and hard and metallic. There was nothing soft there.

'Now if you had a wife to give you an alibi,' said the iron voice. 'But - '

'Where are you taking me?'

The car hesitated, or rather gave a faint whirring click, as if information, somewhere, was dropping card by punch-slotted card under electric eyes. 'To the Psychiatric Centre for Research on Regressive Tendencies. '

He got in. The door shut with a soft thud. The police car rolled through the night avenues, flashing its dim lights ahead.

They passed one house on one street a moment later, one house in an entire city of houses that were dark, but this one particular house had all of its electric lights brightly lit, every window a loud yellow illumination, square and warm in the cool darkness.

'That's my house,' said Leonard Mead.

No-one answered him.

The car moved down the empty river- bed streets and off away, leaving the empty streets with the empty pavements, and no sound and no motion all the rest of the chill November night.

AFTERWORD

by David Wellington

As I write this, I'm sitting in a darkened room, lit only by the light of the screen of my laptop, in the early days of November. I envy you, dear reader, because by the time you see this the presidential election of 2016 will already be over. You will have survived the incredible tension of these last few days of a campaign that has dragged out over years. You won't be checking the polls every few hours, watching your candidate gain or lose fractions of a percentage point. You won't be petrified over the idea that maybe this isn't really over, that there could be an actual tie in the electoral college.

Maybe you'll think of the presidential election of 2016 as a historical footnote. Or maybe you'll remember how scared we were, we poor denizens of the past, who had to watch the country tear itself literally in half. Maybe you'll take pity on us. As we must take pity on you. Because no matter what future you inhabit, you're less than four years away from having to do this all again.

No matter how scary this election seems, it's only part of a pattern. Every four years we are presented with this same choice between two candidates, one unthinkable, one barely tolerable. The political engine that runs this country has decided that scaring the hell out of the electorate is the only way to maintain their grip on power, and so we get to do this over and over and over again. The real issues facing this country are ignored, put aside while we watch a map get splattered with blue and red.

It isn't over, not for me. Not for you. It's never over.

Horror fiction presents us with terrors beyond anything an election can bring, but horror fiction works because it has one quality that real-life fears lack. It ends. You turn the page and there's no more story. Even the bleakest, most nihilistic story at least has an ending. You get to feel that familiar chill down your spine, as you imagine a world where the horse-race of American politics is actually the work of nefarious aliens, or baby-eating monsters. You get to panic, just a little, thinking of how we would justify our actions if the dead were watching us, or if we got the thing we say we want most, for the (arguably) great leaders of the past to claw their way back into our lives. Your heart races, your palms sweat… and then it's over, and you get the release, the relief, of endorphins flooding your system. "Thank God that's over," is the unofficial motto of the horror reader.

But… is it? Is it over?

Good horror fiction draws on real-world frights. It has to be relatable, believable on some level. That's the real power of horror, in the end. By drawing on things we're actually worried about, it makes us think about them. Yes, you get your quick neurotransmitter hit of catharsis and relief. A good horror story, though, doesn't let you off that easily. It leaves that hook stuck in your brain. It leaves you thinking, long after you've put the book aside. No, of course, you say, those political robocalls aren't coming from an elder deity of slaughter, that was just a story. But the robocalls have invaded your life, and you know they've changed you. Made your world just a little worse, right?

It's never over.

The stories in this anthology run the gamut from the absurd to the chilling, and I hope they will stick with you. I hope they'll leave stains on your soul, keep you up at night… I hope they'll make you think.

The final terror of politics is that we know, in the end, we did this to ourselves. We got ourselves into this mess. We're the ones who enact the dark ritual every couple of years, we're the ones who go into a dark cave on a Tuesday and put our mark on the wall, the mark of our complicity. Our acceptance of the dark deeds done in our names.

Many people in this country don't vote. I tend to think that's less because they're lazy than that they don't want the responsibility. Everyone in this country complains about politics and the government. Well, that's our God-given right as Americans, of course. We need, though, to always remember that whether we vote or not, we are making a choice. An endless series of choices, which led to the blighted post-apocalyptic landscape we see when we look out our windows.

That's the power of this book, of these stories. To remind us of that basic fact of democracy, the one we can never escape. We put this knife to our own flesh. And then we pressed down. Hard.

Don't forget to vote, in whatever election is coming up. Make sure you vote for the right candidate. If that choice scares you, then you know you're on the right path. It means you understand just how much is at stake.

Then, when you realize just how badly you blew it, when your chosen representative disappoints or appalls or frustrates you—vote again.

It's never over.

McDonald's

THE AUTHORS:

Jeff Strand (Introduction) is the four-time Bram Stoker Award-nominated author of such novels as BLISTER, DWELLER, and CYCLOPS ROAD. He lives in a swing county in a swing state and he voted, so don't blame him!

Paul Moore (The War Room) is a filmmaker who has written and directed four feature films, most recently *Keepsake* and *Requiem*. He is also the co-owner the of movie production studio Blind Tiger Filmworks. His first short story, *Spoiled*, was published in the well received anthology *Appalachian Undead*. He followed that with the story *Things* in the anthology *Drive-In Creature Feature*.

Ray Garton (The Blood of Patriots and Tyrants) has been writing novels, novellas, and short stories in the genres of horror and suspense for more than 30 years. He is the author of *Live Girls*, and more recently has written the paranormal thriller *Vortex* and the collection *Wailing and Gnashing of Teeth*. Visit his website at *RayGartonOnline.com*.

Jason V Brock (Return of the Gipper) is an award-winning writer, editor, scholar, filmmaker, and artist whose work has been widely published in a variety of media (*Weird Fiction Review* print edition, S. T. Joshi's *Black Wings* series, *Fangoria*, and others). He describes his work as Dark Magical Realism. He is also the founder of the website and digest *[NameL3ss]*; his books include *A Darke Phantastique, Disorders of Magnitude*, and *Simulacrum and Other Possible Realities*. His filmic efforts are *Charles Beaumont: The Life of Twilight Zone's Magic Man, The AckerMonster Chronicles!*, and *Image, Reflection, Shadow: Artists of the Fantastic*. Popular as a speaker and panelist, he has been a special guest at numerous film fests, conventions, and educational events, and was the 2015 Editor Guest of

Honor for Orycon 37. A health nut/gadget freak, he lives in the Vancouver, WA area, and loves his wife Sunni, their family of herptiles, running their technology consulting business, and practicing vegan/vegetarianism.

Dale Bailey (Death and Suffrage) is a winner of both the Shirley Jackson Award and the International Horror Guild Award. He is the author of *The End of the End of Everything: Stories* and *The Subterranean Season*, both out in 2015, as well as *The Fallen, House of Bones, Sleeping Policemen* (with Jack Slay, Jr.), and *The Resurrection Man's Legacy and Other Stories.* His work has twice been a finalist for the Nebula Award and once for the Bram Stoker Award, and has been adapted for Showtime Television's Masters of Horror. He lives in North Carolina with his family.

G. Ted Theewen (The Governor's Executions) lives on the Illinois/ Wisconsin state line. When he's not writing, he's making ice cream for his youtube channel, *Ice Cream Every Day.* His work has appeared in *Infernal Ink Magazine, Inner Sins*, and the anthology *Floppy Shoes Apocalypse 2: Cherry Nose Armageddon.* His humor blog can be found at www.tedscreepyvan.blogspot.com

Thomas Breen (GOTV) is a former journalist who covered local, state, and national politics. His fiction includes *Orford Parish Murder Houses* (2016), along with stories published in a number of anthologies and periodicals. Find him on Twitter @TJBreen.

Lisa Morton (The Fool on the Hill) is a screenwriter, author of non-fiction books, award-winning prose writer, and Halloween expert whose work was described by the American Library Association's Readers' Advisory Guide to Horror as "consistently dark, unsettling, and frightening". Her most recent releases include the non-fiction books *Adventures in the Scream Trade* and *Ghosts: A Haunted History* and the short story collection *Cemetery Dance Select: Lisa Morton*. Forthcoming books include *Hallows' Eve*, an anthology of original short fiction co-edited with Ellen Datlow, and the novel *Animals: Flesh and Fur*. Lisa lives in the San Fernando Valley and online at www.lisamorton.com.

Simon McCaffery (How I Learned to Stop Worrying and Love the Wall) was born in the waning months of JFK's administration and witness to one of Nixon's final motorcade appearances before resigning to avoid impeachment. His short stories have appeared in *Lightyear, Black Static, Other Worlds Than These, Appalachian Undead*, and many others. He lives in Tulsa, Oklahoma.

Nick Mamatas (Willow Tests Well) is the author of several novels, including *The Last Weekend* and *I Am Providence*, and his short fiction has been published in *Best American Mystery Stories, Year's Best Science Fiction & Fantasy*, and many other anthologies and magazines. His political and cultural reportage has appeared in *Clamor, In These Times*, and the *Village Voice*.

John Palisano (Seeds) writes in non-fiction, short fiction, novels, and screenplays. He hasn't written a speech for any politicians (that he can mention). Say 'hi' at: www.johnpalisano.com

Kevin Holton (The Tie-Breaker) has published poetry and prose with Siren's Call Publications, Thunderdome Press, and Crystal Lake Publishing. When not writing, he's the North American Representative at *Game Time Reviews*. He is also a student, voice actor, and amateur Batman who can be found at www.kevinholton.com or @KevinJLHolton

William F Nolan (Year of the Mouse) writes mostly in the science fiction, fantasy, and horror genres. Though best known for coauthoring the acclaimed dystopian science fiction novel Logan's Run with George Clayton Johnson, Nolan is the author of more than 2000 pieces (fiction, nonfiction, and poetry), and has edited over twenty-five anthologies in his sixty-plus year career. He was a key member of The Group, a collective of authors in the 1950s and '60s, which also included Richard Matheson, Charles Beaumont, John Tomerlin, and by extension Ray Bradbury (as mentor). He has won numerous awards in his long career, including the World Fantasy Convention Award, and two Bram Stoker Awards. A vegetarian, Nolan resides in Vancouver, WA.

David Perlmutter (Your Own Damned Fault) is a freelance writer based in Winnipeg, Manitoba, Canada. He holds an MA degree from the Universities of Manitoba and Winnipeg, and is a lifelong animation fan. He is the author of *America Toons In: A History of Television Animation* (McFarland and Co.), *The Singular Adventures Of Jefferson Ball* (Chupa Cabra House), *The Pups* (Booklocker.com), *Certain Private Conversations and Other Stories* (Aurora Publishing), and *Orthicon; or, the History of a Bad Idea* (Linkville Press, forthcoming). He can be reached on Facebook at David Perlmutter-Writer, Twitter at @DKPLJW1, and Tumblr at The Musings of David Perlmutter (yesdavidperlmutterfan).

Sarah Langan (Love Perverts) is the award-winning author of the novels *The Keeper, The Missing,* and *Audrey's Door* (HarperCollins). She's at work on her fourth novel, *The Clinic*, and lives in Los Angeles with her husband and daughters. Find her on Twitter @SarahVCLangan.

Sunni K Brock (Gadu Yansa) is a published poet, writer, and talented vegetarian cook. If she had spare time, she would spend it working with genealogy, doing crafts, shopping at the farmer's market, and conducting experiments on controlled randomness.

As one-half of the team of JaSunni Productions, LLC, her main functions are editor and sound technician. She is also a guiding force behind the company's vision and direction along with her husband, Jason V Brock. She enjoys spending her days working alongside Jason, tending to their pet reptiles, and aggravating friends on Facebook.

Joseph Rubas (Feast) is the author of over 200 short stories and several novels. His work has appeared in *The Horror Zine* and *Nameless Digest*. He is also the editor of *The 3rd Spectral Book of Horror Stories*. He currently resides in New York State.

Bobby Wilson (Hyper-Pluralism) lives in China where he teaches English and writes. His work has appeared in the *Longridge Review* and *Unlikely Stories*. In his free time he struggles through Chinese literature, plays basketball, cooks for his wife and plays with his cat. Find him at www.bobbywwilsonjr.com or on Twitter @chewingbones.

Anthony Ambrogio (That Hot Summer Night in Healey's Bar Two Weeks Before the Election) has written extensively for film magazines (*Video Watchdog, Midnight Marquee*) and film books (*Eros in the Mind's Eye; We Belong Dead; Peter Cushing; You're Next! Loss of Identity in the Horror Film*—the latter two of which he edited for Midnight Marquee Press). His stories have appeared in *The Fear Finder, Stillwaters Journal*, and the anthology *Brief Grislys* (Apocryphile Press, 2013).

Nicholas Manzolillo (Everybody Listens to Buck) is a Scituate, Rhode Island native who currently resides in Manhattan. His writing has appeared in *Thuglit: Last Writes*, The New England Horror Writer's Anthology: *Wicked Witches, Deadman's Tome*, and *Out of The Gutter*. He is currently earning an MFA in Creative and Professional Writing from Western Connecticut State University.

Hillary Lyon (Getting Out to Vote) lives in southern Arizona, where she is the founder of and editor for Subsynchronous Press. She has lived in France, Brazil, Canada, and several states in the U.S. Her stories have appeared recently in *365 Tomorrows, Night to Dawn, Eternal Haunted Summer*, and numerous anthologies. When she's not writing, she's hand-painting cigar boxes and furniture in the colorful dia de los muertos style.

Mark Allan Gunnels (Take Me to Your Cheerleader) loves to tell stories. He has since he was a kid, penning one-page tales that were Twilight Zone knockoffs. He likes to think he has gotten a little better since then. He lives in Greer, SC, with his husband Craig A. Metcalf.

Curtis VanDonkelaar (The Sixth Street Bus Holds an Election) has appeared in journals such as *Passages North, the Vestal Review, Western Humanities Review, MAKE, Hobart, DIAGRAM*, and others. He is an eight-time finalist in national fiction contests, and has been nominated for the *Best of Net*. He is finishing a novel about life, death, and music, all very new ideas in literature and human experience. Go to *curtisvandonkelaar.com* for more to read.

Luke Styer and Skip Johnson (The Candidate)

Luke Styer is a native of West Virginia, where he reads, plays tabletop games, and watches movies. This is his first professionally published story.

Eugene Johnson is a filmmaker, author, editor, and columnist of science fiction, fantasy, horror, and supernatural thrillers. Eugene has written and edited in various genres. His latest anthology *was released in 2016*, and his anthology *Appalachian Undead*, co-edited with Jason Sizemore, was selected by FearNet, as one of the best books of 2012. Eugene's articles and stories have been published by award winning Apex publishing, The Zombiefeed, Evil Jester Press, Warrior Sparrow Press and more.

Ray Bradbury (The Pedestrian) (1920-2012) was the author of more than three dozen books, including such classics as *Fahrenheit 451, The Martian Chronicles, The Illustrated Man, Dandelion Wine*, and *Something Wicked This Way Comes*, as well as hundreds of short stories. He wrote for theater, cinema, and TV, including the screenplay for John Huston's *Moby Dick* and the Emmy Award-winning teleplay *The Halloween Tree*, and adapted for television sixty-five of his stories for *The Ray Bradbury Theater*. He was the recipient of the 2000 National Book Foundation's Medal for Distinguished Contribution to American Letters, the 2007 Pulitzer Prize Special Citation, and numerous other honors.

David Wellington (Afterword) was born and raised in Pittsburgh, Pennsylvania. He attended Syracuse University and received an MFA in creative writing from Penn State.

In 2004 he began serializing his novel Monster Island online. The book rapidly gained a following, and was acquired for print publication by Thunder's Mouth Press.

Since then, Wellington has published more than 15 novels, and has been featured in The New York Times, Boing Boing and the Los Angeles Times.

You can find him online at davidwellington.net.

A NOTE ON THE STREET ART FEATURED IN THE BOOK:

I imagine political street art has existed since the beginning of time. There is quick and simple art, like a stenciled anarchy symbol, to complex murals that can cover an entire wall or even a building. Street art challenges the political structure, expressing dissent and encouraging the viewer to consider difficult issues. A key component is that it is public, accessible to everyone and anyone. It is the unfiltered voice of the artist speaking to the people. It is also, by nature, temporary. As a photographer, my goal is to document street art before it disappears, immortalizing the message. The art you see in this book was captured on the streets of Los Angeles, California and Krakow, Poland.

- Aleks Bieńkowska

THUNDERDOMEPRESS.COM

Charity Anthology

Proceeds from this anthology will be donated to the Horror Writers Association Hardship Fund, which offers low-interest loans to writers in times of dire need. This anthology is in no way endorsed or supported by the HWA.

In addition, some proceeds may also go to at-risk marginalized communities in times of need.

Made in the USA
San Bernardino, CA
16 January 2017